Sacred Betrayal

Sr. Christine Kresho

PublishAmerica
Baltimore

ISBN: 1-60474-145-7
PUBLISHED BY PUBLISHAMERICA, LLLP
www.publishamerica.com
Baltimore

Printed in the United States of America

Dedication

To the Sisters of St. Joseph of Baden, PA, to the Spirit Sisters of Our Lady of Grace Catholic Church, and to all women and men who hope for rebirth for the Catholic Church so that all the People of God will live, work, and minister as partners with God.

Chapter 1

Clenching the morning newspaper in his large manicured hands, Archbishop Robert Garrote's frenzied roar propelled him back and forth as he paced in front of his huge mahogany desk. Another article publicizing the **Cry Justice** assembly in his diocese. Their fall meeting always took place the first weekend in October. He studied the photo. *At least she managed to avoid getting her picture taken this time. How dare they continue to question so much that we hold untouchable,* he growled to himself as he punched the intercom button for his driver and assistant, Father William Owens.

Father Owens marched down the long, polished-to-perfection hall to the archbishop's study. He held his head high, grinning to himself, his straight hair, combed to perfection and too black to be natural. His pale complexion, narrow nose, and rigid thin lips combined to present a face of steadfast allegiance. He tapped a staccato knock on the door, and slipped inside. Having read the paper at 6:30 that morning he congratulated himself. *I am so prepared for this. I do wish she had been in that picture, though.*

Hearing the muffled click of the closed door, Archbishop Garrote waved the newspaper and bellowed, "Those radicals are going to bring disaster on my church! Did you read this? What a way to begin a Monday. Do you know what I wish I could do?" His rage had turned up the usual ruby color in his cheeks to a glowing scarlet making his coarse wiry hair look even more white than usual.

His cold brown eyes rushed in an erratic back-and-forth flash from the newspaper to Father Owens. His stare searched the soul of the priest standing in front of him. *I know he hates to be called Bill. Such a silly idiosyncrasy, but since I am beginning to think of him as a son, I'll have to ask him someday why he thinks Will makes him more of a man.* "Will, do you understand how much I want this group stopped?"

Smothering his internal glee, Father Will spoke his calculated words with appropriate compliance. "I understand. You have my full support. It's people like you who will save our Church and return it to its proper supremacy. I am here as your servant. You can count on my loyalty." Having crafted his answer with great care he heard the answer he expected.

"Thank you, Will; I needed to hear that. You always seem to know what to say. I do want to save the Church; it is my daily prayer."

"And you will succeed, Archbishop."

"Now, what did we agree upon; I'll call you Will, and you'll call me—"

"Bob. You will succeed, Bob." His external smile was polite; his insides beamed with abandon. He enjoyed being so appreciated. He was grateful to be this close to power, a power that would change this archdiocese and make it an example for the whole church. Others would marvel at what he and the archbishop were destined to accomplish.

Taking a deep breath the archbishop settled into the comfortable black leather lounge chair near his office window. When the duties of his office wearied him, as they so often did, he would swivel that chair and try to find peace *looking out at God's wonders*, he told himself. *Where is the joy I felt when I first went to the seminary? I was so fired up, so happy to be ministering to God's people. Why are things so different now?* He motioned Will to the chair facing his desk.

Looking into the dark eyes of this eager, zealous priest he said, "Let's talk about what we can do to turn these people around." He slapped the desk. "Or should I just excommunicate them?" Regret stuck in his throat as he pushed aside the memory of a bond broken now for three years.

"Well, excommunication may get rid of them for you by pushing them into another diocese; there they would continue their protests and accusations, and may even get more publicity because of it. You know that some of your brother bishops agree with them, and have their own chapters of **Cry Justice**." He stopped short of mentioning one more devastating detail. *All in good time*, he promised himself.

"You're right, of course. But I, I am the faithful Shepherd. After all, we possess the true path to heaven and I am determined to save the Church from these wolves." Another pang of regret punched him in the stomach.

Still clutching the newspaper, his face churned with frenzy as he stood and shook it in front of Will's nose. "Look at some of these things they are saying about us: that we should sit down with those who disagree with us and talk with them, listening to their concerns. What kind of nonsense is that? We know we are right; they should listen to us! And they say that all religions have truth to share; but we know that we have all the truth, so why should we waste time with those who think they have something to tell us? Why don't they understand that it was better before; when obedience meant something?" He caught his breath as he recalled a conversation, a long time ago, when he and she defined obedience as a listening to the Spirit within.

He slumped into his chair; his 6'3"powerful frame ready to cave in, but suddenly he walloped the solid arms of his well-padded chair with his powerful fists. The lure of former days when his power was unquestioned brought a sudden light to his eyes. "We will not give in! Let's discuss some practical ways of dealing with this."

This is proceeding just as I dreamed. Stay calm; this is not the time to get so excited I make a mistake. I have prepared myself well, Will reminded himself. "Archbishop; I mean, Bob, I know that you are aware that there are at least a half dozen priests in the diocese who agree with you. Why don't you invite them to a meeting with you? In addition to offering some expedient recommendations, I'm sure they would appreciate being 'on your team,' so to speak."

"That's a splendid idea, Will!" said the archbishop his chair vibrating under a second wallop. "And the sooner, the better. Let's see, I don't have anything pressing on my schedule next Tuesday. Why don't you call these loyal servants of the Church and invite them here for dinner on Tuesday at 7:30. Then talk to Annie and have her plan the meal and tell her to make it extra special; the best steaks and the best wine; and she makes fabulous desserts; have her bake several of her exceptional pies. After dinner, we'll talk strategies. Go now, and check my liquor supply; make sure we have enough for a drink or two before dinner, and more to keep the conversation going afterwards. And by tomorrow, let me see our guest list, just in case I have someone to add. See you at 10:00 tomorrow." His eyes drifted away toward the window, just for a second. As Will stood to leave he said, "And Will, thanks!"

Closing the office door with his customary decorum, Will's contentment with himself bloated his vacant soul. He saw himself skipping and clapping with reckless self-assurance. Ever since he came to work for the archbishop three years ago he had been waiting for such an opportunity; how sweet the thought that what goes around comes around. He vowed he would never let go of the pain he felt that day when he first walked into the archbishop's office. Having been transferred from Sacred Heart Parish, where he been embroiled in a contentious situation, he knew then, that God would allow him the revenge that would justify him in everyone's eyes.

Even now, three years later, he chafed at the thought of the three Sisters who worked in that parish. Though the pastor, Father Edward McShane, thought they could do no wrong, Will could see that their plan was to assume virtual control of the parish. *How could Ed have been so blind*, he still asked himself. *Were you so intimidated because one of them was the Archbishop's sister? I guess I can understand that. Now, you will have a chance to redeem yourself, Ed, I promise. They were so clever, those three, in how they planned parish events and made it seem that you were in charge, but I, although only the associate, could see through all their posturing. I knew how much they wanted the esteem and deference that comes with parish leadership.*

How poignant the memory of his farewell party; he could see through all that pretense. Now he would be instrumental in restricting not only their revolutionary activities but also the actions of other like-minded nonconformists. The expectation of things to come enlivened his steps. As soon as he got to his computer he called up the diocesan database he had set up last year. In thirty seconds he loaded the file he had named Faithful Ones. With the list on his screen he dialed the first number. Both feet tapped the floor as he listened to the second ring.

Chapter 2

At Our Lady of Lourdes parish Lucy, the parish secretary, had just finished typing the last line of the pastor's letter in the bulletin as she picked up the phone. With her lips still forming her greeting, she heard, "Father James Miller, please." She recognized the voice, but didn't pretend.

"Just a moment, I'll put you through."

"Jim, this is Will Owens. How are you today?"

"Just fine, Will. And you?"

"Even better than fine, thank you. I'm calling to extend to you an invitation from the archbishop for dinner next Tuesday at 7:30. We are calling together the priests that are unwavering in their devotion to the true Church. As you are aware, there is much going on throughout the archdiocese that troubles the archbishop. Your dedication to Church discipline is appreciated, and so the archbishop would like you to be part of a committee that will help to reverse the insubordinate trends that are becoming commonplace these days. I'm sure you read this morning's paper."

"I am in total agreement with your assessment of matters. I will be most happy to be available to the archbishop. I'm marking my calendar now. Thank you for calling."

"Thank you, Jim. We look forward to seeing you on Tuesday."

Although I have always disliked something about that Will, he knows the right people to call. I wonder if I was his first call. Enjoying a self-congratulatory grin spreading across his face Jim acknowledged the recognition he was sure had prompted the phone call. He had been quite outspoken for some time now regarding what he considered opposing forces in his own parish.

To prevent those who insisted on using prayer to further their own agendas he had ceased inviting people to offer their personal prayer petitions during the daily Masses. He remembered how angry, Tom, one of his older parishioners had become because of that change. Tom had insisted at least once a week praying for the Church hierarchy to recognize all the vocations to the priesthood. Father Jim knew what he meant by that. He could not understand how someone Tom's age, having grown up in a time when obedience to authority was the standard, would keep pushing the envelope on women's ordination.

Tom sure has issues, he thought. Tom made it a point that every time there was an execution in the state he would pray for the conversion of pro-lifers. *How can they call themselves pro-life,* he had argued to Father Jim over and over again, *and also be pro-death penalty.* Even though Father Jim didn't favor capital punishment, he hated that logic; after all some of his friends in the pro-life group even believed that killing abortion clinic workers was justified.

War was another of Tom's problems; even though most of the bishops supported the just war theory, Tom never let a conversation about patriotism end without his comments, and he had so many, about Jesus, the gospel, and peace. A veteran, yet he swore he learned from war that war is never the right answer. *He is right about that, but it sure doesn't make him popular with the military people.*

Father Jim wanted peace above all else, especially peace in his own little piece of the world. *All I ever wanted was to serve you, O God,* Father Jim prayed. *I have given my life to your church; is it wrong to be pleased that I may be recognized for my loyalty? Why can't all my parishioners just accept the rules; how often I tell them they do not belong to a cafeteria religion where they can choose what they want to believe.*

He had a sudden urge for a cup of coffee. "Isn't this a great day?" he said as he walked past Lucy.

Smiling she nodded her agreement. It was always a good day when Father Jim was happy which wasn't often, these last three or four years. She noticed a twinge of fear tying a knot in her stomach. *I should call Jeanie later and find out if Father Ed got a call from Father Will Owens. She was so glad when he left Sacred Heart.*

Walking to the window Father Jim saluted the sun with his half-filled cup of coffee. He shook his head and smiled again, as his eyes drank in the bright blue sky with its one puffy white cloud. Such a surge of satisfaction he had not felt for a long, long time; not only had his loyalty won the attention of the archbishop, but he would also have a significant role in bringing order and discipline back to the Church. He felt pretty certain that he knew who else would be there next Tuesday.

Father Michael Lynch, associate at St. John's, tucked the morning newspaper under a stack of files as his pastor stopped by his office. "Good morning, Charlie. Hope you had a good time yesterday afternoon; it was a perfect day for a boat ride. Long drive to get there, though." He was certain Charlie had seen the morning paper before breakfast; certain, too, that he was proud his name had been listed as one of the outspoken members of **Cry Justice.** Mike found it difficult to live and work with a pastor whose views were so opposite his own.

"Yes, we had a great time. And I never mind a long drive when I'm going to be with friends." His eyes moved across Mike's desk stopping for a deliberate second on the stack of files. He smiled and let the silence hang in the air.

Mike was grateful when his phone rang. "A busy day begins," he nodded to Charlie as he said, "Father Michael Lynch here. How can I be of service?"

Turning away Charlie walked towards his office. *Someday he will be ready for real service; life has to knock some truth into him first. Maybe knock some weight off him, too. What a pompous jerk, God, forgive me. No doubt that phone call is from Will Owens, another one who has a lot to learn.*

"Yes, I did see the article, Will. How's the archbishop handling it?"

As Will explained the archbishop's plans, Mike struggled to rise above his envy at Will's position. *I would not have wanted to get where he is the way he did, but I sure wish I were there.* His heart jumped a beat as he heard Will tell him that he and Mark West, his classmate and the associate at Nativity were the youngest to be invited to the archbishop's dinner. Will's next words swelled him with pride.

"You are among the chosen ones, Mike. Next Tuesday, 7:30."

"Tell the archbishop he can count on me. It's time for us to take back our church."

Hanging up the phone, Will tapped his fingers on the desk. *He would do anything to have my job. I know Mike does not like me, but he is so good at pretending; in the end he will prove useful to me.*

Within the next hour he spoke with Fathers Nick Perry and Ed McShane; both were pastors looking forward to retirement; they were weary, they told him, of trying to keep it all together; both were pleased to think they still could have some influence. *Ed was very pleased that I called him. He did not mention it, but I know he is sorry for what happened. I am sure that if he had it do over again, he would have chosen a different route. I am positive that by now he has seen the Archbishop's sister and her friends as the manipulators they are. I'll give him a chance to make it up to me; all can be forgiven, Ed.*

He had left a message for the pastor at St. Agnes, Father Joe Moreno. At 5:30 an adamant Father Joe returned his call. "I've tried so often to reach out to the members of my parish that have joined **Cry Justice**, but their intensity scares me. I am gratified to be offered a chance to connect with like-minded leaders who can offer me some reassurance that I am is right."

Father Pete Rogers from St. James parish was starved for support. "Will, I have felt so isolated for my views; my associate and I have had some testy and exhausting discussions about the direction of the parish. I am so elated at the prospect of putting together explicit guidelines that will curb all this experimentation and discussion. I long for the old days when my flock of sheep accepted my leadership without question."

By 6:00 Will was printing his list of faithful priests. He gazed at it for fifteen minutes, abandoning himself to the wild satisfaction that swirled inside him. *Time to quit,* he said to himself. Standing up he glanced at his list one more time before slipping it under his desk pad. *Until tomorrow morning.* He patted his desk pad. Inhaling a deep reflective breath he tasted how delighted the archbishop would be with him tomorrow morning.

Chapter 3

After Mass and breakfast that Monday morning Sister Frances Mary Garrote walked to her office, her mind a jumble of anticipation mixed with an unyielding sadness. Her position as spiritual director and administrator of Sophia's Blessings Spiritual Center was a constant source of gratitude for her. Mouthing her daily *Thank you, God; thank you, Sophia, Spirit of Wisdom* she opened her office door. Sister Jennifer hurried towards her waving the newspaper in her right hand.

"Did you see the paper? At least your name wasn't it in this time."

"That should make my brother happy. Come in if you have a few minutes." The dance in her brown gold-speckled eyes faltered this morning.

Dropping herself into a soft blue cushioned chair Sister Jennifer studied the face of her friend as Fran settled into the dark blue tweed chair at her desk. She knew that their move from Sacred Heart the summer after Father Owens went to her brother's office was a time of great hurt. Fran had accepted it because he had told her of the embarrassment it had caused him. She accepted the fact that being the sister of the archbishop made political demands on her, but she had also made it quite clear that he had no right to ask her to compromise her conscience.

"When was the last time you spoke with him?"

Fran's weak smile could not conceal her pain. "You mean, a real conversation? He speaks to me at public functions when he cannot avoid me, but talk? No, we have not talked for a long time. Even before the mess at Sacred Heart. But at least, then, we would have dinner together sometimes, and I even thought he listened to me once in a while."

"He will come around one of these days, you'll see. I'm sure some of what you've said has rubbed off on him."

"He is a good man, I know. But somewhere, along the way, he became obsessed with the fear of losing control. With Will Owens there, I'm afraid I could lose him forever."

"Oh, I'm sure that will never happen. It's true, you know, what they say. Blood is thicker than water. Come on, now, we know that Will Owens has ice water in his veins."

"Jennifer, how awful." Even with her hand covering her mouth she could not stop the wholehearted laugh that escaped. "I remember what a good teacher once told me; it rang true then and I have always believed it—that we all need an uncharitable friend."

"A what?"

"An uncharitable friend, the one who lets us say anything, even the unkind stuff, and does not love us less. I'm so glad we don't have to pretend with each other."

"You know what I think we need? How about you, Joan and I watching a movie tonight? The retreat group will be gone by 11:00; we'll have the afternoon to get ready for tomorrow's group. I think we need a good comedy; I'll stop at the video store when I go shopping this afternoon."

"Sounds good. Leave the paper here, if you're finished."

Waiting for her computer to load, Fran turned the pages for the continuation of the **Cry Justice** story. *Why doesn't he understand how much these people love the Church, and Jesus?* She, Jennifer, and Joan had been at the meeting, but she had managed to dodge the reporters this time. She spotted Jennifer in one of the pictures; *I wonder if she noticed this.*

A light knock on her door told her that Joan was stopping by to offer her own words of wisdom. *Thank goodness for my friends.* "Come in, Joan."

"I just wanted to check if you had seen the paper."

"Yes, did you see Jennifer in this picture?"

"No, I don't think she did either. I know you worry about your brother every time there's publicity about these meetings. I am sure you do not need to be reminded of this, but he is your brother first; he was your brother before he became the archbishop, and he's your brother now. He does love you. I think that he wishes he could be beside you at these meetings."

"Now, what makes you think something like that? He was so upset with me when I told him I was joining **Cry Justice**. Since that day our relationship has never been the same."

"I remember him before he was the archbishop. My sister, Karen, was in his first parish when he was an associate; 1970 seems like another lifetime, but I remember Karen telling me how impressed she was with him. He was so outgoing and pastoral; always greeting the people on Sundays before Mass; he started small faith-sharing groups and he used to pray with them every week. I can't believe that all that holiness is gone."

"You're right; I do remember how enthusiastic he was in those days. We had the same hopes and dreams for the church in those days. We talked one time about the real meaning of obedience; now he seems to have forgotten all we shared. Somewhere, the power trip took over his life."

"God has not forgotten; I promise you that you will see him turn back to the real person trapped under all that clout."

"I hope I'll be alive to see it. I miss him, you know. When we were growing up I sometimes worried that he needed power because I was the older sister; and even worse, I was a twin, so he had me and Tess to deal with. My mother used to tell the story of how he always had to stand on a chair when we had our pictures taken so that he was the tallest. It never seemed to matter to him when Tim came along three years later; the competition was always with me and Tess; and it was only in his mind. We were never competing against him for anything."

"Don't give up on him; in my opinion, you should be more concerned about Will Owens."

"Oh, I am. I said that to Jennifer. Instead of letting go of all that happened at Sacred Heart he uses it to feed his need for revenge. Such a sad way to live for someone who is not even 40 years old. Let's not talk about him anymore. Jennifer said we all need to watch a comedy tonight."

"Sounds right to me. I'll make the popcorn. Now, try not to worry so much about your brother. One of these days he will be calling you. I have to go; I'm still working on the schedule for next year's retreats, and next month's newsletter. And tomorrow the *Baptist Women of Bright Promise* will be here; this place will be rocking with their joyful singing." Winking, she said, "Your brother will be singing with them some day."

Chapter 4

Having checked his watch twice Father Will Owens relished the three minutes before 10:00 Tuesday morning. At 9:59 he rapped on the archbishop's office door. With no effort to hide his satisfaction, he held up his list of seven names in front of his chest, bowed and positioned it in front of the archbishop.

"Good Morning, Will. Right on time." The archbishop's eyes raced back and forth, his left hand fidgeted with the stubborn shock of white hair and his mouth tightened in a rigid smile. Wetting his lips, he said, "Excellent job, Will. I think we are on the verge of something extraordinary, don't you agree?"

"Wholeheartedly. I am sure that God will bless your efforts, Archbishop."

"There's one name I thought I would see. What about Charlie Fletcher?"

"I would have agreed with you about four months ago, but I have been hearing some disturbing reports about him. It seems that when he was on a retreat last year, he had a dream that confused and alarmed him. He claims that after praying over it, he decided that he was being called to change his ways and to him that meant he was to embrace all these dissident people as messengers from Jesus."

"I would never have expected Charlie to be swayed so easily. A dream, you say? Tell me he didn't go to Sophia's Blessings for his retreat. Has he done anything irrational?"

"I've been keeping close tabs on him; I have several friends in the parish, but all that has happened so far is that he's become very popular; his Masses are crowded they tell me, but of course, that's to be expected when you give people what they want. They don't want to hear the difficult commandments; they don't want to listen to anything that would limit their freedom. But as far as I can sense at this point, he hasn't broken any church laws."

"By your silence about his place of retreat, I know you are trying to spare my feelings, and I appreciate that. My sister has lost her way for now, but I am praying that she will come around. I guess that is her way of dealing with the problem you all had at Sacred Heart. She never lets a failure keep her down."

"Interesting choice of words, Archbishop; I mean, Bob. I didn't think your sister ever admitted failure."

"Oh, she doesn't, but that's what it was. She likes to call it God's way of pushing her into new work. But she was wrong, and I told her so. Anyway, it also brought you here, so God does bring good out of these painful situations."

Will managed to force a smile in agreement. His insides bristled with loathing as he remembered the wound he would not allow to heal. He also trembled with ecstasy; not only did the archbishop denounce his sister, he counted it as a blessing that Will was with him.

"I am sorry to report to you about Charlie; I know he was a good friend of yours."

"Well, I thank you for being so perceptive and discerning. We'll have to pray for Charlie that he will come back into the fold. He always had a way with people; his talent for persuasion would be of great benefit to our cause. I'm saddened to think we'll be on opposing sides."

"Maybe he'll have another dream!"

After sharing an uninhibited laugh, they began discussing the particulars for their Tuesday gathering. "As they arrive," said Archbishop Garrote, "we'll usher them into the large parlor and begin with drinks. Do we need to order anything?"

"No, you are well supplied in that department; I couldn't see anything lacking."

"Good; we'll engage in somewhat casual conversation until about 8:00, when we'll go to the dining room for dinner. Then I'd like to direct the conversation to specifics. First, we'll discuss how we will ban the **Cry Justice** meetings, and if we can do that, most of our problems will be solved. The second issue will be how to deal with the priests who disagree with us. What do you think?"

"Sounds like a plan. Are you prepared to guide the discussion with any proposals of your own?

"I have my own ideas, of course, but I want this to look as though it is coming from the group. That way we can be confident of their motives. But with my understanding of your inclination in these matters and your grasp of the possibilities, each of us can direct the conversation to a proper course of action, if we see the need. You have perfected the knack to be subtle, right?"

Will understood that as an order, not a question. "Arch... Bob, I am happy to do whatever it is you need."

"It's settled then. Now we have to leave for St. John's. The superintendent is meeting with the school principals. It won't be over until after lunch. I hope they serve something besides chicken salad sandwiches this time! It's a ten minute ride; we can continue talking in the car."

As Will stood up he again thanked the archbishop for his courage, and walked to his office with a heightened appreciation and gratification for his own role in this cherished cause. Grabbing the car keys, he ran to meet the archbishop in the garage.

Will was not part of the meeting, but was always invited to visit with the students in their classrooms; today he chose to remain in the car. He was so lost in his imaginings of what was to come, he was surprised when the archbishop was getting back into the car.

"I'm even more convinced we can waste no more time bringing the Church back to discipline."

"What happened?"

"Nothing overt. But the new one in the office, Sister Sharon, the assistant superintendent, asked about speakers from **Cry Justice**. She wanted to know if the office should give out a list of speakers to the principals for their home-school association meetings."

"I trust you put her in her place."

"I've learned to play a game when it comes to the schools office. I keep silent and study the notebook I always take with me. The superintendent knows that when I do not offer an opinion, I am not pleased. When I am unhappy, Sister Louise knows that I will curtail her authority; she wants control over decisions, such as selecting Religion texts. So, she chooses what she is willing to fight about. Sharon's question was not worth it. I wish you could have witnessed her response of 'That won't be necessary, Sister.' But I know Sister Louise; I have no doubt that she'll take Sharon aside later and they'll find a way to do it."

"Such a lack of respect, Archbishop. I mean, Bob."

"I know, Will. It's all part of that women's movement stuff. But they have to know, that even if it is working in the world, it's not going to change the Church." They shared a moment of such glee Will screeched the car to a halt as the light turned red.

"Good thing we're almost home, Will. You're losing your concentration." Again they laughed.

After parking the car in the garage, Will hurried to his office. He reviewed his meeting with the archbishop and prayed a quick prayer of gratitude for being in this place at this point in time. With a huge red circle he marked next Tuesday on his calendar; the "Day of Deliverance," he said aloud as he added an exclamation point inside the circle.

A request for a hospital visit was on his desk when he returned. He pushed it aside. Expectations for Tuesday so enticed and stimulated him that he abandoned himself to the pleasure of anticipation. Surges of gratification fought to overcome moments of panic. *Be prepared; be over-prepared, if necessary,* he told himself. *We must succeed. Nothing is to be overlooked.*

He set up a computer file to maintain his list of issues and resolutions he hoped to secure. He named and saved his file, Redeemers.

I know the Archbishop's most fervent desire is to suppress **Cry Justice***. Terminate it; the protests will end. Peace and power will reign again; obedience and the assurance of salvation will replace the questioning and the controversies endured by the faithful for years. If there is even a remote possibility that the archbishop will weaken, I must be ready to make the hard decisions, maybe extreme and daring decisions. But I will not fail, O God; I promise.* He clutched at the soft padded arms of his chair as a rush of righteous satisfaction rippled through his body.

Of course, I have no intentions of sharing my Plan B with the archbishop; he might consider it excessive, but when all is over, he will understand that times like these demand valiant men who are willing to sacrifice themselves for the cause. He added some scenarios to his *Redeemers* file, and glanced at his watch. *I can't believe it's almost 5:00; I didn't even get hungry today. O God, may the remaining hours and days until Tuesday go by as quickly. I am your obedient servant.*

Chapter 5

"Joyful praises to our God!" The fervent happy sound of songs and clapping hands brought smiles to Sisters Mary Frances and Jennifer as they walked through the hall.

"Such energy at 10:30 in the morning. Joan was going to join their prayer service," said Jennifer. "I'll bet she is on cloud nine."

"Don't you just love their name, the *Baptist Women of Bright Promise*? Such a great attitude! I hope some of it rubs off on me. Charlie Fletcher called me last night; he has a feeling that yesterday's article on the **Cry Justice** meeting is prompting a response from my brother. I'm so worried that Bob is going to do something extreme."

"If Charlie thinks something is up, it is. I never met a man with such a developed intuitive sense."

"That's one of the reasons all the women relate so well to him. I asked him to come for lunch today; I knew you and Joan would be OK with that."

"I'm glad. Ever since he made that retreat last year, he's been a different man. It's a pleasure to talk with a priest who is so committed to the gospel."

"I know. You don't have to play any games with him. I think this place is a refuge for him; here he can express his views on all the issues and know he is safe. If the church is ever going to change, some of the reasons will be priests like Charlie."

"Here comes Joan. Look at her; she's almost skipping with joy."

"Joan, I've invited Charlie Fletcher for lunch."

"That's great. I bet his intuition is telling him something important about your brother. Did you hear us singing? Aren't they great?"

"Wonderful. You will get your work done in half the time this morning. I'll see you both at lunch."

As Fran walked toward her office, Jennifer pulled Joan into a conference room. "I am so worried about her. Whatever Charlie is going to tell us will break her heart, I know."

"We survived Sacred Heart together; we'll do it again, no matter what. God always saves us. Just think, if we had not come here to Sophia's Blessings, and Charlie had not made his retreat here and had that wonderful dream, he wouldn't be coming here today for lunch. Besides, I told Fran yesterday that one day her brother will become the good person he was years ago. We may have a lot to go through before that happens, but I believe that God has not given up on him."

"You are so positive, O Woman of Bright Promise! I just hope you're right."

At 12:15 Charlie knocked on Fran's open door. "I hear that lunch is being served at 12:30."

"Charlie, come in." The light in her eyes and the quickness of her smile hid the uneasiness she had struggled with all morning.

Charlie was 57, the same age as her brother, about the same height, but in much better physical shape. His liquid blue eyes and his gray wavy hair were the perfect combination for his gentle yet powerful smile; the years had not compromised his strong jaw and made his handsomeness quite compelling.

He kissed her cheek. "Fran, thanks for this invite. I was hoping you would have time today. How I need the peace of this place."

"You know you can come anytime."

"Yes, I do, but I can't always see you. Did you tell the other two?"

"Of course. They can't wait to see you. I'm sure they are in the staff dining room right now."

Singing and clapping erupted the quiet. "Who is here?"

"That's the Baptist Women of Bright Promise. And that joyful noise is coming from the retreatants' dining room; they sing their grace before meals; and after, too. The kitchen staff loves it when they are here. They always sing a thank you to them at the end of the meal. Don't worry, the staff dining room is down the hall; we'll have our privacy."

"They have given themselves a great name. All of you are women of bright promise, too. I hope you know that."

"I try to believe it, Charlie. But there are days when I tell God that we could use more help."

"And what does She say?"

Fran gave him a good-natured push into the dining room.

"Hi, Jen; Joan. I was just telling Fran that you all are women of bright promise."

"We agree," said Jennifer. "Here, Charlie, sit. We're so glad you're here."

Charlie surveyed the round table covered with a pale blue tablecloth; in the center was a small glass vase with yellow, white, and lavender silk flowers. Near the flowers he saw his favorite bread, marble rye in a basket with wheat, pumpernickel and also white rolls. A platter of sliced turkey, roast beef, and ham was next to a plate of tomatoes on lettuce; a bowl of coleslaw, a small tray of raw carrots, cucumbers, celery sticks and no potato chips; the little things they remember—when he was there for the retreat he mentioned how he avoided those salty temptations. He eyed the dessert over on a side table; somehow he knew it would be another favorite, Dutch apple pie. "Why don't you say grace?" Charlie bowed to Fran.

She extended her hands to him and Jen and when their circle was complete, she began: "O God, we remember how you changed ordinary bread and wine into your body and blood. Bless this food and bless us; change us so that we may be bread for others, broken and shared with all who seek truth and love. Give us wisdom so that we may have courage to proclaim your goodness. Amen."

"I liked that, Fran. I mean, to ask for the courage to proclaim God's goodness. Too many prefer a God who punishes because that is how they define justice." He noticed their wide smiles. "Preaching to the choir, I know. You do inspire me." He took two slices of the marble rye bread on which he spread a light layer of mayonnaise. Some turkey and ham, a generous leaf of lettuce and two tomato slices; "A work of art, isn't it?" he said.

Fran smiled but her struggles of the morning kept her focused on Charlie's comment. "I'm sure you agree, Charlie, that some people in authority need the image of a punitive God because it keeps people in line, or so they hope. I believe that a loving God is more demanding, if we understood what unconditional love requires." Fran took the wheat bread and passed the basket to Jen. She moved the coleslaw closer to Charlie.

Jennifer was eager to get beyond the theology. "I think the God of unconditional love is what the **Cry Justice groups** see. Why do you think that message is lost on the leadership?"

Charlie glanced at Fran. "You know that Bob and I were quite good friends."

Fran nodded.

"I have not spoken to him for a few months, now. I have a sense that he knows I am not *in his fold,* so to speak."

"What makes you think that?"

"That's why I mentioned to you last evening that I think something is brewing."

Jennifer and Joan leaned into the table. Fran took a quick sip of her iced tea, the fingers of her right hand turning white as she tightened them around her glass.

"Yesterday morning Mike Lynch received a phone call; the rest of the day he was flying high. At supper he told me that next week he needs to switch his day off from Thursday to Tuesday. I figured he had been invited to a meeting with Bob. I'm still on good terms with Ed McShane; I think he now regrets all that happened at Sacred Heart."

Fran, Jen, and Joan looked at each other without a word.

"Anyway, I called him after supper. Poor Ed; he loved the church of the past, and I know he loves God with his whole heart. But he needs to do something that will make him a name in the diocese. He told me once that he felt so old, and he could not believe that God would be pleased with him for the little that he had done in his ministry. I tried to tell him all the good he's done, but it's true, he has not been recognized, and he wants to do something that will assure him a lasting memory. Something to talk about at his funeral is the way he put it."

"Oh," said Jennifer," I feel so bad for him. He is a good man; we had no problem with him, other than being a bit spineless."

"So," said Fran, "what did he tell you."

"There is a dinner at Bob's on Tuesday; I'm sure we all know who will be there. I started to worry when Ed told me that Will Owens was making the calls. I know the loyalty game that Will plays. I'm afraid that he is gaining control over Bob."

Fran's glass shattered as it hit the floor. Tea and ice cubes spilled over the table and onto the floor.

"Oh, Fran, I am so sorry. I should not have been so blunt."

"It's OK; I have had the very same worry." She mopped up the spill with her napkin. "Is there anything I can do? Besides pray?"

"I got Ed to promise me that he will tell me what goes on next week. Ed is their weakest link; as much as he loved the Church of old, he loves God more. He is not a blind follower. Plus, I think he is suspicious of Will. Come on, now, let's finish this delightful lunch. I'm looking at that apple pie."

Charlie placed his hand on Fran's and gave it a tender squeeze. "Try not to worry. You know that God will bring good out of this."

Fran forced herself to nod in agreement; she believed that he was right, but when it came to her brother she found it difficult, if not impossible, to stop worrying.

Chapter 6

Awake at 6:00 Will paced his bedroom floor. When the sun first peeked above the horizon, he stretched his arms toward his window, and roared, "Deliverance Day. At last!" He dropped to his knees. "O God, this is our day. Be with us and deliver us from those who would destroy your church."

When he arrived at his office he struggled to contain his elation. He swung open his door and gazed at his exquisite wall clock, its bold black Roman numerals, its gold hands pointing to 9:00. *Ten hours and counting.* Tremors of exuberance made it difficult to concentrate on anything but the evening dinner. He noticed the note he had shoved aside yesterday and decided to spend an hour making that visit. Before returning to the office he decided to stop for a bite to eat; he and Bob had told Annie not to worry about getting lunch for them, but to concentrate on preparing the dinner. Back in his office he checked his watch several times each hour and grumbled at the slow march of time.

At 5:00 he strolled into the kitchen to offer Annie his help. She fought the urge to hoot at the implication that she needed or even desired any help, *especially yours,* she thought. She gritted a smile as she shoved him out of her way. *Besides, you make me nervous. There is something I dislike about you, Father Will. O God, forgive me.* With a quick muffled gasp, she blessed herself twice.

Walking into the dining room he nodded his approval: the elegant gold-rimmed china, the gleaming silverware and the sparkling crystal goblets, the oblong table covered with a subtle cream linen tablecloth. He imagined how the guests would gloat over his good fortune. A horizontal centerpiece of yellow and white roses had been placed between two slender yellow candles. A bit *ostentatious, but fitting the occasion,* he thought as he drank in the display and got lost in his vision of what would take place around this table. He checked his watch again—5:30; he tapped it twice—still 5:30.

He returned to his office, sprinted around his desk and plopped into his chair. Drumming his sweating fingers on the edge of his desk he inhaled several fast quick breaths. Deciding to review his notes again his eyes flashed back and forth over his computer screen. His mind invented varied scenarios. He drank in the picture of the archbishop smiling at him as they accomplished their desired objectives. His eyes glazed with triumph as his heart pounded with a fickle rhythm. Gulping a mouthful of air, he held his breath, and exhaled. He repeated this procedure until his heartbeat relaxed into a regular cadence.

The doorbell jerked him back to reality. *The first honored guest is here;* he switched off his computer. Sliding along the shiny floor he skidded into the wall. *Get a grip, Coordinator of Redemption.* He opened the door to welcome Father Jim Miller. "The first one called is also the first to arrive."

Intent on his hopes for the evening, Father Jim brushed aside his annoyance with Will's predictable charm. "I'm looking forward to talking with Bob."

Will noticed a blue Avalon pulling into the driveway; tasting his eagerness he ushered Father Jim into the parlor, hurried back to the door and opened it just as Fathers Mike Lynch and Mark West arrived together. With a gripping handshake he drew them inside. His peripheral vision revealed four more cars turning into the driveway. *"All have arrived."*

He flashed a quick glance at the clock; how perfect that it was 7:25. Leaving the door open he pointed Mike and Mark towards the parlor. He turned to greet Ed, Joe, Nick, and Pete and led them to join the others. Each one had a drink in his hand when Archbishop Garrote entered the room carrying his.

"Good evening, and welcome," he proclaimed lifting his glass into the air. Every priest returned the gesture with a vigorous "Good evening, Archbishop!"

"As you were!" said Archbishop Garrote. "Talk, talk! Soon we'll go into dinner. Annie has outdone herself; I know you will enjoy yourselves this evening."

He turned to Father Jim Matthews who was closest to him and said, "Jim, tell me, how are you? You seem tired."

"That I am, Bob. I can't tell you how much this means to me, to be invited here to talk about how to save our people. Our church is splitting into pieces, Bob. Nothing's sacred anymore; everything is questioned. And I used to believe that I could depend on the nuns to keep everyone in line, but now, they're running around after every liberal cause they find. They abandoned the classrooms, they dress like every other woman out there, and wonder why they're not getting vocations like they used to."

"So, Jim, you feel strongly that we need to find a way to stop the conflicts, the agitation, and ...."

"Absolutely! Sorry, Bob, for not letting you finish, but I ask you, where are the rules, the discipline that kept us together? It's disappearing day by day."

The archbishop nodded as he continued to listen to Jim. At the same time his ears were picking up words and phrases from other conversations. He was overjoyed as he heard the words curtail, stop, restrict, limit, and obey floating around him.

At 8:00 a tinkling bell hushed their animated discussions. "That's dinner!" said the archbishop. He turned and walked towards the dining room; the seven guests followed Father Will, standing tall and smiling, leading the way. With the archbishop at the head, Father Will showed Jim his seat to the right with Nick across from him; next to Jim he placed Ed with Pete next to Nick. Joe came next, facing Mike. And last was Mark, with Will facing him. *Placing myself at the bottom of the table will impress everybody here, especially the archbishop,* he thought. *Besides, it is necessary that Bob looks like he is the one in charge.*

The archbishop offered a blessing and before they began to pass the food, he lifted his wine glass filled to the brim and said, "I am grateful for your presence here this evening." He clinked his glass with Jim's, all the priests did the same across the table and to the one on their left and the one on the right. The archbishop picked up the steak platter, made his choice and handed the platter to Jim. Within minutes all the food had been passed around the table; no one took time to admire the feast of steak, garlic mashed potatoes, gravy, and asparagus. Forks and knives in hand, and as if the archbishop had given the nod, each one carved his steak first.

Annie had been standing in the doorway, and now asked if anyone wished coffee at this time; in unison they all said, "Later." Annie turned and walked back to the kitchen; she hesitated just for a moment to let the swinging door touch the palm of her hand, stretched out behind her With a soft sigh, she wilted into her chair at the kitchen table to eat her own dinner.

The archbishop finished chewing his second bite of steak, took a sip of wine, and spoke. "I've called you here this evening because I see in each of you unwavering loyalty to our faith, impressive strength of character, and unquestioning obedience to the Holy Father." His eyes skimmed the table and rested on Will. "I think we all agree that our church is in a crisis. I encourage you tonight to share your thoughts on how we can save our people from the evil that has found its way into our church. Please, feel free to speak your minds. I am here to listen." Turning his eyes first toward Jim Miller he focused his cool determined eyes on each priest, one at a time, around his table.

Self-righteous excitement filled the air as the guests stole glances at each other. Lips were licked and throats were cleared. Father Jim grunted, "I'll begin. I was saying earlier, there are no rules or order anymore. I feel sorry for the people who are trying to live the values they grew up with. But various groups trying to change things are constantly bombarding them. It runs the gamut from those who think kneeling is out of fashion these days to inclusive language and women's ordination, just to name a few."

"You are so right!" Everyone's eyes shot towards Mike at the end of the table. "When I became a priest I saw myself leading people to God. But now I find myself distressed over getting them to even listen to me and come to church on Sunday." He looked first at Joe sitting across from him; it was no secret that Joe's ardent desire was to be named a bishop.

"At my Mass every Sunday," said Joe, "I say, 'Will the real Catholics please stand up?'"

"That's a good one!" said Mike leading the applause. Heads nodded in agreement.

"There's no respect for the priesthood," said Mark. "When I was growing up, that's what encouraged my vocation. I saw how important the priest was; whenever we had a question about sin, he was the one we went to. Now, they listen to anyone who tells them what they want to hear. There's a Sister Rose Marie in our parish; she's always having get-togethers at her apartment, notice, I didn't say convent, and the people just flock to her because she allows them to question everything in the church today. They claim they are gathering for prayer, but I see that as just an excuse to cover up all the underhanded conversations that are taking place there. But I don't know how to stop her; too many people love her."

Bitter memories hammered Will; just like Fran, and Joan and Jennifer. He struggled to maintain his façade of peace. *You will have your reward,* he told himself; *for now, center all your attention on this night.*

"And," said Pete, "that's why we can't get them to return; people like Rose Marie have held out to them the possibilities for change and even urge them to work for those changes. And when they're frustrated because priests like myself refuse to go along with their liberal ideas, they either stop coming to church or join others who think like they do."

"And where do they find those like-minded others?" asked the archbishop.

What a clever question, thought Will. He marveled at the archbishop's shrewdness in directing the conversation.

Without hesitation, they shouted their answer in unison: "**Cry Justice**."

Will was overcome by zeal. Screaming he leaped from his seat. "What shall we do about that?" His cheeks were flushed with glee, his eyes flashing with commitment.

The archbishop dropped his fork. Every head turned to Will; he cringed at all their eyes fixed on him.

He doubled over and grabbed his wine glass. Rising up to his full height, he said, "See, what you have done already, so quickly. You have pulled my deepest yearnings right out of my soul!"

The silence was brief; Will fought to keep his smile on his face and his hand from shaking. The lights flickered. "A sign," said the archbishop. They all joined in a polite laugh.

Will sat down, his smile still pasted on his face. He bashed himself for stepping out of the quiet supporting role he had designed for himself. His eyes met those of the archbishop. He looked away. *Now he thinks I've gone overboard. How could I have been so stupid? What if I've ruined it all?*

The archbishop cleared his throat. He lifted his glass. "Let's drink to that!" As the glasses were raised, their eyes met again. *Is that a look of forgiveness,* thought Will. *O God, I feel like a child. I have to recover; this cannot be the end. It was just a moment; they will soon forget. They must. They must.*

Taking another moment of solemn eye contact with each priest, the archbishop said in a low, steady voice, "You all seem to agree that **Cry Justice** is a problem."

"We do!" The shout rocked the room.

"Well, while Annie is cleaning off the table and bringing in the dessert— hope you all like apple pie!—think about what we could do together. Let me see your enthusiasm."

That last sentence gave Will the final clue he craved. *All is well,* he convinced himself. *He's going to work from the enthusiasm angle, and soon my moment will be lost in their eagerness to settle their own scores. But be careful,* he reminded himself. *Do not get carried away again.*

The archbishop rang a small silver bell. As Annie entered the dining room, the conversation, as if on cue, turned to idle topics and jokes. The archbishop thanked her for the wonderful meal, and the others applauded adding more words of praise. Annie bowed with her usual gracious smile, placed their dirty dishes on her cart, and wheeled it out to the kitchen hoping no one noticed how fast she was walking.

She returned with two large apple pies. Amid more applause, she was frightened by the emptiness overwhelming her. None of their eyes met hers as she poured each cup of coffee; she forced herself to control the coffee pot in her unsteady hands and tried to dismiss the cold tremors in her heart. Back inside her kitchen she held onto a chair. She wheezed as she glanced at the knotted bulging veins in her hands, and took two slow deep breaths. She filled the dishwasher and wiped the kitchen counters. *What's wrong with me,* she muttered to herself. *These are the leaders of my church; why do I feel as if I am losing someone I love?*

How ridiculous she said to herself as she remembered how the tone in the room changed when she came in. She had not even tried to listen, but how could they think she had missed the **Cry Justice** shout. She had not been to a **Cry Justice** gathering, but she was on their mailing list. When she read their newsletter, she felt such warmth and goodness. *Isn't that how Jesus would want the church to be?* she asked herself.

She slumped down at the table in the middle of the kitchen to pray and wait until they were finished. She knew all the priests by name that were seated around that table; she didn't have any particular opinions about any of them; except she said to herself, *I've never been fond of Father Will; ever since he came to work here, I've had my suspicions about him. Try as hard as I can, even in my prayers, I just can't find a reason to like him. And the archbishop; there was a time when he seemed to be the ideal priest; now he's always so sad and so upset. I think he misses his sister, but he'll never admit that. I hope that someday he won't regret all this lost time.*

About a half hour later she heard the bell again, and the Archbishop's "We're finished in here, Annie. Thank you again. Feel free to leave as soon as you are through with all your chores. Good night, now."

"Good night, Archbishop," said Annie. She lifted the hem of her apron and wiped away a tear that made its lone escape down her cheek.

The archbishop invited everyone into the parlor for more drinks and conversation. An hour later Annie heard their laughter as she closed the back door on her way out. She scolded herself for thinking that Father Will's laughter sounded so appalling. "Forgive me, God," she said half out loud. A warm embrace engulfed her; she relaxed for a moment in its comfort but was puzzled by the accompanying foreboding.

Amid the laughter in the parlor a plan was emerging. All agreed that getting the rebels together called for an ingenious set up. Father Joe spoke what was on everyone's mind. "How can we get everyone to attend something sponsored by the Archdiocese?"

"How about a huge assembly?" said Father Mark.

"But they won't come," said Father Jim.

"They will if we appeal to their sense of justice!" said Father Will. He chided himself for the sarcasm he knew was in that statement but hoped it passed unnoticed by everyone else.

Father Ed had not been part of the shout, though he conceded **Cry Justice** made him uneasy. He supported the archbishop because he had always supported his superiors. The undertone of Will's comment revived his qualms about his motives. "And what do you suggest?" he asked.

He had shifted his body and looked Will in the eye. The question hung in the air. *That's the same chilling question he asked when I told him that Fran and her two cohorts were taking over the parish. I must choose my words with care now. I need him to go along with this.* Will met the eye contact test; he smiled more that he should have as he said, "I am here to listen more than suggest. It seems that we agree on the need for everyone to come together. My humble question, Ed, is 'what would stir their hearts to hope that we are willing to listen to them?'"

"I think I have that answer," said Father Joe. "The role of leadership calls us to reach out to those who have lost their way. If we label it something like A Call for Reconciliation and Possibilities, the reconciliation word will tell them we want to heal our differences, and possibilities will suggest that they can talk about what they hope will come to pass."

At this the archbishop was not able to contain his satisfaction. "What a splendid title! I like it. How does that sound to everyone?"

Affirmations of "Great idea!" and "Excellent!" and "God bless the Church!" rumbled around the room.

Will glanced at Ed who had turned his attention back to the archbishop; he breathed a silent *thank you. I will have to watch him closer than I expected; I had hoped he would be more agreeable. I'll have to work much harder to win him over.*

Now the archbishop abandoned his reserve and immersed himself in details. "Let's choose a date, a time, a place, speakers; let's have a fabulous dinner and arrange media attention; let's make a list of those we'll be inviting. "Oh, hell! We know who we're going to invite!" The room exploded in laughter. He waved his hand toward Will. "My exceptionally capable assistant has compiled a directory of **Cry Justice** members; I would be willing to bet he has not missed a name!"

Exceptionally capable assistant! Will's heart beat so fast had to gulp a quick breath to keep from fainting. Bowing his head to the archbishop he stole a glance at Mike Lynch. *Eat your heart out, Mike.*

With their energies at optimum levels, they got to work. No one noticed the time until they were getting ready to leave; Father Jim pointed to the clock. "I haven't been awake and working past midnight since I was a very young priest."

Father Will made copious notes, though he knew it was to convince them he cared what they said. However, he relished a moment of supreme satisfaction. His mind was spinning in a delicious turmoil at the realization they had chosen him to be the coordinator of the event; he framed his appreciation in self-effacing words to each of them as they left. He knew that even if he got a mere two hours of sleep that night, he would have an endless power supply to begin work first thing in the morning.

After everyone left, he and the archbishop shared one more drink. Each was lost in his own gripping thoughts as they raised their glasses one more time. Each one smiled, not so much at the other, but each to himself as they said goodnight.

Chapter 7

Will tossed and turned all night, his own snoring waking him up four times dazed from muddled dreams. Each time he woke up he found the blue sheet and white thermal blanket twisted around him; he hated that sheet set, not because blue wasn't his favorite color but because his mother had purchased it. He refused to consider it was her way of expressing her love for him; he imagined her ambitions for his life to be opposite his own.

He squinted at the large white numbers on his digital alarm clock. He yawned, counted the hours till morning, and snickered. *Coordinator of Redemption,* he chanted over and over. He conceded that he would use a more modest title in public, but in his bed this night his body squirmed with the pleasure of power.

At 4:20 he could no longer remain in bed. He thanked God for the zealous energy that inflated his whole being as he bounded out of bed. By 5:00 he had showered and dressed. Going into the kitchen he was annoyed at the slow steady dripping of the coffee. Swinging open the refrigerator door, he stared at the eggs, then at the orange juice. Even the thought of his favorite, cinnamon swirl toast, did not tempt his taste buds this morning. He tapped his foot and his fingers watching the coffee's last drip. Grabbing his mug of black coffee, he walked back to his small living room and settled down at his computer.

He looked at his watch; 5:15. *By 6:45 I could have a draft of the invitation designed and sent to my office computer, and still have time to walk over to the cathedral to say the 7:00 Mass.* He knew what he wanted; he had seen it three times during his disturbed sleep. Using a bold Gothic font he typed, You are invited to A Call for Reconciliation and Possibilities. He chose the color green; *for hope,* he whispered to himself with a grin.

At 6:30 he studied his work. His pleased-with-himself smile lit up his entire face. The green letters and a blue border on white were striking. Inside was all the relevant information. The group had decided on the first Saturday of

November, the 9th, three weeks and four days away. The afternoon would begin with registration at 1:00. *The first thing I'll do when I get to my office this morning is contact the events coordinator at the Cloister Royale.* Choosing the most imposing hotel in the city made such perfect sense to him. He could picture the registration taking place outside the grand ballroom. The ballroom itself would have the perfect atmosphere with its round tables suggesting the sharing of ideas; he laughed out loud at that thought.

A stage would be set up for the keynote presentation at 2:00 by the archbishop followed by a question and answer period with a panel. At 5:00 a cocktail hour would take place in the area outside the ballroom. By 6:00 the ballroom would be set up for dinner; he could visualize on the stage the head table with the archbishop and the chosen guests. *Chosen by me, of course,* he muttered. *I know who will be there and where they will be seated.*

He wondered if Evelyn Lane would agree to design the art work; she was a parishioner at Sacred Heart and he hoped she did not remember the gossip about him; no name had ever surfaced during that whole mess, not even when he and Father Ed had that awful final discussion. He was certain she did not have a clue about the wild desires he fought off in her presence. She had come to his farewell party but he was too angry that day to pick up any hints about how she felt that he was leaving. Now he fantasized how she would react when seeing him again. *Maybe this will be the way for us to do something great together for God,* he mused. *What miracles we could work together, my dear Evelyn, and how much pleasure I would have teaching you how to give yourself to God's delight.*

He was sure she could design something for the invitation cover that would symbolize both the reconciliation aspect and the idea of future possibilities. *A trap, to be sure. This looks quite good, I must say.* With one click he sent it to his office computer, stood up, stretched, laughed aloud, and headed for Mass.

Five people were present for Mass; two men, one always in a business suit, the other much younger one always reminded Will of someone he once knew. He seemed to carry a heavy burden; Will made a mental note to get to know him better over the next few weeks. People with burdens often shared their problems with Will, and he found ways to use them to advance his own agenda. They were in his debt forever, convinced he was responsible for their peace of mind.

Three women, one of them Annie, and two other professionals were there every morning, also. When he first arrived here three years ago, this Mass was filled with many older women and men. He had often counted more than thirty people at this early Mass. The numbers began dwindling about a year ago. Will told himself they switched to the 8:30 Mass because they wanted to sleep in. He wondered if Annie knew any of them. *Why should I care, anyway, what Mass they attend*, he thought as he looked out on this small gathering. *The time will come when they will revere the Coordinator of Redemption. And it will come soon. Then they will be eager to be at my Mass.*

He spoke a few well-chosen but mundane sentences for his homily. How he wished he could tell them about their coming redemption.

After Mass he hurried to hang up his vestments, his eyes darting towards the hall when he heard footsteps. *Oh, please, don't let it be someone who wants to talk this morning.* The footsteps passed by the door. *Thank goodness.*

When he got to his office, he arranged a 2:30 meeting with Ms. Barbara Collins, the events coordinator at the Cloister Royale. He smiled to himself as he began to call Evelyn; there was no need to look up her number; he had tucked it away years ago, hoping for the day he would need it. Her company was called **Designs for You**. His mind swirled with perverted implications and his fingers tingled as he heard the ring on the other end of the line.

"**Designs for You**; how can we serve you today?"

"Is this Ms. Evelyn Lane?"

"No. I'm Alicia, her administrative assistant."

"May I speak to Evelyn?"

"She's with a client right now; if you leave your name and number, she will get back to you."

"This is Father Will Owens at the Cathedral; I would like to discuss a project with Evelyn, at her earliest convenience."

"Of course, Father; I'll give her the message."

"Do you think she will call me today; it's very important that I talk with her today. This morning, if possible."

"I'll tell her."

Will looked at the clock; it was 9:30. *Her business must be growing,* he thought. *She used to answer the phone herself. I hope she's not too busy to take care of me.*

He reviewed his draft of the invitation. After experimenting with several fonts, he decided he liked the Gothic font he had first chosen. He printed a hard copy and glanced at the clock; it had been an hour since he had called Evelyn. *I wonder why she still hasn't called me? What if she doesn't want to see me?*

At 11:00 he stared at his phone. *Why, Evelyn? What did I ever do to you? And to think I had great hopes for you, for us.*

At 11:28 his phone rang.

"Father Owens; it's Evelyn."

"Oh, I thought that maybe you had forgotten about me."

"Never, Father; I just had a demanding client, and I still believe in making the customer happy."

I hope that goes for me, thought Will. "We, that is, I have been chosen to coordinate a big event we are holding in the Archdiocese, and I have drafted an invitation I'd like to share with you. When could we meet?"

"Why don't I drop by on my way to meet my next client; I have to go by the Cathedral anyway, so it won't be a problem. How about 12.30, or is that your lunch time?"

"That would be fine. Would you like to have lunch here?"

"Thank you, Father, but I keep energy bars in my car for these busy days. I'll see you soon, then."

Will paid no attention to anything until Betty called him at 12:28 to say that his 12:30 appointment had arrived.

"Thank you, Betty. Send her in." When Will had first met Evelyn, five years ago, she had just started her own design company. Single, 24 years old, with silky blonde hair and ocean blue eyes, she looked like a master artist had designed her. Will had enjoyed the shudder of excitement that swelled within him that day. Now he felt the wetness on his hands and the throbbing in his chest. He cleared his throat as he looked up when she tapped on his open door.

"Come in, Evelyn. How good to see you again." He surrendered to the pleasure she stimulated within him. As she walked toward his desk and seated herself in the chair facing him, his eyes scanned her from top to bottom.

Setting her briefcase on the floor, she smiled; a slight smile. He had hoped for more. "Father Owens, I hope I can help you."

"I'm sure you can. And, please call me Will."

She nodded; he had hoped again for more. "It's not a big project this time, but I remember the stewardship campaign you did for us at Sacred Heart. That was such a fantastic job."

"Thank you, Father Will."

Without taking his eyes off her, he reached for his printed copy. Would she be impressed with what he had done, or would she change everything? Why did he all of sudden feel so inadequate? He slid his design across the desk. Her hand was pulling it closer to her. His fingers pulsed with the urge to touch her.

He jerked his hand back to the edge of his desk. She picked up the printed invitation.

He scrutinized her face as she studied his design. He became aware of irritation churning within him.

She looked up; he stared into her eyes. A momentary dizziness spun within him as he was sinking into their watery depths.

"This is quite good, Father. It won't take me long to get this ready for your final approval."

"What? I mean, really? Thank you. Do you really think it's good?"

"Yes, Father, it's fine. I'll have a proof ready for you tomorrow." She put it in a folder, scribbled a few notes, and placed it in her briefcase. She stood, reached out her hand. "Have a good day, Father. I'll be in touch." He could feel the stickiness in his hand, the intense craving to pull her close. Her hand turned limp; he let go. Turning toward the door she walked out.

He looked at his watch. 12:45. It was all over in fifteen minutes. He stared at his hand, despising the gratification he had anticipated. Even her praise for his work taunted him; he was positive her words were a mere condescension. *She does not know that she is working for the Coordinator of Redemption. They will all know soon enough.* He sneered at all his imagined critics.

Turning back to his computer he printed another copy of the schedule for his meeting with Barbara Collins. *Maybe the events coordinator will recognize my importance.*

I better go for lunch, he thought, though he did not have an appetite anymore. He forced each footstep to the dining room. He strained to put on a pleasant face as he tried to dismiss the cloud that hung in his soul.

The archbishop was finishing his soup; holding his spoon in midair, he waved Will to his seat. "You're late. Will." Annie was standing watch at the kitchen door; she brought him a cup of her homemade beef barley soup.

"How was your morning, Will?"

"Couldn't have been better, Bob. The designer said she will have the invitation proof ready by tomorrow."

"Who is it? That one from Sacred Heart? She did something for us here at the cathedral when she first started her own company. What was her name? She did a good job, as I remember."

"Her name is Evelyn Lane." Just saying her name chilled him to the bone. He took his first sip of the soup. "Yes, she did an excellent job with our stewardship campaign at Sacred Heart, too. I'm sure we'll be happy with her work. This afternoon I'll be meeting with the events coordinator at the hotel."

"Well, it sounds as though you have everything well organized. Good job, Will."

Enjoying their roast beef sandwiches, they reviewed the previous evening. By dessert time, warm satisfaction had dissipated Will's dreariness. He smiled at Annie as she poured his coffee, and even praised her for her chocolate oatmeal cookies.

On her way back to her kitchen, Annie asked God to forgive her nasty thought.

At 2:15 Will parked in the hotel garage and headed for the hotel lobby. Not long ago he could feel the awesome respect inspired by the priest's collar and the black suit. These days the stares were sometimes awkward, and other times even worse. An angry surge bubbled up within him when a woman with a child pulled the little boy closer to her. Will managed a smile as he walked toward the concierge. He was directed to take the elevator to the mezzanine floor where the offices were located. "Ms. Collins' office is the first one on the right," she told him.

He hesitated for a moment outside her door; checked his briefcase for the invitation printout with its schedule, and knocked once on her door.

"Welcome to Cloister Royale, Father Owens." She stood and extended her soft slender hand.

A familiar exhilaration spread throughout his body. In an instant he swallowed the vision before him: long red hair tumbled over her shoulders framing her face in its radiance, one seductive curl begged his eyes to unbutton the black silk blouse that caressed her ivory skin; he reveled in the craving he felt as he fantasized tasting her supple, generous lips. Her coaxing green eyes hinted at promises that wiped out any lingering regret from the morning.

She motioned for him to sit in the chair in front of her desk as she pushed back her hair with the nonchalance of a child who shoves aside a priceless work of art. *She could not be that oblivious to her allure,* thought Will. He clenched his shaking right fist as he reached into his briefcase. He pressed it against the inside soft leather until his hand was steady; he pulled out the schedule and positioned it on the desk in front of him.

"Ms. Collins, on the phone I mentioned to you the date of November 9th and you said that was acceptable. Here I have a schedule of events for our day." He slid the paper across the desk.

"Please, call me Barbara." Her smile invited him to the delight and the agony of unfulfilled desires. As she scanned his work he allowed his eyes to roam over every inch of her. He returned to her eyes and caught his breath as she frowned. "Oh, Father, I owe you an apology. I misunderstood; I thought you were speaking about the evening of November 9th. We have another event taking place here until 4:00 that same day."

Such incompetence, he wanted to scream. Despair crashed in on him. He watched her hand sliding across the desk; he froze his where it was. He felt the honeyed warmth of her palm trickling over his hand. Her words penetrated the swirl in his head.

"Father, I have another idea. I can fix this for you." She removed her hand.

"What? What did you say?" Both his hands were on her desk; he realized he was standing and leaning into her.

She laughed. "Father, relax."

"What? Oh, of course." Embarrassment stung his face; he sank back into his chair.

"You are devoted to your cause, Father. But I have an idea of how we can do this."

"I'm sorry if I startled you. Yes, you are right; I am devoted to this cause." *She's playing with me, I know. And they wonder why men assault them. She enjoyed that. She will regret it if she doesn't make it up to me.* "How are you going to fix this?"

"We acquired another hotel several months ago, the old historic Covington Place, near the lake. It has a conference center, just renovated. No one has used it yet. I will arrange for all the events to take place there, except for the cocktail party and the dinner, which will be here. We'll have the cocktails at 6:00 rather than 5:00 and the dinner at 7:00. We will even provide a limousine for the archbishop and for you, and an escort so that all your guests will arrive in a line behind you, all at the same time. Picture this: all our lights along the driveway will be lit; we will add the spotlight from the top of the canopy. The ten-foot evergreen tree in front will have one thousand white twinkling lights, which will go on when your limo, followed by your parade of guests, approaches the intersection. When you arrive at the door, a band will play as you enter the lobby. You will be escorted to the area outside the ballroom where the cocktail party will be; the dinner will be in the ballroom as you planned. At 6:30 you alone will be permitted into the ballroom so you can make sure that everything is just the way you want. Then you can bring in the archbishop so that you and he can stand at the head table to welcome all your guests. What do you think?" She leaned forward.

His resentment melted away as her eyes magnetized him. "You may have my interest." He hoped his tone sounded detached; he waited for her response.

She reached out toward his hand again. He stiffened but did not pull away. "Father, I do apologize; it was my error. But, please let me do this for you. I will cut the price for the dinner in half, including the wine. And there will be no charge for the limousine." She patted his hand; a gentle tap twice. *She's treating me like a child. Just like my mother; they're all alike.*

With a brusque swish of his hand he said, "Maybe I should just look into another hotel. Since I will have to contact the designer now with these changes, I may as well change the location, too."

"Who is your designer, Father?"

"Ms. Lane."

"Evelyn? I know Evelyn; we went to school together. If you will allow me, I'll call her right now. I can give her all the information, and you won't have another thing to worry about. After all, you have much more important work to do, right? And again, this was my fault. Father, do I have your permission to do this for you?"

Her penetrating eyes destroyed the wall rising within him. He released a quick smile. "If you insist, Barbara."

"Stay here, just in case I need to clarify anything." She picked up her phone. He chewed the inside of his cheek as he watched her fingers touch the buttons,

He heard Evelyn's voice on the other end. Commotion stirred within him. He listened as Barbara confessed her mistake; he nodded as she corrected each part of the schedule. He strained to hear but failed to pick up Evelyn's response when Barbara said he was a dedicated man. When they shared a girlish giggle he fought to squash the irritation clawing its way into his throat. Barbara's voice became lost in his turmoil; a knock at her door as she finished her conversation prevented him from another embarrassing reaction.

"I will be with you in a minute," she said to the woman at the door. She stood, took Will's hand in hers as she pressed her left hand over his. His rigid fingers relaxed under her gentle pressure. "All is well; Evelyn will have a proof ready tomorrow. Father Will, thank you for allowing me to be of service to you. And you do forgive me, right?" Her eyes scorched his soul both melting his anger and stirring up his longing for approval.

"Of course, but it's God who forgives; I am only his humble instrument." He somehow felt justified reminding her of that. To himself, he promised, *You will never forget that the Coordinator of Redemption has entered your life.* He brushed by the woman at the door, unaware that her appearance had saved him from himself.

As he was getting off the elevator he collided with a familiar face. "Oh, excuse me, Father. I wasn't looking where I was going."

"I know you; you're at my Mass every morning."

"Right; I'm Adam Wetzer."

"You mean…didn't you attend Sacred Heart School?"

"Yes, how did you know?"

"I was there, too. You don't remember me?"

"No, Father; I am so sorry. If I knew then what I know now…"

"What do you mean?"

"I needed a friend back then, and I am so impressed now with your dedication to morning Mass…"

"Adam, if you ever need a friend now, I am here.

"I would like that very much. Maybe we can talk someday soon. But now, I'm running late."

"You work here?"

"Yes, I'm a waiter."

Chapter 8

Tuesday morning Father Will doodled on his note pad while visioning himself at the dinner on November 9th. Noticing that his scribbles looked like fireworks, passion burst throughout his body; he chose to enjoy it as fervor for his church while images of Evelyn and Barbara glided past him.

Evelyn's surprise thrilled him; she had said it was professional courtesy but he was sure it meant much more. She had given him credit for the design—to think that one hundred seventy six members of **Cry Justice** would see his name printed on the invitation. The printer completed the job on Friday and the invitations would be arriving in today's mail. The faces of those who had chosen him as coordinator flashed before him; how he delighted in their gushing approval complimenting him on the design and stunned by how much he had accomplished in so short a time.

The invitation requested a phone or fax RSVP by November 5th. Barbara had said he could give her a count for the dinner as late as the morning of November 9th. He wanted the satisfaction of counting his triumphs before that.

Jolts of excitement vibrated through him as he thought of how many more times he would have to talk with Barbara before the event. She had kept her word to make it up to him, and he enjoyed testing her with his extra requests. She had outdone herself trying to please him.

When he had asked about having a small gift for everyone as they signed in at the registration table, she had suggested an exclusive designed chocolate. When she showed him the sample the next day he was awed.

The **Cry Justice** symbol had been imprinted in all its vivid colors onto the top of a three inch chocolate square; each chocolate would be sealed in an elegant box with the symbol again imprinted on the box. A keepsake, she had said, after they have eaten the chocolate.

He found himself mesmerized gazing at a gold chalice with hands of men and women of all colors reaching towards it. Stimulated by the glowing expectation he saw in her face as she waited for his approval he had convinced himself that those enticing green eyes were filled with admiration for him.

She had promised him pens, folders, and notebooks for the afternoon session; imprinted napkins for the dinner. An ice sculpture for the cocktail party. His anger at that first meeting had slithered into the corner where so many other rages had settled.

He had no doubts that most **Cry Justice** members would be grateful for this opportunity to meet with the archbishop. Even those who had doubts about a positive outcome would feel obligated in conscience to show their commitment to the Church.

His more serious concern was the archbishop himself. Even though he expressed so much anger about **Cry Justice** gatherings, even though he had condemned his own sister for her part in them, Will knew the archbishop's weakness in confrontation. He so wanted to heal the division in the archdiocese that he might agree to endless meetings with these people, hoping he could convince them to change.

"I know they will never be satisfied," Will said aloud to himself. Paralyzing thoughts plagued him. *What if they persuade him to attend one of their meetings? I remember hearing how liberal he was in his early years. What if they arouse his old tendencies? I am sure Frances Mary would have more influence than I if his former ideals were ignited. But, that's not going to happen. I will make sure of that.*

He turned to his computer, and brought up Plan B. *The first thing to plan is the seating at the head table. I think I'll put Ed McShane next to the archbishop, and Frances Mary next to Ed. They should be seen in public this way. Frances Mary may not drink the wine because she always said it went straight to her head, so I will have to make sure a sleeping pill is in the water also. I'll put Charlie Fletcher on the other side of her, so either Ed or Charlie will have the embarrassment of dealing with her. Jen and Joan will be at opposite ends of the table so they will be too far away to protect her.*

He had requested Adam to be one of the servers. Talking with him yesterday Will could not have hoped for more. He laughed out loud every time he thought about how Charlie would go down in disgrace.

After ridding himself of Frances Mary along with Charlie, **Cry Justice** would crumble under the weight of the scandal. Everything would be set in motion at the dinner on November 9th.

Two green envelopes in the morning mail with *Invitation Inside* caught Dolores Weber's attention; then she noticed the archdiocesan return address. *One for Father Charlie and one for Father Mike. Must have something to do with that meeting Father Mike went to last week. Eye-catching envelope,* she said to herself with a raised eyebrow. She knew Father Charlie would tell her what it was about, but he was busy with the Foley's this morning. Their daughter must have run away again; that meant an hour and a half of consoling, supporting, and encouraging. He wouldn't have a chance to look through his mail until after lunch. *I can't wait that long,* she thought. She had Our Lady of Lourdes parish on speed dial.

"Lucy," she whispered; have you sorted today's mail yet? Did you see a green envelope from the archbishop?"

"Yes, Father Jim mumbled something like *good job* when he saw it. Do you think it has anything to do with **Cry Justice**?"

"I'm sure of it, but Father Charlie is in a meeting, so I won't hear about it until this afternoon. I'm going to call Jeanie and find out if Father Ed got one, too. I'll call you back." Sacred Heart parish was speed dial number 2.

"Jeanie, did Father Ed get a special envelope from the Archbishop?"

"He did, but when he saw it he looked more troubled than happy. But, listen to this. I called Sister Frances Mary. She and Sister Jennifer and Sister Joan each got one, too. It's an invitation to **Cry Justice** members to meet with the archbishop."

"That means I might have one when I get home this evening; you, too. And Lucy. I can't wait to tell her."

"You know that she and Annie, the archbishop's cook, are good friends. Annie is on the mailing list, but she hasn't come to the meetings because she's afraid the archbishop might ask her to give up her job."

"I didn't know that. What do you think has brought this about? Do you think the Archbishop has had a change of heart?"

"I feel awful saying this, but no, I don't. And I don't trust him, not since Father Will works there. It's just my intuition, but the gut feeling I got when I saw Father Ed's worried face was dread. I remember that same look three years ago when we had that mess here between Father Will and Sister Frances Mary. He didn't believe Father Will then, but he didn't have the guts to stand up for the Sisters either. It was all about jealousy; Father Will always has to be in charge."

"That gives me the chills. If I hear anything from Father Charlie this afternoon, I'll let you know. Right now, I have to call Lucy back."

Dolores was glad that her phone had been quiet this morning. She pressed speed dial 1 again. "Lucy, Jeanie found out from Sister Frances Mary that the green envelope is an invitation to all **Cry Justice** members to meet with the archbishop."

"So that means I will get one, too."

"Right. Jeanie also said that you are friends with Ann Bradley, the Archbishop's cook, and that she never came to the meetings because.."

"That's true, but she used her first name when she put herself on their mailing list. She goes by her middle name because she never liked Florence; too many people called her Florrie. And there's another Bradley in **Cry Justice**, no relation but they are friends, so she used that address. Isn't it a shame that she's so afraid?"

"Well, I can understand her fear of losing her job at her age. But I'm glad to hear she's able to get the mailings, anyway. Do you think she would give you any inside information about their meeting last week?"

"Never, and I would not ask her; Annie never tells tales, even when it would make her look important. But now that you mention the meeting, she did say something out of the ordinary last week, and I didn't give it much thought till now."

"Can you tell me? I mean, do you feel all right about sharing that? I don't want you to betray her friendship."

"Well, I'm telling you now because I'm upset. She said that her heart felt cold, sad like when you are afraid you're losing someone."

"What do you think that means?"

"I'm not sure, but it reminds me of the way I felt when my sister found out she had cancer. I remember feeling so desolate because I knew she was going to die, and I couldn't stop it."

"Oh, Lucy, I'm so sorry. Maybe you should give Annie a call about what we know so far, so she can be prepared."

"I will. Plus, I'm going to encourage her to attend this gathering with us. If there is some kind of death waiting for her or us, we will need to face it together."

Chapter 9

The dramatic red sunrise on November 5th brought Will to his knees. His arrogance in assuming this beauty as his personal confirmation of God's approval brought to his lips what he considered a prayer of gratitude.

This was the day he would make a final tally of those who would be attending A Call for Reconciliation and Possibilities. As of yesterday he had 95 responses; more than 54 percent had already committed themselves to his control. The gluttonous taste of power wiped out his appetite for breakfast. Frances Mary's response had arrived the first day; how he enjoyed snaring his most hated adversary. Also in her envelope were the responses from Jennifer and Joan. The crowning satisfaction of that day was seeing Charlie Fletcher's signature. *How appropriate,* he thought, *that they all arrived the same day.*

Still in his pajamas, his hair disheveled, he threw some cold water on his crusty eyes, checked himself as he passed the mirror and rushed downstairs to his computer. Waiting for Plan B to show up on his screen, he chewed his bottom lip in delicious anticipation. He knew it was up to him to slip the sleeping pills into Fran's drinks, but he would need help with other parts of his plan.

He roared out loud now, grateful that Adam's troubled story was the result of a distraught young boy's memory. I can just imagine Charlie Fletcher's face when I remind him that Adam was an altar boy at his first parish. He'll give me that dazed look of his knowing that I am aware of something and puzzled about why and how I'm going to use it. *"I know, I know,"* he grumbled to himself; *"Concentrate, Will. The dinner will be the beginning of the end, but the afternoon sessions will have to go well, so that everyone stays."*

I'm sure the archbishop will share with me today his entire presentation. I knew he would go along with my suggestion that he concentrate on his willingness to listen. How he gobbled up these opening lines of mine: My brothers and sisters in Christ. I have called you together to begin walking a path to reconciliation. I want to be a shepherd, but the sheep recognize the voice they know. I see this gathering as the first of as many as necessary until I hear your voice and you hear mine.

Sometimes I marvel at Christ's choice of words. Sheep; sheep are so stupid. I know that this will be the only meeting with these troublemaking wolves. And my sheep—my sheep will be led by my voice—the true shepherd who knows how to bring an end to these wolves. The archbishop will come to know I am more than his extremely capable assistant; I am his savior.

Will checked the clock; he could not afford to get so caught up in his excitement that he would be late for Mass. Not even the slightest imperfection in himself would be tolerated; after all, the Coordinator of Redemption had many duties to fulfill. Taking a moment to relish the treat his imagination gave him he saw the archbishop's face change from its sorrowful why to a glowing acknowledgement. After the deed was done, the archbishop would realize that the difficult decisions he had made justified his methods; losing his sister would be accepted as the ultimate sacrifice for God's glory.

Tomorrow I will call the panel members; I do not want to give them too much time to plan their agenda. Frances Mary, Joan, Jennifer, and Charlie must be there to protect the illusions of reconciliation and possibilities. I'll suggest to the archbishop that he appear on the panel, but before the questions begin he should put himself in the audience as a listener. That will endear him even more to the wolves—maybe even convince them to be sheep! Plus, it will lessen the chance that anyone will notice the friction between him and Frances Mary.

I'll need some of our chosen ones on the panel. Pete Rogers would come across as one of the obedient sheep, but his views are too well known and disliked, so he is not a good choice for the panel. Joe Moreno would not be able to downplay his aspirations to the bishopric. However, he would be a good plant in the audience; I will feed him some questions to get the discussion going. Ed Collins; now he's wimpy enough to be welcomed by the rebels, and it will be a good preview for the dinner episode. Mike Lynch just might work out; he'll compromise any convictions he has just to impress the bishop. Mark West would be another younger member and that would look good; and he does not like to alienate anyone, so he will be a good fit on the panel. Jim Miller is too well known for his strict adherence to Church law. Nick Perry is too tired to pretend that he cares what these people think; I hope he just keeps quiet.

Will checked the clock again—it was time to get dressed and head to the Cathedral. His thoughts poured themselves out, becoming more exacting and stirring the darkest places in his soul. *The afternoon has to live up to the theme of reconciliation and possibilities but my plan depends on getting everyone to the dinner.*

Joe could begin the panel discussion with the question of Catholic identity. I'm sure everyone has heard about his famous 'will the real Catholics please stand up' question. If he asks them to name our shared beliefs, that will raise the hope on both sides on the reconciliation idea.

I would be foolish to think that someone like Frances Mary would let that go on for very long. She would be the one to raise one of **Cry Justice's** *favorite issues, like women's ordination, resignation of bishops who are accused of protecting the pedophiles, or inclusive language. Any one of those could ruin the afternoon.*

In the sacristy as he robed for Mass, Will thought about Adam sitting out there as usual. He had to admit that he did not understand how Adam kept coming to daily Mass believing all he had told him about Charlie Fletcher. Trying to get his mind on his homily, other thoughts continued to distract him.

Maybe the bishop question could work to my advantage if Joe could be convinced to bring it up. After all, any resignation would further his aspirations. And if the others will allow this problem to be discussed without getting too emotional, this could be an area where we gain some agreement. Even I have no trouble giving up a few bishops for the sake of redeeming the whole church.

With an hour for the panel, those two topics should fill up the time. If the other issues are raised, the archbishop could suggest that they will be studied and discussed at the next gathering. He laughed at how believable that would sound.

He looked at his watch. *Time to lead the faithful in prayer.* He noticed a slight glimmer in Adam's eyes as he greeted the morning congregation.

Chapter 10

Will went straight to his office after Mass; then realized he was hungry. Annie always had her coffee and a piece of toast after Mass, so Will decided to join her. Tiptoeing into the kitchen, he watched as Annie finished pouring her cup of coffee and was reaching for the milk. When she looked up and saw his face she dropped the carton on the counter and milk began gushing its way towards her and onto the floor.

Will grabbed the carton and some paper towels. "Here, let me, Annie. Sorry if I frightened you. You look as if you've seen a ghost."

Annie tried to laugh and hoped he did not notice her shaking hands. "A ghost…Oh my, no, Father. I just didn't expect to see you."

"I was so busy this morning I forgot to eat. It's a wonderful day, Annie. Be happy." He poured himself a cup of coffee and grabbed Annie's toast." Do you mind, Annie? I just have so much to do today. I'll see you at lunch."

"By all means, take it," Annie said as Will left the kitchen. Taking a deep breath she realized she no longer wanted coffee or toast. Her trembling hand reached out to a chair, and she slid down to its cushion. Her body shuddered as she thought about what she had seen. *Not a ghost, Father, but you were enclosed in the darkest cloud I've ever seen—in fact, no cloud above the earth was ever so scary. O God, what does it mean? Please, God, do not abandon your people.* Tears began to fill her eyes. She tried to stand as she heard the archbishop.

"Good Morning, Annie. Are you all right?"

"I'm fine, thank you." *Thank God, the archbishop looks normal.*

"You'd tell me, if you weren't, wouldn't you? If you need to take the day off, we'll manage. I'm headed for Mass now, but think about what I said. I'll see you in about a half hour."

"I'm sure I'll be OK." She smiled. *He seems different today. Happier, but how could that be if he's listening to….*The image of Father Will exploded before her; she stifled a scream as she saw him being swallowed by the dark cloud; in an instant it was gone, but warm tears flowed down her face. Wiping them away she was stunned by her own cold face. *Maybe I am getting sick,* she tried to convince herself. A tender embrace hugged her. She turned to see who it was. No one was there, but warmth wrapped her entire body in comfort she had never felt before. *O God, thank you; I know you are here, I believe, I believe.* For a full ten minutes, she rested in the calm. A quiet energy filled her, and by the time the archbishop had returned from Mass he heard her humming.

"Oh, Annie, you look so much better; I'll see you at lunch."

Annie whispered a prayer as he walked to his office. *"God save you."*

Opening his door Bob walked to his window and gazed at the bright sunny scene; the trees were bare except for a few leaves still holding on; a gray squirrel stopped, gave him a quizzical stare, and went scurrying up the tree. The evergreens lining the edge of the lawn were standing straight and tall. He recalled a time, so distant now, when he and Frances Mary had walked along those evergreens—they were five feet tall then—sharing the excitement of the first meeting of **Cry Justice**. They were on the same wavelength then; *we were like those trees, Fran, full of life and potential.* He turned to his desk and found himself staring at the sculpture Fran had given him that day—designed and sculpted by her own hands. He remembered their intense connection as they discussed its symbolism—the circular church embracing the light, open windows and doors, the sign proclaiming that all are welcome here. *What happened, my dear sister? I want you to come back; I miss you.*

Dismissing the ache in the pit of his stomach he turned to answer the knock at his door. "Will, yes, come in. I know we have much to do today."

"Good morning, Archb...Bob. I thought you might want to share your speech with me. After all, you are giving the keynote address, so to speak." He hoped that did not sound as patronizing as it was.

"Of course. Those opening sentiments you gave me—about being a shepherd and this being the first gathering until I hear their voices and they hear mine—those are powerful words. I almost felt some guilt, though, because I know I am not interested in hearing what they will want to say."

"But, of course, you are; what you know about those people is what you have gathered from the newspaper; I think they are even more dangerous than reported. So you need to hear their own words and be convinced that they are committed to changing our church to meet their needs."

"I hadn't thought about that. You may be right."

Will nodded. *This is even easier than I thought it would be. But I can't let him be examining his conscience like that or he will start listening to them.* "You, we, must remember our desired end—to save the church. We may be called to make some difficult decisions."

"Your eyes are on fire when you say that. You do realize this will take some time, although I am as impatient as you are to dismantle **Cry Justice**."

"Yes, of course. I just mean that some behaviors may cause you personal sorrow, but I know that your love of the church will overcome any reluctance you may have to continuing the process."

"Are you trying to prepare me for ... Are you trying to suggest that my sister might...." The Archbishop's eyes darted from Will's face to the floor and back again.

"You worry too much, Bob. Of course, you know your sister better than I; do you think her sense of justice is stronger than yours? Do you question her love and loyalty to you?"

"No, of course not, but she believes so much in the work of **Cry Justice**. I even think she prays that I'll join her someday."

Will squashed his inner howl of panic. It was not a fear that God would listen to her prayers; his real dread was that the Archbishop's zeal would not sustain him through Plan B. "And I'm sure you pray for her. Whose prayer do you think God will answer?" His intense eyes brought a poignant smile to the Archbishop's face.

"I have always been a bit wary of believing that I knew whose side God is on."

Another sign of weakness sighed Will. "God is on the side of right. How could he not be pleased with you, who are so devoted to his church?"

"You do have a way of simplifying the truth."

Feeling his heartbeat calming down Will realized that he dare not relax his attention to the archbishop. "You are stronger than you know, Bob. You will have all you need to conquer this enemy while enduring the sacrifices God will ask of you."

"I find myself thanking you again for your support. We will make this work, even if we need to meet every month, right?"

"I am at your service, Bob." *But there will be no monthly meetings; you will come to see how right I am.*

Chapter 11

Dialing Charlie Fletcher's number, Will laughed at the vivid picture in his mind of the dreamer. *Charlie, you're so gullible.*

"Good morning, Will; what can I do for you?"

"Good morning, Charlie. I'm calling to ask you to be on the panel for our gathering, **A Call to Reconciliation and Possibilities**."

Charlie opened his mouth but said nothing. *Don't be judgmental, Charlie; maybe he has changed; after all, you do believe God's grace is always at work.* Charlie took a deep breath. *I wonder why,* he felt like saying, but instead, "Thank you, Will. I am looking forward to this first step for our church in this diocese."

Just what I expected from you. "I'm glad to hear you say that, Charlie. The archbishop does love the church, you know."

"As we all do."

"Yes, of course. *You haven't a clue. How I long for the time everyone sees your fall from grace.* The archbishop and I thought it would be best if he gave a brief welcome, introduced the members of the panel, and then opened the floor for questions.

The archbishop and I—what a frightening picture; I know he'll use that line on Fran, too. "That's fine, Will. I'm sure the archbishop will set the atmosphere, and after the first question, we'll have no problems getting a discussion going." *And, I'm also sure you'll have a planted question in the audience, but we'll handle it.*

"By the way, Charlie, do you remember Adam Wetzer? He was an altar boy in your first parish."

"Yes, I do; haven't seen him for years now. I always thought he was too serious; I tried to get him to relax and have some fun."

Thank goodness you're as clueless as Adam. "You'll see him at our gathering; he works at the Cloister Royale. And, by the way, he comes to my Mass every day here at the cathedral."

I wonder what that's supposed to mean. "That's great, Will. Anything else about the panel?"

"No, just come about fifteen minutes before registration; that way I can give all the panel members any final details."

"I'll be there."

Feeling less satisfaction than he had anticipated, Will hung up the phone. *Now, let's get Fran.*

Hearing Will's voice on the other end of her line, Fran shivered. "Good morning, Will." She tried to block out the frigid image of icicles stabbing at her heart. Seeing the light blink for her other line she said, "Just a minute, Will. I have another call."

I'll bet it's Charlie. "Don't keep me waiting too long, Fran. This is important."

O God, help me to stay calm. "Hello, this is Sister Frances Mary."

"Fran, it's Charlie."

"Oh, Charlie, Will's on the other line."

"Call me back; and remember, who is your strength. We're in this together."

"OK, Will, I'm back."

"Thanks for not keeping me on hold, Fran. I'm calling to ask you to be on the panel for our diocesan gathering."

O God, why do I feel such dread in my soul? "I am very willing to contribute to the call for reconciliation, but how would my brother feel about my participation? In public, I mean." *Why do I feel like this is a set-up?*

If you only knew what your brother will learn about you! "Your brother and I agree that your participation would be a positive thing. Your relationship with the archbishop is a topic of conversation throughout the diocese, as I'm sure you are well aware." *That should get her right where it hurts!*

O God, help me. Say nothing, Fran, don't take the bait. "If Bob wants me there, I will be there."

"That's great, Fran. Charlie Fletcher will also be on the panel, so I hope you understand how determined your brother and I are to live up to the goals of the gathering." *And I will make sure that this will be the end of your trouble-making!*

"As I said, I'll be there." *Why am I afraid that something so wrong is going to happen?*

"Fifteen minutes before registration begins, Fran. See you then." *Oh that felt good. I'll bet she's calling Charlie right now.*

Will cut short his scorn as Ed McShane said, "Good morning, Will."

"Good morning to you, Ed. I'm calling to request your help in making our gathering day a success for the archbishop." *I sound so self-effacing! Just in case, he's not supportive of me, how could he refuse the archbishop!*

Very clever, Will; you know I won't say no to the archbishop. "I'm always ready to serve my Church."

"I know you are. I would ... the archbishop would be pleased to have you on the panel for our gathering."

Your true colors are showing, Will. "Of course. What would I be required to do?"

"Just be yourself, Ed. Questions will come from the audience, and I know your answers will further the goals of the day. Check in with me fifteen minutes before registration."

Why am I getting so uneasy about this? "Fine, Will. I'll see you then."

I'm nervous about him; I hope I haven't made a mistake inviting him into our inner circle. Will completed his panel membership with calls to Mike Lynch and Mark West. His uneasiness about Ed McShane nagged him. *I'll have to be very vigilant about him.*

Chapter 12

Will tossed and turned from midnight on. *November 9th! November 9th; it's here! The day of salvation; my day to save the church!* He twisted and rolled from side to side; at 2:00 he leaped out of bed and fell to his knees. *Your church, my God; our church; I am your servant. Bless this day and all that I will be called to do; I will not shrink from what must be done. I know your power and I feel it within me. The enemies will be overcome, today. Today!*

Sweat trickled down his face, mixed with unrestrained tears; more sweat oozed down his scrawny back. Will could not remember ever being so excited. Heaving deep rasping gasps of air he calmed his thumping heart. Burying his face in the tangled blue sheet and shoving the blanket to the bottom of his bed he laughed with a vengeance that filled him with a sizzling rush. He propelled himself upright pulling the sheet off the bed. Hopping and tripping into his bathroom, he dropped the sheet and tore off his navy silk pajamas. *I need a warm shower.*

Sudsy water flowed over him, soothing his whole body in its delight. *Thank you, God,* he whispered, and was startled to see standing before him Barbara Collins, her teasing green eyes peering into his trembling soul as she tossed her red hair and smiled. Gasping and grabbing for her, his whole body shook and burned with hunger; she vanished. Before he had time to recover, Evelyn Lane was caressing his face, her soft pink lips coming closer and closer. Pulling her sleek blonde hair toward him, he caught his breath and she was gone.

Quivering as clear warm water spilled over him he shouted, "Barbara! Evelyn! Both of you, you will be saved. I am your savior. You will belong to me; you will be mine." Closing his eyes, he threw back his head and soaked up the excitement pulsing within him. Calling out their names over and over he reveled in his visions again and again.

Will had no idea how long he indulged in his fantasies; a squirt of cold water jolted him back to reality. Turning off the water he shivered, reached for a fluffy white towel, and stepped out of the shower. Catching his reflection in the fogged mirror, he gave himself a satisfied smile.

Stumbling into his bedroom, he glanced at the clock on his nightstand. *4:20 and I am so ready for this day.*

Dressing in fifteen minutes he bowed to himself in the mirror. He had bought a new suit for today; now he admired the superior perfection of its lines and enjoyed the power it promised. He pulled on his priestly collar to loosen its curious grip on his throat.

Glancing at the clock he counted the hours before Mass. Annoyed that he was getting drowsy he walked to his living room and dropped himself into his favorite lounge chair. *Maybe I could close my eyes just for a few minutes.* His head nodded forward and Will slipped into a deep sleep. Awakened by his own snoring he shot straight up from his chair. *Oh my gosh, what time is it?*

Will panicked when he realized Mass was in five minutes. He raced to the cathedral, vested for Mass, and strolled to the altar at 7:30. *Perfect,* he thought with great satisfaction. Seeing Adam in his usual place brought back all his hopes for the day. *I can do no wrong; I thank you, God, that Your grace has accomplished so much within me.*

The archbishop was scrambling eggs when Will came into the kitchen after Mass. Saturday was Annie's day off, and the archbishop enjoyed cooking; good therapy, he always said. Will and he ate together because there was no 8:30 Mass as the archbishop always took the Saturday evening service. Today, however, the evening Mass had been canceled. "Will, do you think I should offer to have a Mass at the end of today's events; it will be rather late, of course, after the dinner, but what do you think?" He opened the oven and grabbed the sticky buns he had made.

Hadn't even thought about that—since the day will cause you and everyone else to forget all about Mass. "Oh, Bob, ... ah, how thoughtful; I'm sure everyone will be pleased to share a liturgy with you."

"I figured you would say that; be sure to take your vestments along with mine because I want you to concelebrate with me."

Will spooned a helping of eggs onto his plate, and licked the caramel off his finger after picking up a small sticky bun. A surge of gratification mixed with remorse overcame him. *That would be such sweet revenge,* thought Will, envisioning Charlie, Fran, Joan, and Jennifer sitting in front of him. *But, my ultimate goal is more important, and will bring me even more satisfaction.* "We said we would leave here at 11:00 today, right, Bob? I'm sure everything will go as planned, but I do want to be there in plenty of time before registration begins."

"I'll be ready. I have so much hope about today, Will. I'm so grateful that you asked my sister to be on the panel. Such an example of reconciliation—you and she; that alone should set a wonderful tone to this day of possibilities!"

Will smiled. *So gullible! But this day will change your mind.* Will finished his coffee, wiped his mouth, eyeing the archbishop taking another helping of eggs.

"I know I shouldn't be eating all this cholesterol, Will, but I get so hungry when I'm excited."

"I'm the opposite. Just enjoy yourself, Bob." Putting his cup and plate in the dishwasher, Will walked from the kitchen. He maintained his usual rigid steps, but he wanted to skip. His head was spinning with thoughts of Barbara. *Wonder if she will be at the Covington, or will I have to wait until the cocktail hour to see her? The Covington is so new, and they have had to hire people for our event, so I'm sure she will be there to make sure everything goes right for me. Your original mistake—ah, your original sin, my Barbara—has been forgiven! And you will rest in my grace, my beautiful one.* The early morning vision tugged at him; but he shook his head; he had no time now for its delight. *Time enough, later, my divine gift; joy will come later, I promise.*

Chapter 13

The archbishop and Will arrived at the Covington at 11:30; Will's eyes darted around the lobby. The glossy forest green and pure white tiled floor was polished to perfection. In the center under a massive crystal chandelier was a large white sign on a tripod with blue and green lettering, **Welcome to a Day of Reconciliation and Promises.** Rising behind it was a huge white chocolate sculpture of a chalice, held by five hands, masculine and feminine. Two immense vases of Stargazer lilies, their crimson spots reminding him of blood, sat in tasteful elegance on two round iron tables on either side of the sculpture. Will was stunned at the flawless beauty of the entire scene, while an unexpected pain of remorse stung his soul, just for a minute.

There she is! You're even more astonishing today, my beautiful Barbara in that luscious cranberry suit; it makes your enticing green eyes all the more exciting. How I wished you understood the greatness of today, and how your salvation will come through me!

"Bob, there's Barb…Ms. Collins; she is the events coordinator I told you about; the one I've been working with to make this day all that it should be. Allow me to introduce you."

Will was three steps ahead of the Archbishop in his haste to get to Barbara. "Ms. Collins." Barbara turned and smiled; Will fought his urge to stare. "I would like to introduce to you his Excellency, Archbishop Robert Garrote."

Will's eyes followed Barbara's graceful hand as she greeted the archbishop; he enjoyed the tingling in his own hands as their hands met. Then she reached towards Will's hand; he was so warm he worried if his face was reddening. Struggling to let go as soon as he felt her grip lessening, he said, "You have done a magnificent job, Ms. Collins; the welcome area is glorious."

"I'm so glad you like it. Didn't I tell you I'd make this work for you?" She smiled and a pulsating rush swept Will's entire body. "Let me show you the registration area."

Will and the archbishop followed Barbara through a hall with plush green plaid carpeting; on the white walls hung large framed prints of Monet water lilies and purple poppies. They came to a spacious square, carpeted in solid green; blue packets in neat rows were arranged on three large round tables in front of signs, A-G; H-N, O-Z.

Drawn to the ostentatious floor vases that stood in each corner of the room, Will stared at the mixture of white Muscadet lilies with their pink brushmarks, brilliant yellow Royal Justice lilies, and crimson Olympic Stars, their dark spots reminding Will of the Stargazer lilies. *Why do I feel a special attraction to those spots? They do remind me of blood to be shed again for salvation?* Complimenting Barbara again on her marvelous work, he hoped his internal gushing was not showing. His mind was screaming, *Bob, isn't this fabulous? Didn't I do a fantastic job?*

He heard the archbishop speaking. "Ms. Collins, I want to express my deepest admiration for all you have done for this great day."

"Thank you, Archbishop. I was inspired by the dedication of Father Owens, here."

Will bowed, belying the jubilant leaping of his heart and mind. *I love you. I love you. You are mine.* Checking his watch he was glad it was already 12:30. In fifteen minutes the panel members were due to meet with him. *This day, my day, is meeting all my expectations.* "The panel members will be meeting me here, soon."

"I have several guides stationed in the lobby; they will direct them here to you, Father. Is there anything else I can provide for you?" She smiled again.

Oh, you will, my love, more than you know. "I think everything is ready, thank you." His desire for her was consuming him; *Coordinator of Redemption* flashed inside his head and he turned his to the figures walking down the hall. *Ah, how fitting that they are the first.*

"Good morning, Charlie, and the same to you, Fran."

"Good morning, Will." That they replied in unison gave Will an unspeakable sense of amusement. Smiling, he eyeballed Charlie from head to toe. *Just perfect, Charlie, that you chose to wear a sweater and khakis, today. You and Fran make an engaging picture together.*

Indulging his satisfaction of payback he watched Ed McShane approach; he, of course, was in his black suit and priestly collar. Ed nodded first to Fran, extended his hand to Charlie, and spoke to Will, who had little time to enjoy the fact that he was the one who had called them together.

Sprinting down the hall with tactless smiles on their faces came Mike Lynch and Mark West. *You two will never get anywhere if you don't learn to put on a proper face. Don't you realize your very demeanor speaks the seriousness of your role?* With one glance at Will, both faces turned into a solemn pose.

"Thank you all for your promptness." Scanning each person standing before him, Will timed his glance just long enough to enjoy his inner smirk. "The archbishop," he turned his icy eyes on Fran, "will give the welcome and opening talk." Passing his scrutinizing look over the others, "You have not been asked to give a speech; you are on the panel to answer the questions and concerns of our faithful ones in the audience. And remember, the theme for our day is reconciliation and possibilities; your personal agendas are well-known; you were invited to show your willingness to listen." He made sure his remarks ended with a determined glare at Fran and Charlie.

Charlie stole a quick glance at Fran. *How pathetic and transparent, Will, and how unfair.*

O God, help me; I know I forgave him once; why do I feel I will need to forgive again? Fighting to look at Will without flinching Fran even managed a weak smile, surprised that a spontaneous prayer for her brother had arisen within her. *O, Bob, will this day be one of reconciliation and possibilities for us?*

Ed also glanced at Fran. *He will never let go of what happened at Sacred Heart; I've always wished that I had told Fran I was sorry I had sided with Will. I know she doesn't hold a grudge, and I don't like what I'm feeling right now.*

Mike and Mark kept their eyes fixed on Will, but their imaginations soared with visions of power and control.

"Now then, I think we all understand the glorious goal of this day." Will nodded. "I see the archbishop is heading for the podium. Please, follow me now to your panel table. Sr. Frances Mary, I think you should sit first, next to the podium, and Ed, it would be quite symbolic if you sat next to Sister. Mike and Mark, I'd like to see you two next, and at the end, Charlie."

As they walked in silence, Fran prayed for a small sign from her brother. *Just a nod would help*, she thought. As she headed for her chair, Archbishop Garrote turned and smiled; then he walked towards her, his arms outstretched. "Thank you, Bob." *And, thank you, dear God.*

Embracing her he whispered, "Fran, I hope this day will bring you back to us."

"And, I hope that you will come to know how much we all love our church, Bob. I've missed our talks." Fran looked in her brother's eyes; making a weak attempt to smile he walked back to the podium. The hope in Fran's heart faded; shivering from a baffling chill she took her seat and smiled at Father Ed as he sat down beside her.

"I'm glad you're here, Fran. I hope we can talk later."

"Good afternoon, brothers and sisters," the archbishop boomed. "I welcome you to this day of hope." Continuing with the speech approved by Will, the entire audience became spellbound; eyes brimmed with hope, heads nodded their appreciation.

They are believing my words. *Just the effect I wanted.* Soon Will heard the archbishop's final sentence.

"And, now, to show that I am here to listen to you, I will be taking a seat among you, as you ask your questions and offer your comments." The deafening applause convinced Will that today was the beginning of the end.

Joe Moreno stood as the applause was coming to its end, and began the afternoon session with Will's question about Catholic Identity. As suggested by Will he directed it to Ed McShane. "Father McShane, do you agree that Catholic Identity is vital for our children today; after all, if they do not know what the Catholic Church believes, why would they remain in the church?"

"I think everyone would agree that Catholic Identity is important for all of us; however, that identity should not mean that we cannot question the direction of the church or her leaders; after all, the very word, catholic, means universal. Our church should proclaim by our words and actions that all are welcome. We Catholics have to be involved with…" His words were cut off by a burst of applause.

That's not what I expected from him! Will felt the first pang of fear that day, but hearing the sustained applause he realized that Ed's response was a perfect fit with the day's theme of reconciliation. *This is what I need to happen this afternoon; if they believe him, they all will be lulled into a false hope. I don't agree with you, Ed, but you just might help me more than you will ever know.*

He heard Joe pushing for more details about shared beliefs and Fran was going on about their common love for the church and for God. Will was pleased with the nodding heads and smiles he saw around the room. He caught the archbishop's eye for a moment, and was certain that gratitude would be the defining emotion marking the day—the defining emotion to be offered to the Coordinator of Redemption. *What could be more glorious at the end of the day than to have the archbishop in my debt;* Will gloated at the impact of the thought.

Other questions and answers were lost in the fog of Will's thoughts about the evening dinner; embarrassment and ugly revelations would bring this day to a fitting conclusion and begin the ultimate dismantling of **Cry Justice**. The church, and what mattered even more to Will, the archbishop would recognize Will as redeemer and savior.

Will was not surprised when Joan brought up the question of women's ordination; *how clever of Fran not to mention it herself*, thought Will. By now the tone in the room had become one of genuine listening to each other; questions and answers went back and forth for an hour. Will was shocked that anger did not take over, but again convinced himself that all was the result of basking in the promise offered in the archbishop's opening talk. The interest level had increased to such a degree that when Will interrupted to ask if anyone wanted to stand and take a break, the answer was a resounding "No, thanks."

Will was not pleased to hear the archbishop throw out a question on what people wanted to see on future agendas. *What is going on with him*, screamed Will. *He is in complete denial that this was just an exercise to begin the end of* **Cry Justice**. *If he keeps talking like this, they might believe him. Maybe he is trying to impress his sister, or maybe he just wants to look good to this audience. Whatever he is thinking, I hope he isn't beginning to believe that* **Cry Justice** *has some validity. Thank goodness, I am keeping my head straight on this.*

Applause followed the archbishop's question. Fran smiled, and offered the first suggestion. Will swallowed the disgust he was feeling. He looked at his watch; at 5:15 he was going to bring the discussion to a close. *Can I survive another half hour* he wondered. *Well, no matter, if the archbishop is losing his head over this, the dinner will put everything back on track—my track!*

Pete Rogers was speaking when Will checked his watch again. *Even the obedient sheep is sounding like a reconciler*, he groaned. "One more minute, Father Rogers, and we must bring this wonderful afternoon to a close."

Peter nodded to Will who shuddered at the spark he noticed in Pete's eyes. *I must be the sole strong one; the only one unwilling to yield to the evil taking over our church. Thank you, God, for giving me the strength to do what I must.*

"Thank you, everyone for your participation, today. I'm sure everyone feels the same excitement that I do. Now it is time to get ready to move to our evening together; and I am hoping that everyone will be coming. At 5:30 the archbishop and I will be in a limousine provided by Ms. Collins." Glancing around the room Will pointed to Barbara at the back of the room. "Ms. Collins has been the driving force working with me to bring about this wonderful day. Please thank her with your applause now."

Barbara's hair tumbled over her shoulders as she made a slight bow. Will trembled as she spoke, "It was my pleasure to serve you. I hope you all appreciate the dedication of Father Will in bringing you all together. We have been most happy to work with him and for you."

His heart soaring with gratitude, he drank in a surge of his earlier fantasies. "Thank you, Ms. Collins." Hesitating just long enough to enjoy his delusion he bowed and smiled to her. "Now, when you get to your cars, please line up behind the archbishop and we will parade to the Cloister Royale. What a marvelous witness we will be! Ms. Collins has promised us a blaze of lights to welcome us." Seeing her smile he felt his thumping heart. *O Barbara, some day soon. How I want to grab you now and take you with us.* He smiled at the audience. "See you soon, at the Cloister Royale."

Chapter 14

"Look, Bob. Look at the lights! Isn't this glorious! God be praised!"

Hearing the music of the band blaring its welcome he said, "Bob, hurry! You must be the first to walk in. Hurry! Hurry!"

"Walk with me, Will. That ice sculpture is more impressive than I imagined. What you have accomplished is beyond belief."

Glancing at the sculpture of the chalice and the icy hands reaching towards it, Will thought, *Just like the ice will melt into nothing, so shall **Cry Justice**. My dream is coming true.* "Thank you, Bob. When everyone gets in, you should mingle during the cocktails. I'll be checking the dining room, so that this fabulous day will continue without a wrinkle."

Searching the room for Barbara Will found her behind the band, her red hair swaying with her body to the music. For a moment the band disappeared and he saw only her. The music faded as he walked toward her. She saw him coming and glided over to him. *Not now,* he heard himself saying. *Not now; I have important work to do.* When she stopped in front of him he was pulled into her fresh fragrance. *Her eyes are still dancing.* He bit his tongue so hard he thought he tasted blood. "I need... I need to get into the dining room as soon as possible," he blurted.

"Of course, Will. Please, relax. Didn't I tell you I would make this day good for you?" She patted his trembling hand. Dismissing his first inclination to draw back he delighted in her warmth. "I'll open the door for you."

"I don't want anyone coming in early."

"Don't worry; I'll lock it again; you can come out whenever you're ready."

"Thank you, thank you so much. I just want everything to be perfect."

"And it will be." She patted his hand again.

Wanting to scream *Don't treat me like a child,* he walked into the room mumbling to himself. *You will see the beginning of my great work; nothing can stop me now.*

Hearing her click of the lock he studied the head table; it passed the grandeur test. Checking the name cards he found them exactly as he had planned. Fran was between Charlie and Ed at the opposite end from the archbishop.

Staring at Fran's filled wine glass, he fingered a tiny plastic bag in his pocket. He swung his head as he heard two waiters push open the door leading from the kitchen. "Thank you for all the work you're doing." Will began a nonchalant walk around the tables, touching napkins, and straightening a fork or spoon here and there, keeping one eye on the waiters. As soon as they went back through the door to the kitchen he darted to the head table. Pulling out the plastic bag, he dumped half of the powder into Fran's water and half into her wine. *Two sleeping pills should cause enough dizziness for a good show before her final exit. And if she takes some wine, it will speed things along.*

"Anything wrong, Father?" Dropping the bag Will looked up to see Barbara coming in the door. At the same time the waiters entered from their door with the salads.

"No, no, absolutely not. I was just checking the name cards." He began walking towards her. "The tables are exquisite, Barbara." He denied himself the pleasure of her eyes by pointing to the decorations. A single yellow rose on each table accentuated the two golden stripes on snow-white table cloths.

"Did you ever think," he said to her "how yellow speaks of cowardice and yet in the rose is so beautiful?"

"That's a profound insight, Father. You are a rare man." She patted his hand.

His hunger for her longed to be satisfied as she yielded to his grasp; the brush of her sleeve snatched him back to the moment. Seizing a napkin he said, "The **Cry Justice** imprint is sure to impress everyone. I am grateful to you, Barbara."

"I'm glad I have lived up to your expectations, Father. I will open the doors in fifteen minutes: I will invite the archbishop to enter first. That's the way you want it, correct?"

"Yes, absolutely. And I will direct him to his place at the head table."

As she turned to walk away, his eyes were glued to the image floating away from him. Skimming his dry lips with his hungry tongue he bent down to pick up the plastic bag. He waved his hand around the chair clawing at the floor; the bag was gone. Poking his head under the table he noticed it lying behind the leg of a chair. Reaching for it he heard Barbara say, "Father, where are you?" He bumped his head in his hurry to answer her. "Father, what are you doing?"

"Oh, just picking up a pencil I dropped." His shaking hand slipped into his pocket. "Everything is fine, just fine."

"I forgot to tell you that the reporters are here—from all three TV channels and the city newspaper."

"Thank you, that's good to know. Thank you, Barbara."

"And I just wanted to say again how impressed I am with what you are doing here, today." Turning away again she slipped through the doorway. He caught a glimpse of the crowd engaged in vigorous conversations, holding glasses that were still full.

Moving to the end of the head table his eyes scanned the entire room. The boxes of chocolate at each place released in him an unexpected delight; *they will devour the chocolate, just like I will see to it that* **Cry Justice** *is devoured—all they will be left with is the empty box to remind them of what they tried to do to my church.*

Hearing the crowd gasp as the doors were opened he watched Barbara bring in the archbishop, and Will waved him to his seat. Murmurs rose as people seated themselves, some picking up the chocolates and nodding to each other, others admiring the overall view. Keeping an eye on Fran, he relished her effort to smile as she passed by him. She looked surprised that she would not be sitting next to her brother. He enjoyed her wince when she saw his name there. Finding her name card she looked around to find Charlie who had stopped to speak to the archbishop. Ed came up behind her, and pulled her chair out; nodding her thanks she sat down as Charlie leaned over to whisper something to her.

A hush came over the room as the archbishop began to say grace. After his Amen, he called for a toast. With his excellent peripheral vision, Will drank with great pleasure as he watched Fran put her glass to her lips. Forks went into salads, and more wine was drunk. Knowing that Fran was not much of a drinker, his eyes darted back and forth checking her water glass. So far, she was still eating salad and chatting with both Charlie and Ed. He saw her starting to reach for water just as a waiter arrived with her plate. She pulled back as he placed her plate on the table. It was Adam; he turned towards Charlie. Will could hear him ask, "Do you remember me?" Nodding Charlie put out his hand; Will enjoyed the shocked look on Charlie's face as Adam pulled away with "Please, no."

Fran's eyes grew wide as she stared at Adam and raised a questioning eyebrow to Charlie. Standing tall and stiff for a silent moment, Adam pivoted on his heel, and walked away. Charlie shook his head; Ed said something Will couldn't hear. The three of them watched the other waiters complete serving the head table.

The whispers throughout the room matched the surprise on their faces, as everyone looked at plates of beef filet medallions in a half circle next to a jumbo crab cake, red bliss potatoes and fresh green beans.

"A culinary masterpiece, Will" said the archbishop. "Will, did you hear me? Wonderful meal."

"Oh, yes, thank you, Bob." *When is she going to take a drink; I can't keep watching her, but she always drank at least one full glass of water with a meal.*

Light banter buzzed next to murmurs of serious discussions with hearty laughs breaking through first in a corner of the room, and passing from one table to another. Will watched as glasses of wine were refilled. He stole another glance at Fran; her water glass was almost empty. And he was surprised to see that even the wine glass was now half empty. *Soon, soon.*

The waiters began collecting the now empty plates. More laughs skipped from table to table along with oohs and aahs as plates of tiramisu were being placed on the tables. Waiters carried silver pots of coffee.

A scream from a table in front of Fran turned everyone in direction of the head table. Fran's head was on Charlie's chest. Camera flashes blinded everyone's eyes. Shoving his chair back, Charlie clutched Fran's face. Cameras flashed again. "Stop it!" shouted Charlie. Ed had grabbed Fran's hands, and was rubbing them. The archbishop was frozen in his chair. Adam appeared again behind Charlie. "What did you do to her? Why are you holding her?"

"Adam, please stop. I don't know what you're talking about. Somebody, call an ambulance."

"Already on its way, Charlie" said Joan. Jennifer stood beside her, clasping her hand. "Is she breathing? Please, Charlie, is she breathing?"

Leaning over Fran Charlie placed his fingers on her neck and shook his head yes. He began whispering in her ear. Another camera flashed.

"Charlie, what happened?" Hovering over Charlie's shoulder was the archbishop.

"Bob, I have no idea; all of a sudden she just passed out on top of me."

Will stood at his place. Shouting over the noise, he said, "Please, everyone, sit down. The ambulance is coming. I'm sure Sister Frances Mary will be fine. She may have just been overcome by the heat; I'm sure this is not serious."

No one even looked at him. He began shouting again, but everyone turned in the direction of the sirens. The doors burst open; three paramedics ran with a gurney to the head table. Cradling Fran's head, Charlie cried as Adam yelled behind him. Cameras flashed again. The archbishop stepped aside as Fran was lifted to the gurney; brushing away a tear from his left eye, and another from his right, he reached for her putting his hand on her arm; with his right hand he made the sign of the cross on her forehead.

His frantic gaze fell on Joan and Jennifer. "Come, Bob" said Jennifer as she grabbed his arm. "Our car is near the door."

Joan stared at Will. "You can come, too." She turned around. "Charlie…"

"Don't worry about me; I'll be right behind you."

Chapter 15

In the waiting room, the archbishop sat with his head in his hands. Jennifer and Joan sat together to his right; Charlie was on his left. Will stood near the wall. The bright lights on the two wooden tables, the scattered magazines, and the subdued noise coming from the TV added annoyance to their anxiety. Jennifer's fingers edged their way to Bob's hand; turning to her, he said, "What if I never get to tell her."

"She knows, Bob; she knows. And she is going to be all right; believe; believe."

He looked at Joan; she nodded a yes, and placed her hand on top of Jennifer's.

Shifting his weight from one foot to another Will planned his response when the doctor would announce that Fran was dead. *He will be difficult to deal with for a while, but he will come to see that this had to be done. With her death and Charlie's downfall,* **Cry Justice** *will crumble.*

"Archbishop Garrote?"

All eyes searched the doctor's face for some sign of hope. "Yes, I'm Archbishop Garrote." He pushed himself to stand balancing himself on Charlie's arm. Joan and Jennifer rose with him, still holding on to his hand.

"Archbishop, I'm Doctor DiMarco. Your sister experienced a critical heart attack. As far as I can tell right now, there was no permanent damage, but she will have to make a serious cutback in her activities. In time, she will recover."

"Thank, God! Thank God! When can we see her? What caused this? You're sure she will be OK?"

"She's sleeping right now, but you can go in. We are not sure what caused this, but we did pump her stomach and sent the contents for analysis."

Choking back his disbelief Will asked, "What do you expect to find?" *How could this have happened; how could she have survived?*

"We don't know what to expect but because this happened at a meal, we have to check for the presence of a poison."

"Poison!" they all cried in unison.

"I don't mean that someone gave her poison; it could be as simple as food poisoning."

"But" Will said, "we all ate the same food."

"Well, she may have had an allergic reaction to something; there's no use speculating right now. I know you'll feel better after you see her. No more than two should go into her room; the others can look through the window."

Dr. DiMarco motioned for them to follow him; the archbishop walked beside him; Charlie, Joan and Jennifer, holding on to each other, followed. Will walked alone. *Thank goodness I found that plastic bag*, he thought. *Even if they find evidence of the sleeping pills, they won't be able to tie me into it. Adam, you may be of more use to me than you know.*

Approaching Fran's room, Jennifer whispered to Charlie. "Let's tell him to go in alone this evening. We will wait until tomorrow." Squeezing her hand he agreed.

Huddling close to each other, Joan, Jennifer, and Charlie pressed their hands on the window. A muffled sob shook Joan's shoulders, as Charlie pulled her closer to him. Wiping her eyes Jennifer prayed in silence, *O, Fran, do not leave us. Please be strong.* Will winced as the archbishop leaned over and kissed Fran on the forehead. Sinking into the chair near her bed, Bob rested his head on her arm and sobbed.

Will waited for five minutes; opening the door he said in a hoarse voice, "Bob, I think you should let her rest. Come now, we should go." Looking at Joan still being hugged by Charlie Will said, "I'll call a cab for us."

Walking with their arms around each other Charlie, Joan, and Jennifer followed the archbishop stumbling down the hall, Will supporting his arm. He twisted his head for one last sneer at the trio staring at him. *How pathetic. I did not succeed tonight, but my mission will be completed. Have no doubt.*

Jennifer's voice was quivering; her body shaking as she spoke to Charlie and Joan. "I was suspicious of this day when we first got those invitations, but the discussions today changed my mind. Now, I feel so awful thinking this, but I can't help it. I can see it in Will's eyes; he's going to use this as some kind of crazy proof that God is punishing Fran for her role in **Cry Justice.**"

Charlie said, "I had an even worse thought; somehow, Will had something to do with this."

"Oh Charlie, please, no," sobbed both Joan and Jennifer.

"I noticed he was nowhere in the room while we were having cocktails. He had an hour to do his evil deed."

"What can we do?"

"I don't know, Joan. We'll have to wait for the report from the doctor. Even then, I don't know how we'll be able to prove anything, but let's agree to be very careful." Joan shivered; Charlie saw Jennifer trembling. "We all need to go home; are you OK to drive?

"Yes," whispered Jennifer, stifling a sob. She grabbed Joan's hand.

"I'll be here tomorrow as soon as I can. Even if we can't spend time with her, we'll be together." Charlie gathered both of them in front of him. "Look at me; God is with us, here, right now. God is with Fran. We will get through this, together."

Walking out the front door of the hospital, the still night air chilled their bodies and souls; an ominous dread gripped them as they saw Will and the archbishop getting into a cab. Turning Will glared at them. *I feel as though I've been stabbed,* thought Jennifer. *I'm afraid to think about what Charlie said.*

When they got to their car, Charlie gave each of them a strong affectionate hug. "You're sure you're OK? I'll follow you home if you want."

"You don't need to do that," said Jennifer. "We'll be fine. Thank you so much, Charlie, for being here. See you tomorrow."

Watching as they buckled their seat belts he stood alone in the cold as they drove away. Even as they waved and put on a brave smile, he could see the tears rolling down their cheeks; he wiped away his own.

Chapter 16

Trudging down the shiny hospital hall, Archbishop Garrote wiped his eyes as he tried to calm down his breathing. He had offered the first morning Mass without giving a homily, knowing that everyone understood. Waiting for Will to finish the second Mass he wept while looking at the picture in the Sunday newspaper. Will had seen it earlier, and reveled in its front page, full color, above the fold placement. There was Fran, sprawled on Charlie's chest; his head bent and his whispering into her ear looked like a kiss. *This is one for my scrapbook and worth an award. I couldn't have done better if I had staged the picture myself!*

The ride to the hospital had been in silence. Now Will walked beside the archbishop, biting his bottom lip to keep from smiling, relishing memories of the newspaper picture. He was quite sure the archbishop had not seen the TV morning news. *Too bad. That was even better than the newspaper.*

Approaching Fran's room, they saw Jennifer and Joan sitting beside Fran's bed. Will was disappointed she was still breathing. Bob thought she looked even more ghostly than last night; the tubes and needles were a blur, and she was so still. He gulped down the lump in his throat as Jennifer and Joan looked up.

Both came out to him. "Go and be with her," said Jennifer. "She may not make it through today." Bob broke down. Joan and Jennifer circled their arms around him.

Will stifled any outward sign of the leap of excitement that energized every cell in his body. *And the sooner this is over, the better it will be; I know he'll feel guilty for a time, but Fran's death and Charlie's disgrace are crucial. Do us a favor, Fran, and don't linger.*

Jennifer said, "The doctor assured us that she can hear; there's always a chance that we can call her back. I can't tell her to let go, I can't say we'll be all right if she leaves us."

"I can't either." Bob wiped his eyes. Lowering his head he clung to Joan and Jennifer as he walked into Fran's room.

Will watched as the archbishop made the sign of the cross on Fran's forehead and sunk into the chair beside her bed. *Bob, tell her it's OK to go; you can see how bad she is.* To his horror, he saw the archbishop jump up and scream. "She squeezed my hand; she squeezed my hand. Here," he said to Jennifer; "hold it. See if she does it again."

Jennifer grabbed her hand, and felt how cold it was. She hesitated turning to the archbishop, but just as she shook her head, she felt it. "Bob, it's true! Joan, call the nurse."

Smacking his mouth Will smothered his gasp as Fran opened her eyes. In an instant Bob was hovering over her while Jennifer and Joan hugged her, tears running down everyone's cheeks. Spinning on his heel Will turned down the hall, colliding into the nurse with "I'm sorry."

Racing into the room, the nurse froze. "I can't believe it. It's a miracle. It's a miracle." Walking over to Sister Frances Mary she stared at the monitor above her head; everything was normal. "Let me take your blood pressure, just to be sure. But I can already tell; you have such wonderful color in your face; I shouldn't say this before I call the doctor, I know, but I can't help it. I've never seen a miracle. You are fine."

Bob looked out the window for Will; Joan and Jennifer, wiping away what were now tears of joy, hugged the nurse. Fran smiled, uttered, "Bob," and reached out for her brother. He grasped her hand, and began sobbing. "Come here," she whispered as she squeezed his hand. "Everything is OK; I'm fine."

"Fran, I'm so sorry, I'm so sorry. Can you forgive me?"

"For what?"

"For being so stubborn, for not listening to you, for being so self-righteous, for…"

"O Bob, there's nothing to forgive. I love you, don't you know that?"

At that moment, Charlie burst into the room. "Fran, Fran!"

The nurse grabbed his arm. "It's a miracle, Father."

"What happened?"

"She just woke up. I'm going to call the doctor, but I know it's a miracle."

Dashing over to Bob, Charlie took hold of his hand, gathering Jennifer and Joan into a group hug. Fran pulled on Bob's sleeve. "Hey, what about me?" Opening their circle they pulled her in laughing and crying.

"You look so wonderful," Charlie said.

"I feel great. The last thing I remember is feeling dizzy. What happened?"

"Well, you collapsed—on me!"

"Oh no, I'm so embarrassed."

Charlie stole a glance at Bob, Joan and Jennifer. *Not a good time to mention the morning paper.* "Oh, Fran, don't be; everyone understood."

A knock on the doorframe brought them all face to face with Will. "Sister, I'm so glad to see you have recovered."

An instant chill nudged Charlie, Joan, and Jennifer closer to Fran.

"Will," said Bob, "thank you for coming in to share this miracle moment with us." He noticed that Will had a newspaper tucked under his arm.

"I was so concerned for your sister, Bob." Turning to Fran he said, "You brought our day to a crashing close." The paper slipped onto her bed.

Lunging forward Charlie attempted to snatch it, but Fran saw the front page. "Oh, no!" She covered her face.

"Oh, Sister, I realize this might be uncomfortable for you, but I think you need to consider that someone may have set you up."

"What are you talking about, Will?" said Bob.

Turning a wide-eyed face to Charlie he said, "Do you remember Adam's reaction to you yesterday?"

Charlie was stunned. "Why; what are you saying?"

"Didn't you think he seemed angry at you?"

"I remember that he wouldn't shake hands with me, but I couldn't understand why. We used to have a pretty friendly relationship."

"Well, it's just my humble opinion, but I think you should find out what he meant. After all, he was in the room during the set-up."

"Are you saying he did something? And why, Fran, if he is angry with me?"

"I'm not blaming him; I'm suggesting that if you have any questions, you might want to talk with him.

Wiping away a tear Fran took her brother's hand. "I can't believe this."

"I don't either, Fran," said Bob patting her hand as he held it in his. "I think this was just an unfortunate, but frightening, episode. Maybe you've developed an allergy or something."

"Your brother may be right," said Will. "Forget that I said anything. I'm sure all you need to think about is getting out of here."

Nodding, Fran shivered and pulled the covers up to her shoulders.

"He's right, Fran." Bob smiled at Will. "Let's concentrate on this miracle, and be happy."

Charlie, Joan, and Jennifer had not said a word, numbed by an icy gloom hovering around them.

"I hear we've had a miracle!"

Everyone turned toward Doctor DiMarco. Smiling the archbishop said, "What can you tell us, Doctor?"

"This is astounding, especially since I just read the report from the lab. Sister, I admit I do not understand; the report shows that you ingested a large amount of a substance found in sleeping pills. That amount would have caused you to pass out, but because you also had some wine, this should have been much more tragic. In fact, in my opinion, you should have died last night."

Joan and Jennifer screamed and held onto Fran huddling close to Charlie. Bob's jaw dropped open; his panicked eyes darting to Fran. Shifting from his spot Will kept his eyes on Charlie.

Doctor DiMarco said, "I'm sorry for being so blunt; I've reported this to the police. I think this was an attempted murder."

Holding onto Charlie Fran was crying. "Who? Why?" Bob squeezed her hand.

"The police said they will be sending two detectives here within the hour. Meanwhile, Sister, you do seem to be a miracle. I would suggest that you get ready to go home; you can feel free to leave as soon as the police are finished with their questions. Good luck to you."

"Should all of us remain here, Doctor?" asked Will.

"Yes, but some of you might want to wait in the lounge."

"I think that is wise. Bob, I'll wait for you. Thank you, Doctor." Will gave one last nod to everyone. "Think about what I said."

Chapter 17

Relieved that the waiting room was empty Will took out his cell phone and dialed Adam.

In Fran's room, Charlie was the first one to speak. "I don't want to bring up Adam's name when the police come. I don't believe he had anything to do with this."

"But, Charlie," asked Bob, "who else would have a reason to want to harm you? I believe Will had a point when he said that Adam seemed angry with you. I think he meant to kill you, for whatever reason, I can't imagine."

"I don't know what was going on with Adam, but from what I remember about him, he just couldn't do something like this. When he was an altar server, he used to tell me how worried he was about his mother after his father had died and wanted me to talk with her. I had known his father from high school. We talked every week for a few months and she seemed ready to accept the hard fact that life had to go on. He used to tell me every day how glad he was that I had helped his mother. He was upset when they moved; in fact, they moved to Sacred Heart, and his mother was doing well at the time. I even thought she was ready for a new relationship."

"Maybe you need to talk with him."

"I'll think about it, Bob."

"May we come in?" The detectives smiled and nodded as they entered the room. "I'm Detective Tom Conroy; this is my partner, Detective Bill Harris. Who wants to start?"

Joan and Jennifer looked at each other and then Charlie; Bob looked at Fran and cleared his throat. "Well, we know that my sister suffered a near fatal attack because of sleeping pills and wine." He cleared his throat again and pointed towards Charlie. "We also know that a former altar server was one of the waiters and seemed to have a problem with Father Fletcher."

"What kind of problem, Father?" asked Conroy.

"I have no idea." Charlie took a deep breath. "However, I just can't believe he had anything to do with this. There were others in that room during the setup."

"Do you have another suspect?"

Bob stared at Charlie. "My assistant was in there, but he had planned the whole day; he was the one who mentioned Adam to us this morning. He was the one who noticed that he had a problem with Father Fletcher, here."

"We will need to talk to him. What's his last name?"

"Wetzer," whispered Will. All eyes shot towards the door. No one had noticed Will standing there.

"This is my assistant, Father Will Owens."

"Father," said Conroy, "do I understand that you suspect this Adam Wetzer?"

"I'm not saying he's a suspect; I mentioned his name because he did have the opportunity, and he seemed to have a problem with Father Fletcher, here; in fact, I thought that maybe he had made an error and had targeted him rather than Sister Frances Mary." He made a slight bow in Fran's direction.

"Father," asked Harris, "do you know this Adam personally?"

"I do; he comes to Mass at the Cathedral every day."

"And yet you think he may have planned to do harm to Father Fletcher?"

"It's hard to believe; he a very intense young man. But I've never asked him about any problems; in fact, I was just as surprised as Father to hear his accusations yesterday."

Charlie broke in. "What accusations? I remember that he didn't want to shake my hand"

"Didn't you hear him say, when Sister collapsed and you were holding her, 'What did you do to her? Why are you holding her?'"

"No, Will. I did not. And it doesn't make any sense."

"All I'm saying is that you knew Adam many years ago. Maybe there's something in your relationship with him or his mother that he misunderstood."

Charlie shook his head. "I have no idea what you're talking about."

Conroy spoke up, "Well, Father, if you do think of something, anything at all about Adam, let us know. Meanwhile, we will have a talk with him."

Charlie nodded as they turned to leave. Pulling out his ringing cell phone Will said, "I'll take this in the lounge."

Charlie watched him hurry down the hall. *He is up to something, I know.*

"I'm glad you called me back. Listen to what I tell you, but do not get upset. I will help you. The police have just left Sister Frances Mary's room; in a conversation with Father Fletcher, your name came up and they are going to question you."

"Why would they question me?"

"Remember what you said to Father Fletcher yesterday at the table when Sister Frances Mary collapsed on him?"

"But I was thinking about my mother."

"I know that, but I couldn't say anything, because I promised you I would not tell anyone; and you have to keep our conversations a secret, too. You can never tell anyone that we talked, do you understand?"

"But what should I say?"

"Tell the police the same story you told me; then they will suspect Father Fletcher instead of you."

"I'm a suspect?"

"The hospital found sleeping pills in Sister Frances Mary's drinks, and your name came up in the conversation with Father Fletcher because you had the opportunity to slip something into her wine and water."

"But I didn't do it; why would I want to hurt her?"

"Well, they think you meant it for Father Fletcher."

"That's crazy; I hate him, but I wouldn't do anything like that."

"Stay calm, Adam. Just tell your story to the police, and let them make their own conclusions. I will help you, but remember, it has to be in secret."

"Thank you, Father Will. What would I do without you?"

"Can you manage to reserve a room in the hotel for a meeting?"

"Well, I'm friends with one of the maids, in fact I think she likes me, and she would do anything for me. Why?"

"If you can get a room, and get Father Fletcher and Sister Frances Mary together—you know how he is with women—I guarantee you that his true colors will be revealed. Get Sister Frances Mary to come first, and I will meet with her for about a half hour, and share your story with her."

"But how will that help?"

"When your name came up at the hospital, Father Fletcher denied knowing anything about your mother; once Sister Frances Mary knows the truth, she will suspect that he had a reason for threatening her—you see, I don't think he meant to kill her; I think he just wanted to make her sick so they could break off their relationship."

"You mean they were…"

"I am aware of things I shouldn't be telling you, but you have to believe I know that Father Fletcher somehow got those sleeping pills into her drink, and you made a convenient scapegoat. Everything will be fine, you'll see. I have to go back to her room now, and take the archbishop home. Remember, stay calm; tell the police your story, just like you told it to me, but never mention my name, ever. And that includes setting up the meeting with Father Fletcher and Sister; if you are ever asked about it, you are to say that Father Fletcher wanted the meeting. No one is to know that I helped you with this. I don't want the archbishop knowing that I kept his sister's relationship with Father Fletcher a secret."

"I understand, Father Will. You try to make sure people believe the best about others. I admire you."

"I know you will be strong, Adam. God bless you."

The conversation in Fran's room stopped as Will walked in. He eyed each one in turn, hesitating just a moment longer on Charlie. Smiling at the archbishop he said, "Bob, whenever you are ready to go home, I'm here."

"The doctor said that Fran could go home after the police were finished. Joan and Jennifer will take her." He looked at Fran, and smiled. "And I'll come for supper, OK?"

"I'm so happy."

"By the way, I didn't call our sister and brother. Knowing Tess, there will be a call waiting for me when I get home. She'll tell me it's her twin radar."

Fran laughed. She knew that was true. "Now that everything is fine, you can tell her and Tim everything that happened; and I'll call them both when I get home."

Motioning to Will he said; "Let's go." Giving a hug to Joan and Jennifer, and shaking hands with Charlie he said. "Thanks, Charlie, for being a good friend to my sister."

"Charlie, will you come for supper, too?" asked Fran.

"I was hoping you would ask."

"In that case," said the archbishop, "would you pick me up? Save Will here, a trip." He nodded to Will, "You need some rest anyway, after all the work you did for yesterday's meeting."

Will managed a smile after biting the inside of his cheek. *You are so weak and such a disappointment; I thought you wanted to save the church. Now you're believing all this reconciliation nonsense.* "Sure, thanks, Bob. Very thoughtful of you. We did accomplish something great together, didn't we? Even though no one got dessert!" He laughed while bowing to Sister Frances Mary.

Fran smiled while a shiver shook her whole body. The archbishop laughed; the others giggled wondering why they felt so nervous.

Brushing past Charlie Will followed the archbishop out of the room.

Fran shivered again as they left. Heading for the closet Joan pulled out Fran's clothes. "Come on, let's get ready to go home. We'll see you about 6:00, Charlie."

"Come on, Charlie, I'll walk you out," said Jennifer.

Nearing the elevator, she said "You don't trust him, do you?"

"I can't put my finger on anything specific, but I thought he was too pleased to bring up Adam's name."

"I thought so, too." She flashed a quick smile. "But, for now, let's just be happy."

Charlie leaned over and kissed her cheek. "See you later."

Chapter 18

The next morning Fran woke up humming a melody from an enchanting dream. *Thank you, God, for bringing us all together again.* Savoring the hopes promised by last night's shared dinner, she allowed her imagination to stir up dreams of the three of them working together at **Cry Justice**.

The ringing phone startled her. Thinking it was her brother, Tim, she hummed again as she reached for the phone. He had been so upset last night she knew he would be checking on what kind of night she had. Surprised by a voice she did not expect she said, "Adam, what's wrong?"

"I need to talk with you. The police came to see me yesterday; I didn't do anything to hurt you, Sister, honest."

"I believe you, Adam."

"Could you meet with me today? I would like to talk to you."

"Of course, Adam. Why don't you come here for lunch?"

"No, I don't want anyone to see me. Could we meet here at the hotel where I work? One of the maids who is a friend of mine said we can use Room 235 until 1:00. I'm afraid to let anyone see me talking with you."

"Adam, that's a strange request, but I don't blame you for anything."

"Please, Sister, I need to see you. Please, I don't know where to turn."

"OK. Adam. I can be there by 11:00."

"Thank you so much, Sister. Just take the elevator up to the second floor, and go to Room 235."

Placing the phone back in its cradle, it rang again. This time it was Tim.

"Hi, Sis. How was your night?"

"I slept like a log. I'm fine."

"Are you going to take it easy today? I don't think you should go overboard for a few days anyway."

"Oh, Tim, don't worry so much. I did have a strange request from the former altar server of Charlie's that I told you about last night. He wants to meet with me today at the hotel; he's afraid to be seen, but wants to talk."

"Fran, I don't think you should do that; if he was responsible for what happened to you, you don't know what he might do now. He doesn't sound right to me."

"I'm sure he had nothing to do with that. And he was so upset; he begged me to listen to him."

"You're a softy, Fran, and I know I won't be able to change your mind. Just promise me you'll be careful. And call me this evening."

"I'll do that, Tim. Now have a very good day."

In his office Charlie was checking his e-mail when his phone rang. "Excuse me, I didn't hear you. Who is this?"

"Adam."

"Adam, I'm glad you called."

"Can you meet me today at the hotel? I need to talk to you."

"What's wrong, Adam? You're welcome to come here."

"No, no, I need to see you in private. I don't know where to turn. I didn't do anything to Sister Frances Mary, but the police came to see me, and I'm scared."

"Adam, I told the police I didn't think you had anything to do with it."

Like I would believe that. "I'm glad to hear that, but I need to see you, here, in private, at 12:00." *That should give Father Will a little extra time to talk with Sr. Frances Mary.* "Please, come to Room 235. I'm afraid I'm going to do something bad. I need your help."

"Adam, take it easy. I'll come. Promise me you won't do anything rash."

"I promise. Room 235. 12:00."

Sitting for a moment his hand resting on the phone Charlie prayed. *I wonder what is bothering him. I better call Fran.*

The phone had rung five times when Charlie heard Jennifer's voice on the other end. "Jennifer, Good Morning. How are you?"

"Couldn't be better, Charlie. Fran had a good night, too. But she's not here; I saw her leaving about fifteen minutes ago."

"Do you know where she was going?"

"No, she just said that something had come up. You sound worried."

"I was wondering if she was OK; I'll call back later."

Charlie looked at his watch; *10:30; if I leave at 11:00 I'll get to the hotel in plenty of time.*

Parking her car in the hotel lot Fran tingled with excitement recalling how well the panel discussion had gone on Saturday. Walking towards the lobby, an unexpected November gust pushed her backwards a few steps. Wind often reminded her of the Holy Spirit; *O dear God, you seem to be pushing me away.* Pulling her purse back onto her shoulder she tucked her hands in her pockets. Noticing an icy chill as she entered the elevator, she hesitated before pressing the second floor button.

Knocking on the door of Room 235 she was surprised that it was unlocked. Nudging it open she tiptoed inside.

"Adam?" She gasped as Will came out of the bathroom. He had on jeans and a pale blue long-sleeved shirt. "What are you… Why are you… Adam called…"

"I know; he called for me because I knew you wouldn't come if I called."

Seeing a large kitchen knife on the bedside table she swung around for the door, but Will grabbed her, kicked the door shut, and shoved her onto the bed. He jumped on top of her and stretched her arms above her head.

"Will, what are you doing? Let me go! Let me go!"

"If only you had died."

"Charlie was right."

"Of course, he was." Pressing his knees on her thighs he slapped her face so hard she gulped for air. With one hand holding her arms together, he reached for the rope he had laid on the bed. He jerked her hands upward and tied them to the bedpost. Feeling his crushing bony body spreading out over hers every muscle in her twisted in vain to dump him to the side. "Keep squirming, Fran; I love the struggle."

Sliding off her he grabbed her chin. "Open your eyes; look at me!"

Fran stared at the ceiling. Slapping her again he said "I told you, look at me!" Her eyes did not move. "OK, have it your way; you always did have to be the one in power. But I ask you; who is in charge, now!"

Hearing his belt drop to the floor Fran bit her lip as she listened to the buttons on her blouse pop off. His fingernails scraped her legs as he pulled off her skirt and panties. He was on top of her again, his bare cold chest pressing against hers. Walking his cold fingers up her back he unhooked her bra. He lay on her for a full minute heaving slow deep breaths. With cold lips he sucked on her ear lobe, whispering, "How does it feel, Fran, knowing what's coming and not being able to stop it?" *Glad Adam gave me an hour; I can enjoy this a bit longer.* He slid his tongue into her ear, and howled as she twisted her head away. "How does it feel, Fran, to be totally in my power? My hands can touch any part of you I want. How does this feel, Fran?" His cool moist tongue licked her ear as he slithered his hands all over her trembling body.

All of a sudden Fran felt his body stiffen. *O God, please help me.* Darkness overcame her, and her body wilted beneath him.

"You, bitch!" He slapped her face from side to side. "I wanted you to feel this, too." Snatching the knife from the bedside stand and slipping off her, he thrust it into her chest. Watching the blood ooze out and over her limp body he roared and stabbed her again and again. When he stopped he stared at her blood on his hand; it ran down his arm, down his leg, and onto the sleeve of his shirt. He wiped his arms and leg with the bedspread. He glanced at the clock by the bed; *in fifteen minutes Charlie should be here.* Grabbing the knife, his clothes and shoes he ran for the bathroom; one shoe fell from his hand; he kicked it across the floor. Roaring with glee as lathered himself from head to toe and sang as the warm water rinsed it all away. Dressed again, he went to the sink, rubbed some soap on the bloody sleeve and rinsed it in the sink, snickering as the water turned red and swirled around the knife.

Hearing a knock on the door he grinned. Wiping the knife clean he pulled the plastic gloves from his pocket. After a second knock, he heard Charlie call Adam's name. "Door's open."

Hesitating Charlie put his hand on the doorknob. *I guess I need to hear what Adam has to say.* He turned the knob and pushed the door open. "Oh no, no, Fran!"

Racing over to her, Charlie held her in his arms sobbing and screaming. Hearing the door close he stood up seeing a blur coming at him. Will sliced his face with the knife. Charlie's head struck the corner of the nightstand as he collapsed to the floor. Still clutching the knife, Will shoved it into Charlie's abdomen. He yanked Charlie's arm to the knife, pressed his fingers around the handle and turned the body over onto the knife. Taking a quick, final glance around the room he opened the door. Seeing no one in the hall, he closed the door, and ran to the elevator.

Chapter 19

I hope Adam is finished with his meeting, Louisa thought walking towards Room 235. *I know I could be in trouble for letting him use this room, but he was so worried about something.* Pushing open the door she screamed; her legs became like concrete poles bonded to the floor. Her yelling became shrieking.

Maria came running from the other hall. "Louisa, what is wrong?" She bolted to her friend gasping for air. Reaching the door, she hugged Louisa and screamed. "Who are they?"

"I don't know. Maria, what am I going to do? Adam asked me if he could use this room."

"Adam could not have done this. We have to call security. Thank goodness everyone else on this floor seems to be out. Let's close this door and I'll call Joe."

Within minutes, Joe Morgan, the head of security came up to Louisa and Maria pressing themselves against the wall. Their eyes were squeezed shut, their lips moving in prayer.

"You found someone dead?"

Their eyes popped open. "Worse," they cried in unison. "Murdered."

"It's good you didn't go in; I'll call the police."

Five minutes later Detectives Conroy and Harris introduced themselves to the three waiting in silence. Looking at Louisa and Maria, Conroy said, "Are you OK about going in here with us?"

Louisa grabbed Maria's hand as they nodded a trembling yes.

Opening the door, Joe gasped. Conroy and Harris shook their heads. Louisa and Maria dabbed the tears rolling down their cheeks. Walking over for a closer look Detective Conroy motioned for his partner. "Bill, look who they are. Father Charlie Fletcher, and Sister Frances Mary."

Bill turned away; after all these years he thought nothing could turn his stomach. "We better get the crime scene investigators here. He turned to Joe who was still standing in the doorway with Louisa and Maria. "Can you tell us anything?"

Louisa looked at Joe and then at Maria. She wiped her eyes. "I know Adam could not have done this."

"Are you talking about Adam Wetzel?" said Joe.

Louisa nodded. She looked at him again. "I know I should not have let him do it, but he wanted to use this room for a meeting this morning. He said he had to see someone in private, but he never said who."

"Is he working now?"

"Probably; he usually works lunch." Louise wiped her eyes again.

Conroy looked at Joe. "Get him for us. Take him to your office. I'll meet you there." Turning to his partner he said, "Wait for the crime scene crew and then meet me in Joe's office."

Pacing back and forth in the kitchen, Adam squashed his cell phone against his ear as he talked to Will. "I thought you would be calling me sooner. I'm working already. Should I come up to the room now?"

"I'm sorry, Adam; I'm afraid I failed you. We may have to set up another meeting."

"Why? What happened?"

"I was late getting to the hotel because the archbishop asked me to meet with him; by the time I got there, I saw Father Fletcher tapping on the door and going in. Within minutes he and Sister Frances Mary were arguing. I waited near the ice machine but when I heard Sister Frances Mary yelling at him I decided I would make things worse if I went in, so I left. I'm sure she will call you, and we can try again to get them together. I'm sorry I disappointed you, Adam."

"You probably were right to leave, but I'm getting scared. I've been waiting since yesterday for the police to ask me about my outburst to Father Fletcher, but nothing yet. Hold on, a minute. Joe, the security manager is coming."

Adam held the phone at his side. "Good morning, Joe. How are…."

"Adam, Detective Conroy wants to see you in my office, now."

"A detective is here. I'll talk to you later."

"Remember, Adam, tell your story, and keep our secret. Call me later."

Adam followed Joe, his hand shaking as he slid his phone into his pocket, his mind reviewing his story and racing with questions he thought the police might ask. *Remember what Father Will said, stay calm, tell your story; keep our secret.*

Flashing a weak smile to Conroy Adam stood in silence.

"Adam Wetzer?"

Adam nodded. Patting Adam's shoulder, Joe left his office, closed the door behind him, and walked down the hall shaking his head.

"Did you have a meeting this morning with Father Fletcher and Sister Frances Mary."

"No."

"Louisa told us she let you use the empty room; that you told her you needed it for a private meeting."

"That's true, but I said that to keep their identities secret. I thought that if Father Fletcher and Sister Frances Mary had some time to talk Father would explain that he meant for her to get sick, not die. And I thought they needed to meet somewhere private so that her brother would not see them together."

"Are you saying that you know Father Fletcher was involved in the attempt on Sister's life? How would you know that?"

"I've known Father Fletcher since I was a child; I just know." *How am I going to keep our secret?*

"So you're saying you're friends with Father Fletcher? And you set up a meeting in this room as a favor for him?"

"No, I'm not a friend, but I thought Sister Frances Mary would get him to admit the truth."

"What truth?"

Adam swallowed and took a deep breath. "Well, many years ago, I was an altar boy for Father Fletcher. He took special interest in me after my father had died, and I was grateful to him." Adam swallowed again. "At first."

"What do you mean by that?"

"Every Wednesday after my father's funeral, Father would come over to our house. Even after we moved to another parish, he kept coming to see her. My mother started to be happy again, so I didn't think anything of it; I was just glad he was helping her live again. She would send me out to play with my friends and tell me not to come back until it was getting dark. When I would come back, he was gone, and my mother would have a special dinner for me; she always said Father helped her make it."

"So when did you start disliking all this?"

"One night when I came home, she was crying. She said that she was all alone again. Every night I would hear her crying in her bed, for about two months. And then, one morning when she didn't get up, I found her dead with an empty bottle of pills beside her bed. She killed herself because of him, and he never even came to her funeral."

"So you would have a serious motive to want to hurt him."

"I admit I hate him, but I think he; maybe he and Sister; maybe he wanted to leave Sister Frances Mary like he left my mother."

"So you're telling us that you believed that if you arranged a meeting for Father Fletcher with Sister Frances Mary, she would get him to admit what he did to her?"

"Yes, because when that happened at the dinner, I thought she was dead, and since he was sitting beside her, I figured he put sleeping pills in her drink."

"Well, Adam, you may have just helped him finish the job."

"What do you mean?"

"Your friend Louisa found both of them dead."

"No! Not Sister Frances Mary! You said both of them?"

"Seems like Father Fletcher killed Sister Frances Mary and then himself."

Reaching out for a chair against the wall Adam's face drained of all its color. *I need to talk to Father Will. I wonder how long they are going to keep me here.*

Conroy waved Bill in to the office as he turned to Adam. "Are you all right?"

"I just can't believe it." Gripping the side of the chair Adam's hands turned white. "I never thought anything like this would happen."

"Well, Adam, we may need to talk to you again. You're free to go. Are you OK to go back to work?"

"I think so. Thank you, Officer." Hanging his head for a minute, Adam took a deep breath and stood up. Nodding to both detectives he opened the door. Watching him walk down the hall they saw him pull his cell phone out of his pocket.

"What did he tell you?" asked Bill.

"That he arranged for Father Fletcher to meet with Sister Frances Mary but he has past issues with the priest. I don't know; the story sounded a little too contrived to me. I'll have a better feel after we have a report from the crime scene people."

On his way back to his office when his phone rang Will hoped it was Adam. During lunch he had trouble pretending to be interested in the archbishop's happy retelling of the previous evening with his sister.

"Hello."

"Father Will, you won't believe the awful thing that has happened."

"Adam, what's wrong?"

"Both Father Fletcher and Sister Frances Mary are dead. The police think that Father killed Sister and then himself. Did you think that was possible?"

"I told you that I heard them fighting before I left. I'm not surprised. Did you tell the police your story? Did you keep our secret?"

"Yes, but I sort of suggested that maybe they were having an affair because of how Father Fletcher left my mother. And I never mentioned your name, honest, but I'm so upset. I liked Sister Frances Mary."

"I'm sorry about that, Adam. But this should clear your name."

"The police said they may have to talk with me again."

"Not to worry, Adam. Just remember, that our conversations with each other are never to be revealed. I will help you all I can, but it must be in secret."

"I know, but I still feel so terrible about Sister Frances Mary."

"Adam, try to think of her as a martyr for the truth and she saved you. That's how she would want you to remember her."

"You always know the right thing to say; that will help me. I believe that God works through you."

"I am his instrument, Adam. That's why you must follow all my directions, no matter what happens next. I will take care of you."

Chapter 20

"No! No! No!"

Hearing thunderous pounding on the archbishop's desk Will raced from his office. He glanced at the police car through the window as he pushed open the archbishop's door. Detectives Conroy and Harris were standing in front of the desk; papers had been flung to the floor. "Bob, what's wrong?"

The archbishop was hunched over his desk, sobbing and holding his head with both hands. "Fran and Charlie; they're both gone."

"What do you mean?"

Conroy broke in, "Right now, it looks like murder-suicide."

Making a credible effort to look shocked and distressed Will said, "Are you sure?" *This is going as planned.*

Looking up the archbishop pounded his fists again on his desk. "That can't be true. I know that is not true."

Will leaned over to the archbishop and whispered in his ear. "Archbishop, I realize how difficult this is." He straightened up, hoping the next part of his sentence would be overheard. "But remember what we talked about at the hospital."

"Are you talking about Adam?" asked Conroy.

Will looked at the archbishop who was wiping his eyes. Hesitating long enough to suggest a reluctance to share damaging knowledge, he said, "No one wanted to believe that."

"We have already interviewed him; he told us quite a story about Father Fletcher wanting a private meeting with Sister Frances Mary, and about his mother and the priest.

"Did he explain what he meant when he shouted to Father Fletcher about what he did to Sister Frances Mary?"

"What do you think he meant?"

"I don't know, but it sounded like Adam knew a terrible secret about Father Fletcher."

"But, Will," said the archbishop, "when you seemed to think that Adam was the guilty one, it was Father Fletcher who defended him."

"I know, but this news is too disturbing. I never wanted to believe the rumors I had heard about Charlie and Mrs. Wetzer."

"But Charlie, Father Fletcher, had no clue what Adam meant."

"Well, that's what he told us. I think this news should cause us to rethink the possibility."

Conroy's partner spoke up. "Father Will, do you have any personal knowledge about this relationship?"

"No. But, at this point it explains a lot."

"To be honest with you," Conroy hesitated and looked at the archbishop first and then Will, "Adam blames Father Fletcher for his mother's suicide; are you sure you knew this priest?"

Groaning the archbishop said, "Detective, yes, I knew Father Fletcher very well; he was a good priest. There is no way he was ever responsible for someone's death, never. And, I know you will discover he had nothing to do with my sister's death and he did not kill himself. We all had dinner last night; everything was fine; in fact, everything was great."

"Were your sister and Father Fletcher involved?"

The archbishop's jaw dropped and his eyes hurled daggers at Conroy and then at Harris, "What the" he gasped; "what are you suggesting, Detective?"

Conroy lowered his eyes, and cleared his throat. "Archbishop, this; the scene. This did look like a tragic end to a lover's quarrel."

Harris hurried to add, "Archbishop, we're just giving you our first impressions from the crime scene. There was a lot of anger in that room."

A tear rolled down the archbishop's cheek as he shook his head. "Detectives, I assure you, my sister and Father Charlie did not have an improper relationship."

Swallowing the pleasure tickling his throat, Will knew his performance was worth an Academy award. Moving closer to the archbishop he put his hand on Bob's shoulder. "Archbishop, I'm here to help." Turning his head to the detectives, he said, "I'm sure the archbishop is only interested in the truth, and will cooperate fully with your investigation. But, he has gone through enough for today; do you need to ask anything else right now?"

Harris shook his head. Conroy said, "Archbishop, we are very sorry for your loss; I hope you realize that finding the truth is our highest priority."

Positioning himself in front of the archbishop Will pointed the detectives toward the door. He nodded to each detective as they left, watching with calm satisfaction as they drove away.

Turning back toward the archbishop's office he glared at the sight of the archbishop slumped in his chair, his head wedged into his chest. *I've got to move him away from this depression; how are we going to save the church if he continues this useless mourning.*

He rapped his knuckles on the doorframe. Lifting his head the archbishop gave Will a feeble wave of his hand. "Will, come in. Pull that chair over here, closer to me."

Dragging a chair next to the archbishop Will set it at a slight angle so he could look into his eyes. "Bob, how can I help? You must believe that Fran is in a better place."

"Will, I don't know how I can go on. I don't know what I believe anymore. I've been sitting here remembering all the consoling words I used to say to others, about how those who have left us are nearer to us than ever, how love never ends, how we all live in God and will see them again. Now I battle so many questions, so many doubts. And how am I going to tell Tess and Tim?"

"Bob, you must go on. Now that Fran sees the truth, she would want you to continue your work."

"What do you mean, now that Fran sees the truth? What are you talking about?"

"Don't you believe that now she sees the error of her ways with **Cry Justice**? Don't you believe that she would want you to tell others the truth?"

"I have a huge hole in my heart. I can't stop crying. I feel as if I'm drowning, and you think I even care about **Cry Justice**? Besides, maybe she was right. What if she was right, Will? Maybe I wasted all those years when we could have been working together."

"But, Bob, I see another version. I think Fran had a change of heart. I think she was killed because Charlie would not let her leave the group after the great meeting that we had."

"Will, it's so considerate of you to try and find an acceptable reason for her death. But I don't think that's why she died."

"Why is it so hard for you to see that? It provides a perfect explanation for her tragic death. Can you understand what this could mean for you, for our church?"

"But it makes Charlie look bad, and I just know there's no truth to it. But, as I said, it's kind of you to try and make me feel better."

"I realize that Charlie was once a good friend. And I know you believe that last evening was some sort of reconciliation and reunion, but your grief may be blocking your judgment. Just think about what I've said and…"

"I'm tired, Will. I'd like to be alone."

"Of course, Bob." Pushing the chair back to its previous spot Will walked out without looking back. Dragging his heels towards his office, Will stopped dead as he heard a howl coming from the archbishop. *O Bob, get over it; she was evil and deserved to die; they both did. I'll put up with your weakness for the time being, but once the funeral is over, my plan will have to go forward, or else.* Feeling the pulsing of his cell phone he pulled it from his pocket. "Adam, hold on, I'm on my way to my office."

Closing and locking his door Will said. "Adam, what's wrong?"

"The police want to ask me some more questions."

"Remember what I told you and keep calm. I have some new information for you, but we'll have to plan how to get this information to the police."

"What is it; will it help me?"

"Of course, Adam. You know I'm looking out for you. The archbishop and I just had a conversation. You liked Sister Frances Mary, and of course, the archbishop is distraught over losing his sister. He's beginning to suspect that Father Charlie might have been trying to convince Sister Frances Mary to leave that group they belonged to; you remember reading about **Cry Justice**, don't you?"

"I heard something about it, but I didn't understand what it was all about."

"Well, the archbishop was very unhappy that his sister belonged to that group with Father Fletcher. He thinks that maybe she decided to leave, and Father Fletcher wouldn't let her."

"And so he killed her! He has some kind of power over women. With my mother—I think he wanted my mother to go with him when he was moved to another parish far away and when my mother said she didn't want to move me again, he just dropped her. Now it's making sense. That's why she committed suicide."

"I think you're right on target, Adam. But now, we have to figure out a way to get this information to the police."

"Well, what if I go to the archbishop and tell him about my mother; then he could tell the police that part. It might help."

"Adam, I'm not sure that's a good idea. You know more about Sister Frances Mary than her own brother; he would never believe that she and Father Fletcher were, you know, involved. So he wouldn't want to hear about your mother and Father. When the police talk to you again, you could tell them how Father Fletcher dominated your mother, and instead of fighting with him, she took it out on herself. Then you could say that's why you thought he did something to Sister Frances Mary. They'll ask you for more explanation, and that's when you would explain that Sister Frances Mary was a strong woman, and wanted to leave **Cry Justice** to support her brother and when Father would not let her leave, they had a fight."

"You make it so clear. How can I thank you for helping me again?"

"Be strong. Remember, the police cannot know that I helped you because I work with the archbishop and it would be terrible for the church to have the police asking the archbishop embarrassing questions. And I know your devotion and loyalty to the church in spite of the pain caused you by Father Fletcher."

"You can count on me. You make up for all that he did to me. I'll never forget your kindness to me."

Chapter 21

"Tess."

"Bob, I was ready to dial your number. I know something terrible has happened to Fran. She's gone, isn't she?"

"Yes." Hearing her scream he sobbed and rubbed away the tears washing both his cheeks.

Gulping for air, she said, "Tell me everything. I know it's awful, but I need to know the details."

How he ached to put his arms around her. "Tess, I didn't see her. I can tell you what the police told me." Talking and crying, he knew that he would have to tell her the detectives' suggestion that this was a love affair gone wrong. Knowing also what she would say, he knew her fist would be clenched like his.

"Bob, you know that can't be true!"

"That's what I told Detective Conroy. But how can I prove it?" Gritting his teeth, he stared at his fist.

"Fran and I had a connection so deep that there could never be a secret between us. Even when one of us didn't want to share, and even when we respected each other's need to keep silent, our struggles were transparent to each other. We understood that the time would come when the words would come out. There is no way that Fran would compromise her values in a wrong relationship and I wouldn't know."

"I believe you, but that won't be enough for the detectives. I can't give them any reason for them to be found together in a hotel room." He tasted the salt as the tears he could not stop trickled over his lips.

"That altar server you told me about when Fran was in the hospital—what was his name—Adam?"

"Yes, but neither Charlie nor Fran thought he was involved."

Tess gasped for more air. "Tim called me this morning and told me he was worried. He had called Fran and she told him about this strange phone call from

Adam asking her to come to the hotel. He warned her to be careful, but she felt she had to go. You know she wouldn't refuse to see him if he made up some story about needing her help." She relaxed her tight fist for a moment.

"So, if Adam was the one who got them to meet at the hotel, maybe he was waiting inside and killed them both." Bob's heart skipped a beat and sank into the bottomless hole that he wished would swallow him whole. Realizing for the first time that he would welcome death right now he imagined Fran surrounded by the whitest light, holding out her arms to him. He sighed. Tess's question pulled him back.

"But, Bob, how could he do that alone? You know Charlie would have defended Fran with his own life."

"But who else could have been there?"

"Where was Will this morning?" Bob's heart began beating rapidly, his clenched hand went cold, and bitter new tears stung his eyes.

"Oh, Tess, please, don't. We had a meeting and then, as far as I know, he went back to his office. You can't believe he's still carrying a grudge because I pulled him out of Sacred Heart. Remember, I asked Fran to leave, too."

"I know." Biting her trembling lip she brushed away a hot tear.

"O God, Tess. Did she ever forgive me for that?"

"Bob, you know that for Fran, family came first; she would never hold a grudge. Even though she and Jennifer and Joan were let go without cause, she believed that God would open new paths, and she would find new life. That's when she would pray the Magnificat—my soul magnifies the Lord, she would say. But when all that happened at Sacred Heart she told me she had written her *Un-Magnificat.*"

"The Un-Magnificat? That sounds like she lost faith."

"It could sound like that, but it was how she worked through the loss. It was an expression of hanging on to the God she wanted to believe in even more. I can remember part of it; I'll say it for you if you want."

Swallowing the massive lump in his throat Bob said, "Please."

"This is how it began: 'My soul wilts before you, O Lord, and my spirit weeps in your presence. Why have you looked away from the misery of your servant? Surely, from now on all generations will call me cursed, for your might has crushed me with sorrow, and terrible is your name.' I can't remember the rest of it, but she wrote it down for me; I'll find it."

"Oh, Tess, I was the one who crushed her."

"She never blamed you, Bob; she understood how hard it was for you."

"But I was upset with her; I believed that all three of them had become a bit too strong. They were designing all kinds of new programs in the parish, and people kept asking where Father Will was, and what was he doing; then the gossip took over and everyone thought he was having an affair. Now I wish I had let her tell me her side of the story."

"We used to laugh about the affair allegations. Fran said Will was too cold to have the hots for anybody. But, Bob, if Father Ed had been a more effective leader he could have stopped it all. Fran told me once that she thought he wanted to be rid of Will and rather than take a stand, he let the gossip escalate so that you had to make the decision. You have to believe she did not blame you."

"How I wish I could talk to her; I'm so sorry for everything."

"You have to remember last night; I know that was her dream—to share dinner with you, to be brother and sister again. But, Bob, I have to tell you this— she always worried how much influence Will was having over you. She was afraid of what he could do."

"But not murder, Tess. He couldn't be responsible for her death. He's so loyal to the church; he's driven to protect the faith."

"Are you sure he's not driven to be in power?"

The memory of Will losing control that night at dinner flashed before the archbishop; he forced it aside along with an intruding uneasiness seeping into his soul. "But, Tess, he's the one who was in charge of the great meeting we had; he planned everything."

"That's what frightens me."

Recalling something Will had said that morning the archbishop became silent.

"Bob, are you still there? Hello? Bob?"

"I'm here. Will said something this morning—he suggested that Fran wanted to leave **Cry Justice**; he said that 'now that she knows the truth'. What do you make of that?"

"Fran believed in **Cry Justice**; the truth she knows now is that your heart was open again." Choking she realized what she had said. "Bob, you know what I mean—that the two of you could share your love for the church again. She wanted…"

"It's OK, Tess, I do know what you mean. I don't think I can talk about this anymore, not right now. And I need to call Tim."

"I'll call him, Bob, if you want."

"If you're up to it, I would be grateful. When do you think you and Tim and your families could come here to be with me?"

"We'll be there tomorrow, as early as possible."

Hanging up the phone Bob saw Will standing in his doorway. *How much had he heard?* "Will, I didn't know you were waiting for me. Is there something you wanted to say?"

"I'm worried about you, Bob; I thought your devotion to the church was unconditional, but you seem so divided now. I thought we were going to convert the church together. What has happened to you?"

"My sister is dead!"

"And you should realize that God has provided you with an opportunity."

"How can you be so cruel? How dare you even suggest that God approved her murder!" Will's face turned crimson with anger, his eyes like stinging arrows. Bob gasped. "Will, what are you doing?"

Will had grabbed Fran's church sculpture from the archbishop's desk, and was holding it high above Bob's head. "How could you be so miserably weak?"

Shoving his chair back as fast as he could Bob surprised himself that he had risen to his feet. He rammed his fist into Will's stomach. Will did not even flinch; he laughed. Bob stared at Will's arms, as if in slow motion, heaving the sculpture at him.

"No! No! Don't do this!"

Bob felt a tug at his arm; he turned and blinked open his eyes. "Where? Where am I? Fran, what are you doing here? Tess? Tim? What is going on?"

The hugs and squeezes were so tight he began coughing for air. "I don't understand." Trying to lift his head he moaned and sank back into the white pillow. "Where am I?"

"Get the doctor, fast," yelled Tim to the nurse who had looked in on the commotion.

"Bob," Fran and Tess said together while Tim grasped his hand. "You've been in a coma since November 9. The limo you were in was hit by a bus as you approached the hotel for dinner. Do you remember anything?"

"Fran, you're here. You're alive." A tear dropped on his cheek.

"Of course, I'm here. Why wouldn't I be?"

"I don't know why I said that. I still don't understand why I'm in this bed."

When the doctor entered the room, the three stepped away from the bed and watched with steadfast eyes as their brother was examined. Turning to them with a broad smile Doctor Gordon said, "He seems fine. Sometimes, these things happen; they just wake up. But I want him to stay here for another twenty-four hours for observation." He turned back towards the archbishop. "Do you remember what happened?"

"Not much that was real, it seems. I remember being happy at a meeting; I remember riding in a limo, and seeing bright lights, very bright lights."

"Those were the lights at the hotel entrance," said Fran. "In fact, they were so blinding the police decided that's what caused the accident. The bus driver couldn't see the traffic light change and ran full force into the side of the limo, the side where you were sitting."

"Will, what about Will? I remember he was in the back seat with me."

Catching her breath as an icy chill clutched at her Fran said, "He's fine. He was taken to the hospital and was let go within an hour. Not a scratch. But he was quite shaken. He's been insisting on completing the work of that day."

"Can you call him? I need to see him."

"Of course," said Fran, her stomach churning.

"But not right now; just stay here and talk with me."

Motioning Fran to a chair next to their brother, Tim and Tess pulled up two more chairs. Fran reached for Bob's hand. Smiling, he said, "So, tell me what's been going on. By the way, what's today's date?"

"December 2nd, Monday," said Tim.

"I missed Thanksgiving."

"Today is our Thanksgiving day," said Tess and Fran together.

"That twin thing never quits, does it?" Winking at Tim he said, "What are we to do with these sisters of ours?"

Tim hugged them both.

"Fran, do tell me what's happened since the meeting day. What did we call it? Something about reconciliation?"

Unable to hide her joy she said, "A Call for Reconciliation and Possibilities."

"And it went well, right?"

"Very well," said Fran patting his hand.

"I bet Will was upset the day ended without that dinner; he had worked so hard to make it special."

Fran hated the icy agitation that rose within her at every mention of Will's name. How she wanted to savor these moments with her brother without these dark and cold intrusions. "You are right about that; he insisted on having it the following week, but the hotel couldn't accommodate him, and besides, everyone from the meeting was so sure you would be back, they convinced him to wait."

Bob found his thoughts floating to a dark memory inside. "Oh, that's good." His voice was so faint Fran had to ask him to repeat it. She was concerned about the distant stare in his eyes.

"Bob, what's wrong? You look as though you've seen a ghost."

"What? Oh, it's nothing. I thought I was remembering something; you know, how parts of a dream sometimes stay with you, but fade away as you try to recall what it was all about. But let's concentrate on being awake! Will will be pleased to know we can proceed as soon as possible."

"That's fantastic! I'm glad I decided to wait."

Fran caught her breath as she turned to see Will at the door. Tim stood and extended his hand. Darting a quick look at Fran, Tess turned her eyes back to her brother.

Waving him closer Bob said, "We were just talking about you, Will."

"It's wonderful to witness this miracle, Archbishop." Will's eyes moved from Bob to Fran lingering on her just a moment too long.

He knows just how to get to me, thought Fran feeling an immediate urge to leave. *At least I won't have to call him.* Standing with a slowness that reflected her reluctance to leave her brother's side she said. "I need to go home for a while, Bob. Besides, I want to share all this good news with Jennifer and Joan."

Grabbing for her hand, Bob caught it and held on. "You'll be back tomorrow, before I leave here?"

"Oh, I'll be back in a few hours with Jennifer and Joan."

"How about Charlie Fletcher? For some reason, I need to see him."

Beaming Fran said, "Of course; I'll call him as soon as I get home." Hugging him she whispered, "I love you, my brother." Embracing Tim and Tess she said, "I'll see you two when I get back. Why don't you get some lunch? I'm surprised that no food has come yet for you, Bob. Maybe Tim can get you some real food. You must be starving." Realizing she was beginning to ramble she sighed. *I need to leave; I hope Will won't still be here when I get back.* "I am leaving," she said with a weak wave of her hand.

"I'll walk out with you, Fran," said Tess.

"Don't forget to call Charlie."

Why *does he want to see Charlie,* muttered Will to himself. *Doesn't he remember how we laughed about the dreamer?* "Bob, how much do you remember about our great day—great that is, until the terrible accident. You must know that I wish it would have been me, not you."

"Oh, Will, don't say anything like that." Shadowy memories shuddered within him. "I thought I remembered beef and a huge crab cake, even red bliss potatoes, but I found out that we never got to dinner."

"That is what we were supposed to have; I must have told you that. But no, we never did get there."

"Pull up a chair, Will. Stay for a while," said Tim. "I know my brother is eager to hear what you have been doing."

Chapter 22

Fumbling through her purse for her cell phone, Fran was two rows past her car when she stopped to chide herself. *Stop thinking about Will, Fran, and concentrate on the good things about today. Bob is back!* Her fingers tingling, her heart throbbing, she punched in their home number.

"Joan, Bob is back! He woke up today; just woke up."

"Oh, Fran, such good news."

"I'm on my way home. I knew you and Jennifer would want to come to see him. The doctor wants him to stay for observation for twenty-four hours. But Will showed up, and I just had to get away."

"I understand; his name chills me from head to toe."

"Here's something to warm you—Bob wants to see Charlie! I was going to call him when I got home, but why don't you do that? I'm getting into my car now. I'll see you soon."

Before starting the car, she broke down in tears. *O God, what is wrong with me? I am so grateful for Bob, yet why do I feel I won't have him for long? I can't bear to lose him again, and, O God, I can't stand Will! Why did he have to show up today? I hate him! I hate him! O, God, forgive me.* She did not remember pulling out of the parking lot, but realized she had stopped at a red light, and was pounding the steering wheel. Wiping away her tears she took a deep breath as the light turned green. At the next intersection she took a quick look in the visor mirror and sighed. *Maybe my red eyes will clear up before I get home.*

Erupting within her soul came the words of the prayer she had not said for years now. *My soul wilts before you, O Lord, and my spirit weeps within me.* Remembering the agony that had inspired her composition of this prayer as well as her new life at Sophia's Blessings she faced her conscience. *I guess I've been in denial about Will. I wanted to believe that I was above holding a grudge.* She wiped away a single tear and continued praying. *Why have you looked away from the misery of your servant? Surely from now on all generations will call me cursed, for your might has crushed me with sorrow, and terrible is your name.*

She turned into the driveway exhaling a sigh of relief. Taking another quick glance in the mirror she sighed again. *They'll know I was crying; and they'll know why.*

The December air cooled her stinging eyes. Looking towards the front door she waved to Joan and Jennifer motioning for her to hurry inside.

"Come, we have some lunch ready," said Jennifer.

"No matter what it is, it will be comfort food," said Fran. Seeing the large Christmas soup mugs with the dancing gingerbread men made a smile spread across her face. She inhaled a slow smell of the delicious aroma of chicken noodle soup. A half sandwich with sliced turkey, lettuce and tomato sat at each of their places.

"Sit down, Fran," said Joan. "I'll fill the mugs."

With her friends on either side, Fran held their hands and said grace. Jennifer and Joan could feel the tension leaving her. "Amen."

"Will's appearance must have been such a downer for you," said Joan. "I'm so sorry."

"True." Sipping the soup, Fran relaxed in its warmth. "But I realized coming home I've been holding such hatred in my soul. Bob seemed so like his old self when he woke up. We were having such a good visit, but after Will arrived, I began to feel I was losing Bob again."

"Fran, you're too hard on yourself. Leaving Sacred Heart changed everything including your relationship with your brother. Will has a terrible hold on him, we all know that."

"Joan's right. How could you not feel what you call hatred? But we both know you. You hate what he has done, not him, and you need to allow yourself to feel that."

"I hope you're right." She took a bite of her sandwich. "This is so good, Joan."

"I'm glad you're enjoying it. I called Charlie; he was so overjoyed to hear about Bob. He said he'll see us at the hospital. He was heading over there within the hour."

"I'll be ready to go soon. I need to freshen up."

"We're ready whenever you are," said Jennifer. "If Will is still there, he'll have to face all three of us, plus Charlie."

"That picture almost makes me wish he will be there." Fran finished her sandwich and drank the last drop of soup. "I can't rid myself of my gut suspicion. I know Will has been insisting on having that dinner, and I don't know why that bothers me so much. As long as Bob was in the coma, no one felt like celebrating, but now Will can use his recovery to get everyone together, and he will come across as a redeemer, or something."

"A redeemer!" Jennifer clutched her heart as if her words had stabbed her. "What a strange image, Fran. It gives me the creeps."

"Me, too," said Joan.

"Enough about Will. I can't wait to see Bob and Charlie together. I just need to run to the bathroom. I'll meet you two in the car."

Walking to the car, Joan dug her hands deep into the pockets of her brown corduroy jacket. She glanced at Jennifer. "Are you worried about Fran? Do you think all this stuff with Will and her brother is too much?"

"She's always managed to grow no matter how challenging the situation, but when Bob was injured, she was so afraid that they would never have a chance to be brother and sister again." Jennifer covered her ears with her gloved hands. "And then to have Will show up while they were enjoying such a gift. Well, I can understand how painful that was."

"I know. And every time his name comes up, I have this dreadful icy sensation crawl all over me. It's so weird."

"I've had that same thing happen to me. I didn't mention it because I thought I was overreacting. Should we tell Fran?"

"No, at least not now, but I think we should keep a close watch. And tell Charlie, when we have a chance."

"Agreed. Here she comes."

"Want me to drive?" asked Joan.

Fran nodded. "I'm getting in the back."

Nearing the hospital, Joan gave a quick look at Jennifer. The frozen stare on her face told Joan that she had seen him, too. She hit the brake as the light turned red. "Sorry; I didn't mean to stop so fast." Gulping a mouthful of air her eyes were directed at Will marching towards the parking lot. Jennifer clenched both her hands.

"Look! There's Will," said Fran. "He's leaving. That's good; I'm not up to facing him twice in the same day."

Chapter 23

Walking into her brother's room Fran's eyes danced with delight. "Charlie, I'm so glad you're here." Hugging her brother first she then turned to Charlie with arms outstretched. She relaxed in his embrace allowing his gentleness to strip away her chills. She smiled at Tess and Tim. "I'm glad you stayed." When Tess hugged her Fran knew that she understood that she was glad they were still there, and had not left Bob alone with Will.

"Bob, it's so good to see you!" Joan leaned over to embrace him. "Welcome back." Looking at Charlie, she smiled and extended her arms to him, and waved Tess and Tim towards them for a group hug.

With a hasty brush of her hand, Jennifer wiped away a tear as she, too, hugged the archbishop. "Bob, we are grateful! I knew this day would come; I'm just glad it came sooner than later." She felt Charlie's hand on her back and turned to greet him. Tess and Tim smiled as they waited for their welcome.

No one said the words out loud but everyone was thinking, *This is like the old days, all of us together.*

Bob's words triggered hums of surprise. "Do you think December 14th is too soon to have dinner? The dinner we should have had on November 9th?"

Charlie cleared his throat. "I'm sure everyone will be thrilled to see you. Can it be done so soon?"

"Will assured me that he could." Bob swept his hand across his eyes, wiping away a strange shadow.

Shivering, Jennifer stole a quick glance at Joan who nodded as their eyes met. Realizing Charlie had sensed something between them, she mouthed "later" to him. Fran missed it all, except for her own chill and her brother's strange look. Attempting a smile for his sake she said, "Bob, I think that will be fine. As long as you are able to be there. Did you remember something? What were you brushing away?"

"I don't know, Fran. I keep almost remembering something, and it feels important, but whatever it is, it leaves me in the dark."

"Don't push yourself; if it's a memory from your dream, it will come when you need to remember."

"What's this about a dream, Bob?"

"Oh, Charlie, I keep having these dark glimpses of something." Turning towards his brother and sisters he said, "Did I say anything just before I woke up?"

"You were tossing and turning," said Fran, "and you cried 'No' twice, and 'don't do this.'"

Bob's lip quivered; his eyes shifted from Fran to Tess to Tim. "I don't know why. I don't remember what was happening."

"Bob," said Charlie, "I'm sure that if you are supposed to remember, you will, when it's time." For some strange reason Charlie found himself shivering. Will's smug face flashed before him, but faded into a dark shadow.

"Charlie's right," said Fran. "Now we need to concentrate on getting you home. You should be ready to leave about 11:00 tomorrow morning."

"I was thinking, if it is OK with you, that I could spend some time at your home, at Sophia's Blessings, before I go back to my place."

Before Fran could find her voice, Jennifer said, "It's way beyond OK; we would love to have you."

"I agree!" said Joan. "We have a small group coming in tomorrow about 3:00 for several days of reflection, so we'll be here in the morning. I seem to remember you like breakfast food anytime, so Jen and I will make you brunch. I still remember how you like your home fries, with lots of onions."

"Thank you, Joan."

"And Charlie is saying Mass for the group at 11:30 for the next three days, and he always stays for lunch. That's a hint—we hope you'll stay with us for at least three days. Won't it be great for all of us to share lunch every day? We promise you will get a refreshing rest, and what wonderful conversations we will have." Joan enjoyed the smile glowing on Fran's face.

"I couldn't ask for more." Bob's gaze rested on Fran; *why am I feeling this cold sadness in my heart, when everything is so good?* "Maybe I will even remember what I saw in my dreams, or maybe they were nightmares."

"I like to think that both dreams and nightmares have messages for us," said Charlie. "Maybe when we are asleep we are most open to the Spirit."

Nodding Bob looked again at Fran. He shivered from a confusing icy sensation as an eerie sentence crossed his mind. *I'll save you, Fran.*

"We're going to let you rest, now," said Fran and we'll be back tomorrow morning; I'll get your room ready."

"And I'll bring you something to wear," said Tim. I think you can make it through one day in some of my clothes."

Charlie laughed. "Tomorrow, after we get you to Fran's, I'll go to your place and get whatever you need."

Bob reached for Charlie's hand. "Thanks, Charlie; I am grateful."

After a round of hugs Fran and Tess said in unison, "Get some sleep." Tim shook his head as Joan and Jennifer gave the archbishop a thumbs up. Heading for the door, Bob saw Fran engulfed by an icy shadow; he felt a bloodcurdling scream straining to cry out, but his voice was paralyzed. *O God, what are you trying to tell me?* He managed a weak wave as they walked by his window.

Hesitating Fran peered into his eyes. Driving away her menacing fear she flattened her fingers on the window. "Love you, brother."

When they got to the parking lot, Fran grabbed Tess's arm and pointed to Will's car. "He's still here."

"Just keep walking," said Tess. "And hope he doesn't see us."

"I see him, too," said Charlie. "Let's not allow anything to spoil this night." Quickening their steps they got to their cars, out of Will's sight.

Will was so involved with his thoughts he missed the entire group. His hands were sweating as he gripped the steering wheel drinking in the delight he was sure would be his. *Little does Bob realize that agreeing to December 14th for the dinner was not his decision; I would have had the dinner that day even if he had not awakened. Barbara has been so wonderful about this whole thing; she almost feels responsible for the accident since it was her idea to have all those bright lights at the entrance. She's ready to do whatever I want. Having to plan a second dinner has been a wonderful bonus.* He had found some reason to meet with her every week since the accident. He felt the familiar throbbing within him.

Knowing his timing had to be right his breathing became rapid and shallow. *When she realizes what I have accomplished, when **Cry Justice** is destroyed, she will know my power; she won't be able to resist submitting to me, her redeemer.* Pleasure bursts riddled his body. Turning the key he reveled in the purr of the engine, somehow finding thoughts about internal combustion complementing his internal explosions.

Recalling how annoyed Fran looked that morning when he appeared in the doorway his satisfaction was swept away by his rage. "You think you have your brother back in your life; well, enjoy it for now, because he will soon be shocked at what happens to you. He'll grieve for a short time, but then he will recognize you had to die. If he doesn't…" Realizing he was shouting he heaved a deep breath. *Calm down, Will. I will succeed; nothing will stop me from saving my church. Plus my Barbara, and my sweet Evelyn. I will be your savior and you will be my favored ones.*

He braked as he approached the red light. *I forgot to check but I assume Bob will be released about 11:00 tomorrow; I can pick him up and still have time before I head for my meeting with Barbara.* Grinning he remembered how stunning she had looked last week; he had noticed that her hair was a few inches shorter, but still as luxurious and maybe even more enticing. His fingers quivered as he pictured them stroking those soft, shiny red tresses. He caught his breath as he glanced at the car clock, its green numbers showing 4:00; his meeting with Barbara was twenty-two hours away. His heart pounding he sped off.

Chapter 24

Awakening at 6:30 Bob opened his eyes, stretched out his arms, and realized his insides were smiling with his face; *my day of freedom.* Even breakfast felt like room service at an expensive hotel.

By 9:00 everyone had gathered in his room. His eyes rested on each face gathered around him as he sat on the edge of his bed, waiting for the nurse to give him the word that he could get going. He looked at the clock: 11:00. Catching his eye Fran felt the twinkle in her own. Her heart was singing while she shuddered from a peculiar chill. Tess squeezed her hand and Fran knew they would be talking about this later. Joan's eyes darted from Bob to Fran to Charlie and then to Jennifer. Her sigh brought all eyes to the clock, now at 11:20. Tim was the one who saw the nurse first. As soon as he saw her nod, he said, "Let's go, everyone!"

With Tim on his right and Charlie on his left Bob steadied his halting effort to stand. "Slow and easy, Bob," said Tim.

"Bob, I'm here! I was aiming for 11:00, but got caught in the traffic."

Choking on the air she had gulped Fran did not look towards the sound of that voice. Joan reached for her hand and Jennifer sighed. Tess bit her lip as she looked at her brothers.

"Will, I didn't expect you. I'm going to spend a few days with my sister."

"Oh, I assumed you'd be ready to come home." *What is going on with him? I can see that I'm going to have to do this alone.* "What about clothes? Should I pack a suitcase for you and bring it to you?"

"I'll be coming by later, Will, for some of the archbishop's things," said Charlie.

Sneer all you want, Charlie; your time is coming. Will looked at the archbishop standing now on his own. *What will the days at Fran's place do to you?* He shuddered, moving closer. "Bob, we have much work to do yet. But I understand. You do need some rest."

"That I do, Will. I'll let you know when you I'll be coming home." With faltering steps and reaching again for Tim's arm, Bob headed for the door. Charlie stayed beside him. Fran swallowed the lump in her throat and slid behind her brother. Tess's warm hand joined hers, and she glanced at Joan and Jennifer as they moved together towards her.

Stepping backwards into the hall Will watched the group file past him. *Pitiful* he smirked. "Bob, I'm meeting with Ms. Collins at 1:00 to set up the December 14th dinner. I'm sure she will be most happy to hear about your progress."

Bob's hushed and brief thank you stung Will; scowling he stared at the chatty group ambling down the hall. *He doesn't even seem to care how important this dinner is, even though my reasons are so far removed from his. He should be grateful that this dinner will make him look like a leader. But, of course, I am the true leader, the savior. How can I even hope that he will understand. Once Fran is out of the way, he may be a bigger problem than I anticipated. Oh well, no problem for me; I'll deal with that when it happens.*

Smiling at a nurse strolling by Will let himself bask in her shy grin; he spun around and ogled her until she disappeared around the corner. Turning back to the hall, he saw no one. Waiting a few more minutes he headed for the elevator. His steps became more spirited as his mind danced with images of Barbara.

He was glad when he got to the parking garage, that Fran's car was on its way out, followed by Charlie's. He ran the short distance to his car, and once seated behind the steering wheel, he heaved a deep sigh as he fingered his keys. *It would have been easier to have the dinner without you, Bob, but then I wouldn't be able to enjoy your mortification when Fran's shameful behavior brings our dinner to a smashing close.*

Pulling up in front of the hotel, he opened his car door and tossed the keys to a valet—a convenient perk—a gift from Barbara. Straightening his black suit jacket, he ran his fingers over his priestly collar, and strode through the door being held by a bellman.

Taking the elevator to the mezzanine floor, he caught his reflection in the mirrored elevator walls. Suit a perfect fit, not a hair out of place, shoes shined to perfection. Anticipating her greeting he turned right to Barbara's office. Addicted now to the familiar flutter in his stomach he tapped a polite knock, opened the door, and was smitten by the vision before him. *How good it will be when you recognize me as the savior I am; your pure love will be my delight when you rest in my faithful embrace.*

"Right on time, Father. Your punctuality is a virtue." Pointing to a soft blue cushioned couch she rose from her navy leather chair. Gliding from behind her desk Barbara sat down next to him. Teeming with a curious mixture of excitement and panic Will felt torn between sliding himself away from her and pressing closer to her inviting body.

"You're very kind, Barbara." How he ached to gaze into those enticing eyes, but she was too close. "I have some good news; the archbishop woke up yesterday and was released from the hospital today."

"Oh, Father, I am so happy." She clasped his hand with such enthusiasm that Will jumped to his feet pulling her up with him. He hungered for her captivating lips but realized he had shoved her away.

"I'm sorry. I'm sorry. Please forgive me."

"Oh, no Father, I am the one to ask for forgiveness. I've embarrassed you. I was just so relieved to hear that the archbishop has recovered. Please, I meant nothing improper. Do sit down." She returned to her desk.

Tormented by desire Will was cold, sad, and desperate. He had known these feelings every time his mother visited him when he was in the seminary. His mother's face flashed before him, shaking her head in disappointment. Summoning up the control that had become so much a part of him he said, "Don't waste a moment regretting it. All things happen for a reason; someday we'll laugh about this."

"Father, I have to admit that you seem to be driven, and though I am not a Catholic, I sense that your energy comes from a deep spiritual reservoir. That's an appealing quality in a man. And so, again, I say that I am sorry if I made you uncomfortable."

Trickles of pleasure seeped into Will. *I wish you could hear this, Mom. You were so unhappy with me when I told you I did not want to marry. And here I am, becoming a savior to this beautiful woman. Will you ever understand why this is more important than grandchildren for you?* "Barbara, your words mean more to me than you know. Now, let's get back to the reason I came." Allowing his eyes to meet hers he paused. Now *it's my turn to be in charge.* "You can come back here beside me; I won't attack you."

"Thank you, Father. You have a sense of humor, too." As she settled in next to him, he detected her subtle fragrance. Her next words encouraged Will's wildest fantasies. "I think we are going to be great friends."

Measuring his words with care Will took both her hands in his. "I believe that, Barbara." With a decisive calm he inhaled her scent, satisfied with his sense of discretion. He placed her hands in her lap. "Now, the date for the dinner will be the same; the archbishop is in full agreement. And I would be grateful for the basic timetable we agreed on the first time."

"Of course; the cocktail party followed by the dinner at 7:00; a half hour for you to check out everything; a band playing as you enter the lobby. Can I do anything else to satisfy you?"

Someday soon. "Of course not, Barbara. I couldn't ask for more."

Chapter 25

Squinting at the bright sun sliding through the blinds Bob's fingers stroked the soft yellow flannel sheet as he became aware of a tear and a smile at the same time. The night had been filled with dreams that he could not remember, and in spite of a fleeting chill, he felt an extraordinary peace here, at Sophia's Blessings. His eyes wandered around the room, soaking in the sheer lace valance touching the narrow white blinds, the pale blue walls, the slim bronze crucifix on the wall, and the velvety blue lounger. As those strange words, *I'll save you, Fran,* crept again into his head, he heard a faint tap on his door.

"I'm awake!"

"Good morning, brother. "How did you sleep?"

"Fine, fine, Fran. Is everyone else up? What time is it?"

"Yes, and it's 8:30. Joan's getting breakfast ready, but we're skipping the home fries, today. Some hot oatmeal, juice, toast; the doctor said you can have some coffee, but to limit it to two cups a day for now."

Bob reached for his sister's hand. "I'm so happy to be here, Fran. I remember the theme of our day was Reconciliation and Possibilities; that has special meaning for us, right? We've been on separate paths for too long, don't you agree?"

"Oh, Bob." She had no other words as she leaned in for a hug. She let the tears wash her cheeks and realized that they were both embraced by a happy God.

Bob patted her back. "Let's go eat."

Walking into the dining room, they were greeted with applause. "Charlie, I can't believe you're here already."

"Fran gave me your key last night, so I've already been to your place. If you find out you need anything else, let me know."

"I guess Will's taking care of everything."

"I'm sure he is."

Bob shook away a sudden and cold fear, and bowed to the smiling faces around the table. "Good morning, Tess, Tim, Joan, Jen. I hope everyone woke up as rested as I did."

"Here, Bob," said Jen as she pointed toward a pulled out chair. "Sit; Chef Jen is ready to serve!"

Oatmeal never tasted so satisfying; its warmth soothed the nervous stirrings Bob felt twisting in his stomach as he looked at the intense eyes and cheerful faces surrounding him. He eyed the apple Danish, the bagels, and the croissants, but chose the wheat toast. Each voice had its own appeal and laughter erupted every few minutes, as Bob kept shoving the shadows away. "Charlie, maybe this afternoon we can talk some more about dream messages."

"I'd like that, Bob. We'll have Mass at 11:30; then," nodding to Jen, "we'll be eating again. Let's talk after that."

Tess and Fran began picking up the dishes; Tim emptied the coffee pot grounds, and Jen was clearing the leftovers.

"Fran," said Tess, "Tim and I will be leaving after lunch." She turned to her brother, "Bob, I'm so glad you decided to stay here for a few days."

"Me too," said Tim.

In the brief silence that followed, Fran allowed her heart to soar in hope while Tess prayed for Fran because she was sure she knew what her twin was feeling. Tim said a prayer of gratitude for life, and Bob recognized a longing in his heart for conversation with his sister.

"Bob," said Charlie, "show me your room; I'll bring your suitcase, and you can tell me what I forgot to bring."

When he opened the bag, the first thing Bob saw was the sculpture from his office desk. He picked it up, held it in front of him, and turned his questioning eyes to Charlie.

"Fran thought you might want it."

"Do you know she made this for me?"

"Yes."

"This was when we both believed in—have I been wrong about **Cry Justice**? Have I lost my way, Charlie?"

"Just a detour, Bob. Sometimes, when people are given power, the responsibilities engender fear."

"Fear?"

"Just my opinion; but may I ask you this—did you become afraid that you might not serve the church, the People of God, worthily?"

"First of all, I didn't think I was worthy to become a bishop. Then I guess I did think I would not serve the people well. I can't remember when it happened, but somewhere along the way that fear that I wouldn't serve them became a duty to save them, and also the church. There was a time when I thought that meant a new vision, but I got scared of giving people too much freedom."

"Freedom is very scary; and maybe God is the only one who trusts us enough to give it to us."

"I never thought about it like that, Charlie. But it sounds right."

"Maybe you should rest a bit for now. We'll talk more this afternoon, if you want."

"Good idea. Thanks, Charlie."

Will finished his breakfast and carried his plate and coffee cup out to the kitchen. "Thanks, Annie."

"You're welcome, Father Will. I thought I'd see the archbishop today."

"Yes, so did I, but he decided to spend some time with his sister. He does need rest."

"I'm glad he went with Sister Frances Mary. She used to visit here often, but—well, I'm just happy that he's there. Maybe they will become friends again."

"Maybe you're right Annie." *And that will not be good for him or for the church.* "By the way, didn't I see you at the meeting that day? I didn't know you belonged to **Cry Justice**?"

Swallowing the panic mushrooming under his piercing eyes, Annie labored to sound calm. "I thought; I mean, I didn't feel it would be appropriate, knowing how the archbishop felt about the group."

"And how do feel now, Annie?"

Why is he asking me all this? Help me, God, to be strong, to say the right thing. "I think that the Day of Reconciliation was wonderful, except, of course, for the accident."

"So you feel that the archbishop was convincing."

"Yes, of course; I don't think he would be dishonest with us. He has a good heart, and once he understands that **Cry Justice** loves the Church, and wants the Gospel message to be preached as Jesus would want." *Why is he smiling? Why am I feeling so cold? Why am I saying so much?* "I mean, I think it was a good day.

"Fine, Annie; that's just what I wanted to hear. Thank you. I'm not making you nervous, am I?"

Shaking her head no Annie couldn't prevent the blush heating her face as she tried to hide her shivering. She attempted to smile. "No, Father; I'm just not used to being asked about such things."

Will patted her arm; Annie hoped he didn't notice how cold she was. "I'll see you at lunch time."

Annie steadied herself by reaching for the kitchen chair as Will turned and left. *"O God, please send your Spirit to the archbishop; help him to hear Sister Frances Mary and become what you hope him to be."* Crossing herself she began loading the few breakfast dishes into the dishwasher.

Chapter 26

Bob woke up in a cold sweat; this was his third morning at Sophia's Blessings. The night had been a terrifying parade of nightmares, but all he could remember was screaming Fran's name over and over and a feeling of betrayal and anguish. Sitting on the side of the bed he prayed. He feared reliving those dark scenes, but understood that he needed to know what message they were giving him. His talk with Charlie the other day convinced him of that. *I should talk with him again; maybe he can help me remember more, or at least make sense of what I do recall. Right now, I better get showered and dressed.*

The smell of home fries helped Bob set aside his bad dreams as he walked into the kitchen. "Smells great, Jen."

"Thanks, Bob. Hey, you look tired this morning. Didn't you sleep well last night?"

"I was hoping it wouldn't show. Where's Fran?"

Jen turned back to the stove and her potatoes. "She'll be here; she went for a morning walk. She didn't sleep well last night either."

A cold shadow rose in front of Bob and disappeared in an instant; gasping he covered his mouth. Jen had missed it.

"Good morning, brother."

"Heard you didn't sleep last night either. Do you think both of us could talk with Charlie after breakfast?"

Fran took Bob's hand. "That's a good idea."

Joan and Charlie came in together. "Let's eat," said Jen. Toasted bagels sat to the right of the fries and scrambled eggs; warm and buttered wheat toast was on the left. Fran sat down next to Charlie and across from Bob. Stifling the scream that exploded within him he stared at two shadows, each holding a knife over Charlie and Fran.

"Bob," cried Charlie. "What's wrong? You look as though you've seen the devil."

"Just a bad night, Charlie. Maybe I don't want to go home!" He tried to smile.

Jumping in, Fran said, "I vote for that!" She glanced at Charlie. "We both want to talk with you after breakfast—about our bad dreams."

"And after Mass, I do have to go home, Charlie. After all, the big dinner is eight days away."

Everyone seemed to eat a bit faster and soon Jen and Joan were clearing the table, telling the others to go. "Let's go to the living room," said Fran.

Bob and Fran walked towards the blue couch; the soft pillows with their green and blue circles offered a calming welcome. Sitting next to each other they watched Charlie push the coffee table to the side and slide the green recliner in front of them. Reaching for their hands, he said. "Let's pray."

The three friends relaxed their hands into each others. "O Spirit of God, we open ourselves to your quiet wisdom. We place our dreams before you; we honor your gifts and we praise you. Help us to see and understand." Charlie squeezed both their hands. "Who wants to go first?"

Bob looked at Fran. She nodded. "I don't remember much; I heard someone screaming my name." Hesitating she said, "In fact, it sounded like you, Bob. When I woke up I just felt trapped, sad, and desperate."

"That's weird. In mine I was screaming your name, Fran. All night long. And when I woke, I felt that I had been tricked and I was also so sad and desperate."

They centered their eyes and hearts on Charlie. Bowing his head he was silent for a whole minute. When he raised his head, tears trickled down both cheeks. Fran reached out for his hand. "Fran, Bob, I'm not sure what to say, but since your dreams are so in sync with one another, I think there is a serious warning here. Dreams are symbolic, and nightmares demand our attention. I can't say who will be a danger to you, but I believe, you must pay close attention to anything that makes you nervous or frightened."

Fran glanced at her brother. *Maybe I should mention how chilled I get when Will is around, but I'm afraid it's my own failure to release all my anger against him. And I don't want Bob to think I blame him for anything.*

"Charlie, remember when I woke up in the hospital? I was screaming at someone but when I try to figure out what was happening, I can't see through the darkness. I think I was about to be killed." Fran gasped. "But this morning—" He covered his face. "This morning I saw a dark figure behind each of you holding a large knife."

"Bob, look at me," said Charlie. "Did you have a sense of who it was?"

"Yes, but not now; in my dream I was shocked to see who it was aiming the sculpture at me."

"Sculpture? You mean the one Fran made; the one I brought you here? You never said that before."

"It just came to me. What does that mean?"

"It might mean that the dream is coming back to you. Even more important is the symbolism—that was a gift from Fran. It was given because you shared something in common then; I mean, I'm sorry; that didn't come out the way I meant it."

"I understand, Charlie." He looked at Fran. "We both understand. Go on, with what you think it might mean."

"Bob, only you can know what rings true. Maybe someone had a different vision for the day, and you changed the agenda. Because you brought about the Day of Reconciliation and Promises, it could mean that you had broken the trust of someone who believed you when you set it up. Maybe the darkness is a sign of your dying to old ideas and being brought to a new birth. Death in dreams is often a sign of new life."

Struggling with a surge of guilt Bob squirmed curling and uncurling his toes. *Am I being called to admit that I was faking it? He shuddered at the memory of how they laughed that night at dinner. I realize I wanted to bring people around to my way of thinking. Now, I am different, but I wasn't honest with anyone, not even Fran, about why I wanted that day. I wanted to change them; I wasn't ready to change myself. Now I know I was wrong. Maybe this is all a punishment.* "Charlie, maybe—what if I'm being punished?"

"Bob, you know we don't believe in a God like that. Why would you think that?"

"Maybe the dark shadow I'm seeing is me, my dark side. Maybe my conscience is calling me to repent."

"Bob, I've known you for a long time; I know we haven't been on the same wave length for a while, but don't we both believe that God can use even our smallest steps in the right direction as a way to real conversion?"

"So you think that even if my motives were not authentic, that God would still bring about good?"

Fran reached over and squeezed his hand. "You remember, what we used to say—if God waited for us to be perfect, nothing would ever get started let alone accomplished. The very fact that your invitation brought you and **Cry Justice** in the same room was a step in the right direction."

"She's right, Bob. As I said, only you can recognize the right interpretation of your dream. I think you need to place these nightmares of yours in God's hands and pray for the light to understand."

"I'll do that, Charlie." He looked at Fran, and smiled because she was still holding on to his hand. "Fran, you know I would like to stay, but I do need to go home this afternoon—after lunch, of course. But we'll talk every day before the big dinner, OK?"

"I would love that, Bob." Releasing his hand she winked at Charlie.

Checking his watch, Bob said, "Now, it's almost time for Mass. Charlie, I'd like to celebrate with you today."

Charlie's grin said it all. Fran was positive she felt her heart jump for sheer ecstasy. During the Mass she blinked away her warm happy tears; it had been such a very long time that they had shared this sacrament together. Dismissing the brief shadows that appeared and disappeared behind Charlie she promised herself she would think about them later. After Mass she hugged her brother and winked again at Charlie.

The smell of steaming New England clam chowder invited them to lunch. "Jen, when did you do all this?" asked Bob as he admired the arrangement of crackers, bowls of salads, and a plate of chocolate chip cookies.

"The miracle of the crock pot," laughed Jen. "And our retreat cook did the salads and cookies for us."

Knowing their days together were near the end, conversation filled every minute. A last cookie signaled a moment of silence and the time to say goodbye.

Fran spoke first. "You'll get him home safely, right?"

"And I'll call you after I get back to my place," said Charlie.

"Fran, I should call Will and let him know I'm coming."

"Of course. Feel free to use the phone in my office." She bit her lip as the now familiar chill ran through her body. Switching her thoughts to the upcoming dinner she did not feel the elation she expected and needed. She and Charlie, with Jen and Joan remained in quiet at the table until Bob came out of her office.

Bob gave her another hug. "Now I'm ready, Charlie."

Fran caught her breath as she watched them walk away. Charlie was being followed by a shadow with a knife.

Chapter 27

Mumbling to himself Will put down the phone. *It's about time you're coming home and I wonder what foolishness you listened to while you were there. At least I'll have a week to see if you have strayed from the course.*

His steps quickened as he headed for the kitchen. "Annie, the archbishop is coming home this afternoon. I know you'll plan something special for dinner."

"Such good news, Father. Of course, I'll get some steak from the freezer."

"And how about a pie; you know how he loves pie! Apple is his favorite, I think."

"Yes, Father." *Sounds like he's trying to impress the archbishop. I wonder what else is going on. I'll be so happy to see the archbishop, but why do I feel so scared?* Crossing herself as he walked away, she prayed, *O God, please take care of us.*

The clock chimed 1:00 as she opened the freezer. That's when she realized a tear had crept out of her left eye. She closed the door, broke down and sobbed. The next chime of the clock brought her back. *I've wasted fifteen minutes; why am I so sad? I must get busy; the archbishop will be home soon. I'll feel better when I see him, I know.*

Opening the freezer again she chose two large steaks. *I'm sure I have canned corn, whole and creamed and biscuit mix and sour cream; I'll make that corn casserole he likes so much. And I'll do baked potatoes.* She hurried back to the kitchen shivering, she assumed, from the cold steaks. *Maybe I should make the pie first; glad I bought those apples last week.* As she rolled out the crust, she heard the front door open. *He's here; maybe I can say hello before Father Will sees him.* She hobbled for the front door, ignoring the pain in her knee.

Seeing Father Charlie, she stood still and caught her breath. Soothing light embraced her whole body. "Welcome home, Archbishop. How wonderful to see you, Father Charlie." *I hope I'm not gushing.*

"Annie, it's good to be home. I think you've gotten younger since I last saw you."

"Oh, Archbishop, you know how to make my day." *It's been a long time since he joked around like that.* "You are the one who looks younger! Doesn't he?" She smiled at Father Charlie.

"Yes, he does. It's good to see you again, Annie." He leaned over and hugged her.

"Annie," said the archbishop, "would it be a problem for you if I invited Father Charlie to stay for dinner?"

"It would make me very happy."

"Welcome home, Bob."

Three excited faces turned towards Father Will. "Charlie, thank you for bringing the archbishop home."

"I've asked Charlie to stay for dinner."

"I would expect no less of you, Bob." *This may be even worse than I thought.* He turned to Annie, "I'm sure Annie can handle the extra work."

"Oh, Father, it's not work when one is happy." *Oh, my, I better be careful of what I'm saying. How did I get so bold?* She found herself giggly with a new freedom. Twirling herself around she was shocked she had no pain. Walking to the kitchen, she saw herself skipping like a young girl.

"Will, maybe we can take this time for you to get me caught up on the plans for the 14th."

"I'd be glad to do that, Bob, but what about Charlie, here?"

"Oh, I'd like him to sit in; you don't mind, do you?"

Will smothered the curse rising within him. "Of course not. Your office, I assume?"

"Thank you, Will," said Charlie. "I know Bob appreciates all the energy you have put into this special gathering."

Don't patronize me! "I am doing what I feel is good for the Church, Charlie. We are all dedicated to do all we can for the good of our people, are we not?"

"True, but I'm sure you realize that we in **Cry Justice** were surprised by the invitation to a day of reconciliation and especially the word, possibilities. We do love the Church and the word, possibilities, gave us much hope."

You don't have a clue what loving the Church means. Forcing a polite smile Will said nothing as he opened the office door.

Bob's eyes darted to the spot where his sculpture used to sit; how glad he would be to put it there again, now that it would remind him of his new connection with Fran. "Will, would you move my chair from behind my desk so we can sit with each other without that desk separating us; we are equals in God's eyes, right?"

O God, what craziness has taken over his soul? "Of course, Bob."

Dismissing a fleeting chill Bob motioned Charlie into the chair to his right. "As Charlie has so kindly put it, I have been on a detour."

I knew it was mistake for him to go to Fran's place. "I'm not sure I understand what you're saying; are you still in favor of the dinner on the 14th?"

"Of course, Will; but now I think I'm ready to listen."

I better make this sound good, because I can see he is a lost cause. "Bob, you don't give yourself credit; remember when we first gathered here to plan a day of gathering, your main purpose that evening was to listen."

"Yes, I remember saying that. Maybe God played a joke on me and took advantage of my words even if I didn't realize all that I was saying." *Because you and I both know that was a ploy.*

How long this night is going to be! "Bob, I've met with Ms. Collins and everything is on track for the 14th. Things will be the same except for the parade of cars and the lights! Don't want to take any chances of putting you in another coma, after all!" Glancing at Bob and then at Charlie, he hoped he had made that sound a bit humorous. Will watched as Bob's pensive face gave way to a half-hearted smile first at Charlie, then at Will. Sweating the ensuing moment of silence Will said, "This time we will have success." *In ways that will put me in charge; you're the one who wanted to dismantle **Cry Justice**, and now you're serious about listening to them. You and the dreamer deserve each other and all that's coming.*

"Success for me will be to convince all my people that I am their true shepherd, listening to them and believing in reconciliation and possibilities. They may not be as open to accepting that I have changed, as Charlie is."

Will squashed the howling rage erupting within him. *Maybe it would have been better if you had not awakened from that coma; no, not maybe, definitely.* A startling thought seized Will's attention—what if Bob was going to put Charlie in charge of the dinner? Panting for air, his heart was pounding so hard he was sure it was going to burst. *I can't let this happen; and I have to show I am in charge. What can I say that won't show my total loathing of both of them?* The room began spinning out of control. Darkness overwhelmed him. Opening his eyes he gaped up at Bob and Charlie standing over him. Moving his arm he was stunned to realize he had fallen to the floor.

"Will, what happened?" said Bob.

"Here, let me help you up," said Charlie reaching down for his hand.

Will groaned as Charlie's firm hand pulled him upright.

"Are you all right?" Bob's eyes searched Will's face.

"I'm fine. I guess I've been so busy I forgot to eat lunch."

At that moment they heard the ding of Annie's bell. "Well, that should be taken care of right now," said Bob.

Ignoring Charlie's outstretched arm Will turned and walked with his head held high. He quickened his steps as the short hall to the dining room closed in on him. Standing in the doorway Annie aimed her smile at the archbishop and Father Charlie. Noticing Father Will's ashen face she surrendered to her compassionate nature. "Father Will, are you not well?"

Forcing a halfhearted smile, Will said, "Oh, Annie, I'm fine and I'll be even better after this fabulous meal you've prepared." His eyes scanned the table impressive in its flawlessness—three gold edged plates, crisp white napkins, sparkling glasses filled with red wine. Wincing as the sight triggered the memory of that Tuesday dinner when all seemed perfect, today he would have to endure a meal with the dreamer. *O God, I know that you demand sacrifices of your most favored followers; the sufferings that afflict me tonight are for your glory and honor, and will prepare me to complete your work though I will now be working alone.*

As Bob took his place at the head of the table he motioned Charlie to his right. His chest tightening Will seated himself to the left.

"Charlie," said Bob, "please lead us in grace."

Will gritted his teeth as Charlie spoke, "O Jesus, we bless and thank you for this time together. When you ate with your disciples, you took ordinary bread, blessed it, broke it, and gave yourself to them. We ask you to take us, bless us, break us, and pass us among your people. Amen."

Standing with the kitchen door open Annie said, "Oh, Father, that was so beautiful." Pushing her cart to the table her heart twirled like a pirouette. As she lifted the plate of grilled steaks Charlie reached for it. "Oh Father, you just relax; I'll take care of this." She placed a boat of mushroom gravy near him, the bowl of steaming baked potatoes and the corn casserole in easy reach for the archbishop.

"You have outdone yourself again, Annie," said Will. "Everything looks wonderful and smells delicious."

"Thank you, Father Will. I was glad to do it." She smiled at Father Charlie and the archbishop. "Does anyone want coffee now, or with dessert?"

"Are we having apple pie?" asked the archbishop.

"Of course, Archbishop."

"That's when I'll have my coffee."

Will nodded his agreement.

Charlie said, "Count me in, too, Annie."

Turning her cart around she waltzed into the kitchen.

Bob and Charlie became engrossed in their conversation. Their sentences swirled around Will whose thoughts were spinning out of control; gripping the hem of the tablecloth he fought to control his seething anger. Chewing his steak he was annoyed with its leathery taste. The potato stuck to the roof of his mouth. He grabbed his water swallowing so fast he began choking.

"Will, what's wrong?" said Bob.

"I'm fine; I'm fine. I just get too excited realizing that our dinner is a week away."

"Will," said Charlie, "I'll be glad to help you."

Oh, you'll be helping me alright; and I am counting the days until your embarrassing downfall. "Charlie, you are too kind; I appreciate the offer. But for tonight, just enjoy your dinner."

"And you, yours. This steak is so tender. Are we having steak at the December 14th dinner?"

"Yes, steak medallions and a crab cake. It will be a dinner never to be forgotten." *In ways you wouldn't dream!*

"Isn't it strange," said Bob "that I can remember that part of my dream, and yellow roses—what could that mean?"

Not the dream thing again!

"Bob, if you don't mind, I would offer this thought; food in a dream can mean spiritual nourishment, and—"

"That makes so much sense, thinking about where I am right now."

What incredible nonsense! He is a lost cause.

"And maybe the shadows you have been seeing are indicating that you have turned from darkness to light."

"Charlie, are you saying that the archbishop has been in darkness? Isn't that a severe judgment?"

"Will, I know what Charlie means; he's not being judgmental at all."

Stunned Will reached for and held on to his glass of wine; he couldn't chance anything negative at this dinner. "What I meant was that it sounded as though your dream was criticizing you; and I'm sure that could not be true."

"You're too kind, Will. I think Charlie's analysis is closer to the candid examination I need to do. But not now! Now is the time for pie! Annie!"

"I hear you!" Annie said. "And I'm bringing the coffee."

Soon this depressing dinner will be over. O God, give your unwavering servant strength. "Annie, thank you! I am sure the archbishop feels renewed and energized because of this wonderful meal."

"Yes, Annie, thank you so much for this wonderful welcome home."

"Archbishop, you know how happy I am to have you home; and, you, for being here today, Father Charlie."

Will this mutual admiration garbage ever stop?

"Thank you all for your kind words." Bowing her gray head Annie's elation plummeted as she saw Father Will captured by a shadow. She heard herself shrieking but when she looked around the three priests were eating pie and drinking coffee.

Rushing into the kitchen she wrung her hands crying *O God, help me!* Immediately an otherworldly stillness wrapped itself around her. Sitting down at the table she laid her head on her arms. Drowsiness crept over her. She was drifting into sleep when she heard the archbishop say, "Let's toast a new day in our church."

"Amen" she said aware that she was filled with an energy she had not known for years.

Watching the archbishop tip his glass first toward Charlie and then to him, Will said, "Looking forward to seeing you on the 14th, Charlie."

"Same here, Will." Charlie turned to the archbishop. "Bob, this has been a most uplifting evening. Next Saturday can't come too soon." Pushing back his chair he said, "It's been a great day."

Finally this long night is over. Hope you both enjoyed yourselves. A week from tomorrow—redemption!

Chapter 28

Will's dream woke him at 12:01 on Saturday, December 14th. He had a foggy memory of Barbara, and though pleasure surged through him, he ached with a vague sadness creeping into his soul.

Tossing and turning for a half hour he labored to bring Barbara's smiling face into focus. Waking again at 2:00 he was grasping for Evelyn's hand; why had she come to him waving the brochure she had designed? *I won't forget you, my Evelyn. Don't worry about Barbara; both of you will belong to me.*

Rolling onto his left side he convulsed in a spasm; he clutched at his back and rolled onto his other side. The pain subsided but he was wide awake. *I better take an aspirin; I must look my best for today.*

At 5:30 he bolted upright as the alarm went off and he heard himself screaming at Adam. *But why was Adam crying and holding on to Charlie? Three dreams this time; every day, at least one, since that dinner with the dreamer. Forget about it; today will be your nightmare, Charlie.*

Exercising with stretches and crunches on his bedroom floor, his body rejected the energy boost he expected. Troubled by his stubborn tiredness he decided that a shower would wake him up and improve his mood. *I don't understand why I am so unsettled this morning; this is the day of Redemption.*

Although his usual Saturday schedule included the early Mass, Will was irritated that Bob had not offered to say it today. *That would have been proof that he appreciated that I've been carrying his load all this time. I hope he enjoys the extra sleep. Wonder if he had any dreams.*

Finished dressing in twenty minutes he stood in front of his mirror grinning at himself. His mood improved as he walked to the cathedral.

Looking out at the congregation he saw that Adam was not in his usual pew. *Where is he?* He checked again after vesting for Mass, but Adam was still not there. He checked his watch and walked to the altar at 7:30. Adam's pew was

125

still empty. As he was ending his homily, he saw the door open and watched Adam slide into the last pew.

He restrained his urge to hurry through the remainder of the Mass. After giving the final blessing he strode with measured steps to the sacristy. Glancing at the doorway several times, he was relieved when Adam tapped on the door frame. "Good morning, Adam. Good to see you today."

"Sorry I was late for Mass, but I was not feeling well this morning; I didn't sleep much last night; kept having bad dreams."

Panic flared up in Will. "What kind of bad dreams?"

"Father Charlie was yelling at me; I was alone; I looked all around for you, but I was all alone. Everything was dark. I ran to my car, but I couldn't get in the front seat; I was tied in the back seat and someone in a dark hood was driving. I kept screaming, and then the car went over the cliff. I looked up and you were standing at the top looking down. I think you were even laughing."

"Oh, Adam, how awful for you." *Can't believe I'm going to offer him some dream interpretation. Wouldn't Charlie be surprised?* "Adam, did you know that sometimes our dreams are just the opposite of what is true? For example, if you admire someone too much, putting him on a pedestal in real life, you may dream of him in a ditch." *I am so good!*

"Oh, I get it; like when I admired Father Charlie so much, and then found out he was so heartless. Maybe the hooded guy was him, driving me over the edge! What could be the meaning of seeing you laughing?"

"Maybe it means that I was glad you learned the truth."

"But it was too late."

"No, Adam, not in real life. I'm here for you, remember?"

"I feel so much better. I was coming to tell you I was not going to work today, and I know this is your big day. But now, I'm ready and raring to go."

"Adam, you have just made my day! So, I'll see you there. I have a feeling this will be a day that will show God's power."

"I'm sure, with you in charge, Father, that will be true. God bless you."

"Thank you, Adam. Go home now, eat a good breakfast and get to work!"

"I will." Adam spun on his heel and headed out the door.

Humming as he left the church, Will headed for the kitchen. *It is going to be a fantastic day!*

"Good morning, Bob; great to see you making breakfast again."

The archbishop was scraping fluffy scrambled eggs from the frying pan on to a large white platter. "I thought we could have a big breakfast and skip lunch. Home fries and bacon are ready, too. But I didn't make sticky buns today. Toast or English muffin?"

"One piece of wheat toast will be fine, Bob. And no lunch will balance out with our big dinner tonight." He poured a cup of coffee for the archbishop and then himself.

"Right. Do you remember we talked about concelebrating Mass after dinner? I know it will be late; I'm sure people will want to talk even after dessert, so by the time we set up for Mass, it may be 10:00. What do you think?"

"Sounds like a perfect plan."

"Good. I'm excited about today."

"Me, too, Bob. When do you want to leave? We should be there before 6:00 to welcome the others. I would like to be there by 5:00. Though I know that Barb—Ms. Collins will have everything ready, I will feel better seeing it all with my own eyes."

"How about if I go with Charlie? In fact, I'm sure he would like to pick up my sister and Joan and Jennifer, and the five of us could walk in together. Wouldn't we be an ideal living symbol of our theme?"

Will stifled the shriek swelling inside him. Yet, an uncanny satisfaction took control as he envisioned the five of them walking into his planned disaster. "Great idea, Bob." *Besides, now I can go even earlier and enjoy Barbara without thinking about you.*

"I think I'll call Charlie and see if he wants to go to my sister's this afternoon; then we will be ready to celebrate this evening."

Will began choking on the last bite of his toast; panting and grabbing his cup of coffee he spilled it on himself. He shot up from the table and ran to the kitchen sink. Gagging he finally inhaled some air. Still bent over the sink he reached for a glass, filled it with water and gulped a mouthful.

"Will! That's the second choking episode, and before that you passed out. What's going on? Are you sure you're not trying too hard to do too much?"

"I'm fine, fine. I just tried to finish off that toast too fast." He drank a little more water. "Do call Charlie; have a great afternoon, and I'll see you at the Cloister Royale!"

"I'm sure you have lots of last minute details you want to check; go; go; I'll do the dishes. Sure you're all right?"

"Yes, yes, I'm fine. Thanks; I do have things I want to check."

"And don't forget to take your vestments for Mass this evening. I'll see you later."

Will walked to his office, his head swimming with his obsession for Barbara and visions of the humiliation that would satisfy two other consuming desires—he wasn't sure which would delight him more—the death of **Cry Justice** or the death of Frances Mary.

Chapter 29

Whistling to himself Will patted his face inhaling the subtle scent of his shaving lotion. Dressing in his finest suit he relished the intense throbbing throughout his body. *Barbara, Barbara although you will be distressed by this evening's events, you will be amazed when you learn the truth. Salvation comes at a great price. I will not allow you to be lost.* He combed his hair, straightened his suit jacket, and fingered his collar, grinning as he studied himself in the mirror. Turning to walk away he was startled by a flash of Adam holding on to Charlie followed by another flash of himself looking down on Adam and laughing.

Shaking his head back and forth he now saw Evelyn running after him. *Why are you coming to me; I promise I will save you, too. But you have to leave me alone, right now. I have to concentrate!* He looked at his clenched fist. *I have to go.* Fighting off shadowy, unsmiling images of Barbara, he rubbed his temples. *Why are all these images coming at me? Why are you testing me, O God? You know I am prepared to do anything to save your church.*

He stood still for a moment, closed his eyes, made a small cross on his forehead, lips, and heart, and folded his hands in prayer. *But, of course, your greatest saints were called to great sufferings; I thank you, O God, for your strength; I will not fail.* Opening his eyes, he strode from his room. He checked his watch; it was 3:00 but deciding he could not wait any longer he grabbed his car keys, whistling again as he headed for his car.

Approaching the Cloister Royale his thoughts returned to November 9th. *How much further along we would be by now if that accident had not happened. Frances Mary would be in her grave by now, Charlie would be disgraced, and* **Cry Justice** *would be in shambles.*

Pulling up in front of the main door he enjoyed seeing the young men in valet parking race to his car imagining their respect to be genuine. Never turning around he did not see their snickers or hear their crude remarks.

Will was shaken when he walked into the lobby; three people were checking in at the desk; two others were sitting on a couch, but there was no sign of his event. Racing to the elevator he hurried to Barbara's office. She was not there. In a panic he ran back to the elevator. Pounding the down button three times he tripped into the elevator when it opened.

Back in the lobby his eyes searched left and right until he saw the concierge at her desk. Running towards her he noticed two workers moving a large mahogany table to the center of the lobby. Stopping and staring he watched as they set it down; his heart leaped as he saw Barbara approaching, her stride so crisp, her posture so confident.

For a moment, everything faded away except her. Gazing at her velvety, flowing hair he yearned to twist it around his fingers and nuzzle his face in its softness. Then he could no longer see her. "Barbara, Barbara."

"Father Will, here I am; what's wrong?"

He swung his head to the left. "Oh, there you are; nothing's wrong. Why do you ask?"

"You're here so early. I know you wouldn't be checking on me, now, would you?"

A searing rush pulsated through his body. Sure her eyes had twinkled with that question he cast his eyes downward and stilled his pounding heart. "Of course not, Barbara."

"I'm teasing you, Father. And I shouldn't do that; I know how important this day is for you. Please relax." Squeezing his arm, her face was uplifted just enough to fuel his wildest fantasies. Will allowed himself a quick glance into her radiant eyes.

"The ice sculpture of the vase, cup—what did you call it—a chalice?" Nodding his head yes, Will was pleased she had paid so much attention to his words. "The chalice with the hands reaching towards it will be brought in fifteen minutes before your guests begin to arrive."

I dream that **Cry Justice** *will melt away even sooner than the ice.* Will sighed.

"Are you OK, Father? Does that time frame fit with your plans, Father?"

"Yes to both questions; I was just wondering how long it takes for the ice to melt."

"Oh, quite a few hours; you won't notice anything during the cocktail hour. I have to go now and see how the chef is doing. Father, if you wish, you could go check out the banquet room; it's 4:30 already."

"How time flies! I think I will go and take a look at the banquet room; then I'll just enjoy the cocktail hour with everyone else."

Reaching into his pocket Will's fingers caressed the tiny plastic bag. Walking in to the dining room, his hand still inside his pocket he stood at the head table. Verifying that the name cards were placed in the exact order he had planned he pictured Fran sitting between Charlie and Ed at the far end of the table, away from the archbishop. *The time is coming, Charlie and Fran; you may walk in with Bob as part of a team, but the time for separation is near.*

Staring at Fran's filled wine glass, his fingers itched with delight as he pulled the tiny plastic bag from his pocket. He swerved his head toward the door as it opened from the kitchen. Seeing two waiters enter he shoved the bag back into its dark place. Standing rigid he eyed the waiters as if they were soldiers in his private army. "You are doing a great job here." Carrying pitchers filled with water to the head table one waiter shrugged; the other gave a token salute when Will gave the next order. "Please fill the glasses at that table and then bring back two more filled pitchers."

Taking a casual walk around the tables, Will touched napkins, straightened a fork here and a spoon there, and kept one eye on the waiters. Convinced they were walking slower than necessary, he stood still. "You have many more glasses to fill before everyone comes in."

As they hurried back to the kitchen he tore back to the head table. Yanking out the plastic bag, he dumped half of the powder into Fran's water and half into her wine. *Two sleeping pills should first cause her such dizziness that she will, I hope, fall into Charlie's chest—better picture than landing on Ed. And if she takes some wine, eternal rest won't be long in coming.*

Gasping as he saw the main door opening, he dropped his plastic bag, and kicked it under the table.

"Father Will, I hope I didn't scare you."

"Oh, Barbara, it's you. I thought one of our guests was coming in."

"Just a few have arrived so far. Is everything set up the way you wanted it?"

"Yes, thank you."

"Are you ready to come back to the lobby with me?"

How I want to do that! "I just want a minute more to enjoy this picture in silence."

As soon as she closed the door, Will dropped to the floor to pick up the bag. *How far did I kick that damn thing?* Waving his hand under the table and around the chair, his breathing became rapid. At last he saw it two feet away to his left; stretching for it he heard Barbara say, "Father, where are you?"

Why did she come back? He bumped his head in his hurry to stand.

"Father, what are you doing?"

"Oh, I dropped a pencil, and couldn't find it." His shaking hand slipped the bag into his pocket. "But I see it now; you're a good luck charm. I'll be there in a minute."

Exhaling a quiet sigh as she left once more he heard the band tuning up; his watch said 4:50. His redemption set-up had taken less than twenty minutes. *But with eternal consequences,* he told himself with a calmness forbidding his conscience any access.

Heading for the lobby the elation swirling through him churned into exhilaration as he noticed Barbara heading toward the band. His eyes devoured her body swaying with the music as her red hair bobbed in perfect rhythm. The music faded as he came closer; she swayed so close to him her fragrance engulfed him. *Even her eyes are dancing. Stay strong, Will; just a little while longer, and she will be yours.*

"Father, is all according to your desires?"

If you knew my desires, you would be in my arms now. "Yes, of course, Barbara. I had no doubt with you in charge."

"So, I've kept my promise."

Positive her smile was asking for a sign of gratitude, he said, "I wish I could find a way to repay you." *And I will, you darling temptress.*

"Father, do not give it a second thought; it is my job, you know, to make all our customers happy."

Oh, so now I'm just another customer. You'll get repaid, and you will make me happy, you luscious creature, designed for my pleasure. A stilted thank you was all he could manage to say. Having lost all track of time the band penetrated his tangled thoughts. The fifty guests already gathered in the lobby burst into applause.

Coming through the revolving door was Bob, followed by Charlie, Fran, Joan, and Jennifer. Once inside Bob turned to Charlie and Fran and motioned for each of them to grab an arm. The applause mounted to a deafening intensity.

"Isn't this all you hoped for, Father? Father Will, did you hear me? Father Will?"

Nauseating; but you will all be shocked by this evening's end. "Huh? Oh, Barbara, I'm sorry; I didn't hear what you said."

"I'm happy for you, Father; such devotion to your church. You seemed to be in a trance; I'm fascinated by your dedication."

131

Gazing into her playful green eyes he expected the throbbing satisfaction he had become accustomed to but he realized at this minute that he had never known such intense longing. His inner emptiness howled in anguish, he felt so cold, and he began to shake. A dismal, dark cloud was overshadowing him, his mother in its midst shaking her head. "I will be her salvation; I am the redeemer; why don't you understand?"

"What are you saying, Father?" Barbara shook his arm. "What's wrong?"

Staring at her hand clutching his arm the cloud evaporated, his mother disappeared, and consummate tenderness seeped into his every cell. Somehow he knew this was a passion beyond Barbara. In his personal darkness he was terrified it was God, but not the God he recognized or wanted—this God yearned for his surrender, and that he could not do. *You cannot be God; you must be the Evil One tempting me into submission. I will serve a righteous Master, who will reward me for my tireless service.* He smiled, reached over with his other hand, grasped hers and lifted it away. "I'm just spellbound." Disappointed by her look of bewilderment, he said, "I'll explain later."

Observing a crowd so enchanted with the archbishop they had not even noticed him, Will walked with brisk determined steps to the archbishop. Motioning for silence, he said, "Faithful people, I present to you, your shepherd."

Thunderous applause erupted. Will heard, "Praise God" shouted from the group to his left. "Thank you, God" came from several people on his right and that phrase echoed around the room. Shocked by a fleeting crushing loneliness, Will responded as he had done all his life—he squelched any hint reminding him of his need for support, human and divine. His overwhelming conviction that he could prove his worthiness to everyone had driven his life for as long as he could remember. He was not about to surrender any plans he had for this evening. *God, you will be pleased with me! I reject the temptation to yield for any reason to any power.*

Will tried for a full three minutes to quiet the crowd. Charlie, noticing his agitation, pursed his lips and whistled. Will's eyes shot at Charlie. *Real class, Charlie.* He saw heads turn, heard delighted laughter, and realized all eyes were fixed on Charlie now motioning them to turn their attention to Will. Bowing to Charlie and clenching the fist he held behind him, Will turned towards the crowd. "Your exuberant affection for our archbishop is appreciated. It is now time to invite you to our long-awaited dinner. Please follow our shepherd into the dining room."

Nodding towards Barbara he opened the center doors. Walking with the archbishop were Fran, Charlie, Joan and Jennifer. Following them Will stopped when he was next to Barbara. "I am grateful for the exquisite job you have done; the delicate yellow rose on the gleaming white table cloths is a perfect complement to the gold stripes." He was struck by a sudden connection between yellow and cowardice. *Clever perspective; reminds me of Bob. Someday I'll amaze Barbara with my unique mind.* "I am positive everyone will be so impressed by the **Cry Justice** imprint on the napkins. You have outdone yourself, and I want you to know I will not forget your attention to my wishes."

"I promised that you would be pleased; I'm glad I succeeded in doing that for you, Father Will."

"I better get inside now. Maybe I'll see you later."

"Wait a minute, Father."

I cannot bear to leave you. "Yes?"

"The reporters are here—from all three TV channels and the city newspaper."

"Thank you; you haven't forgotten a thing, Barbara."

Walking towards the head table, he noticed several people examining the box of chocolate at their places. *Go ahead, devour the chocolate, just like I will see to it that **Cry Justice** is devoured.*

What he saw happening at the head table perturbed every inch of his body. Hurrying towards Bob who had Fran's name card in his hand he said, "Bob, is there a problem?"

"I'm glad you put me at the end of the table rather than in the center; takes away some of that hierarchical air. But I want to sit between Fran and Charlie. You didn't have any reason for putting them so far away from me, did you?"

"Of course not. I just thought you wanted to be seen as your own person."

"You think too much, Will; I want people to see that my sister and I and Charlie are on the same side now. You don't mind sitting where Fran was supposed to be, right? And you had Mark West on the other side of me; I'll move the name cards."

"No, I'll do it. You just enjoy yourself."

Looking at the wine glass that was supposed to be Fran's Will swung his arm as he replaced the name card knocking over the wine glass. The red wine spread over the white tablecloth. Adam appeared at his side staring at an ugly blood-red blotch..

"Father Will, what can I do?"

"Adam, how clumsy of me. If you can get a large white napkin, I'm sure we can cover this and no one will even notice."

"I'll do it right away; don't worry; everyone is paying attention to gathering their friends together at their tables; no one is even looking this way."

"Now it's my turn to say that you know the right thing to say."

"Father Will, you know how I feel about you; I would never let you be embarrassed. You've worked too hard for this night. I'll be back in a second, and with a new glass of wine."

"How about a fresh glass of water, too. I like lots of ice."

"No problem, Father; I'm so glad to be of some help to you."

Adam, you have no idea how much help you will be. "Thank you, Adam."

In less than a minute, Adam returned with the napkin, the wine, and water. "Lots of ice, just like you asked, Father." He handed the wine and water to Will and with amazing speed, moved the plate to his right, placed the napkin over the spill, returned the plate and took the wine and water from Will's hands. "There you are, Father."

"Great timing, Adam. Looks like everyone is seated."

As the archbishop began to make the sign of the cross, a hushed respect settled into the room. "Good and gentle God, your Son, Jesus, at his last supper, gave us a sign of service by washing the feet of his disciples. We ask you to bless us this evening, as we take new steps in being servants to and with one another. Bless also this food given for our nourishment and enjoyment; bless all those who prepared it and those serve it. We praise you, our God of peace and reconciliation."

A vibrant and jubilant Amen flooded the room.

Lifting his wine to give a toast the archbishop raised his glass to the right, to the left, and in front of him. "To a future of working together as church, listening and respecting each other."

A despondent Will watched as Fran sipped her wine, all his hopes for this evening gone. The flashing lights of the photographers were painful as he compared reality with what he had hoped would be on tomorrow's front page.

The flashes of light sparked a passing moment of fear and darkness in the archbishop. He looked at Fran who was putting her glass down. Startled when he heard himself saying *I saved you, Fran, like I promised, h*e looked around. No one had heard anything; *why are those words echoing in my head?*

Looking at her brother Fran said, "This is a wonderful evening." Noticing a shadow cross over his face she said, "But you're distracted; what's wrong?"

"I think I had another flashback from my dream, but all I remember is darkness, and strange words come to me. But let's talk about it tomorrow; this evening is too special to be disturbed by my murky worries." He picked up his fork and took a bite of his salad.

Will was distracted, too, as he watched Bob, Fran, and Charlie chatting and laughing. As the waiters walked to the tables carrying plates of steak and crab, red bliss potatoes and fresh green beans Will stared at the meal he had so anticipated; now he wanted nothing more than to be finished with this entire night.

Placing a plate in front of the archbishop first, then Fran, Adam said "I'm so glad to see you, Sister Frances Mary. Do you remember me?"

"Of course, Adam; you were in eighth grade when you and your mother moved to Sacred Heart. How are you?"

"I'm fine, now."

Leaving he came back with a plate for Charlie. Will could not take his eyes away from that end of the table. He wished he could hear what Adam had said. He grinned as Charlie nodded, offered a handshake, and Adam backed away.

Staring at Adam and Charlie, the archbishop arched one eyebrow as his eyes asked for an explanation. Fran bit her lip and reached out for Adam's hand; he stiffened and walked away. The highlight of Will's evening was the shocked look on Charlie's face. *You did well, Adam; I see that you will be of great use to me.*

"Charlie," said Bob, "how do you know that young man?"

"When he was seven or eight, he was an altar boy in my first parish. He and his mother, Liz, moved to Sacred Heart a month after his father died. I thought it was too soon to leave a parish where she had so many friends, so I visited her very week. I knew Jim, her husband; we had gone to high school together, so I guess she trusted me."

"I feel as though I know him, too, but I can't remember where I've seen him before. "

"You did come to Sacred Heart for Confirmation," said Fran.

"I guess that's possible, but something bothers me. Was he troubled when you knew him, Fran?"

"His mother did commit suicide."

"What did you say, Fran? I don't ever remember hearing about that. In fact, the last time I talked with her, she told me that she had found someone who had helped her understand that God wanted her to be happy. About a month later, I was transferred to the far end of the diocese, and never heard from her again. I wish I would have tried to call her."

"Charlie, do you think that Adam somehow blames you? There's no way you could have done anything."

"Well, tonight is not the time to ask Adam about it; but I will call him tomorrow; maybe we can meet next week and I can find out what's upsetting him."

Hearing Mark making a comment about the fabulous dinner to Mike Lynch Will groaned to himself. *Just loud enough to make it seem like a compliment to me but those two have no idea what is important. They're both so transparent, and so jealous of me.* Remembering how even Pete Rogers had been caught up in the mood of that fateful November day, Will had little inclination to converse with him either. *To be stuck between Pete and Mark rather than being in my rightful place next to Bob is a severe penance, but the Redeemer must suffer; glory will come later.*

Sitting in sullen silence looking at Nick Perry so relaxed next to Ed McShane Will tried to raise his mood by thinking about Barbara. What stuck in his throat was her comment about satisfying all her customers. His hunger right now was bottomless and no fantasy about Barbara or Evelyn gave him any gratification.

Joe Moreno and Pete were engrossed in eating, drinking, and laughing. Wondering if he were the only one who remembered that Tuesday night dinner when all this had been planned, Will realized that no one was as driven as he was. *O God, I thank you for giving me the grace of perseverance; I will bring them all back to the truth, including Evelyn and Barbara.* He drifted inside to his place of lonely pleasure and suppressed the howling emptiness pleading for recognition.

Will was never as glad to see dessert as he was tonight; the evening would soon be over. Then he remembered—Bob had planned to say Mass with this group. At least that would provide some payback; he would be the one concelebrating. Everyone would see him with the archbishop offering the Mass.

He toyed with his tiramisu. Adam poured his coffee and moved the cream pitcher within easy reach; Will nodded, smiled and then noticed that Charlie was watching him. For an instant he felt a strange gratification but wondered why the archbishop was also looking at him. Bob's eyes were wide open, as if he had just seen some revealing message. Dismissing the tingling warning that floated around inside Will finished his tiramisu and picked up his coffee.

Chapter 30

Realizing that the archbishop was planning on saying Mass, the waiters hurried to clear the tables. Will went out to his car to get his vestments, as well as the hosts and wine knowing Bob had brought all the other items needed.

Walking back to the hotel, he starred in the scene only his imagination could invent: all eyes on him, amazed that this dinner had taken place because of his planning yet envious of his place beside the archbishop. Recognizing that his reputation throughout the diocese had been tarnished by his removal from Sacred Heart he knew that he had been judged and condemned by many. He accepted that Fran was exempt from such criticism. Being related to the archbishop meant privilege, but worse, he heard himself groan, *it's because she's a woman. Men are the chosen of God, and especially myself— called to be his Coordinator of Redemption.*

Walking back into the dining room, he came to an abrupt standstill. Why was Charlie vested for Mass? Gathering all his strength, he headed straight for the archbishop.

"Will, I forgot to mention to you this afternoon, I asked Charlie to concelebrate with us. I think this will seal our intentions with everyone here."

It seals your fate, that's for sure. "You are correct, of course, Bob."

During Mass Will searched for eyes looking at him; he was so ready to offer a smile of recognition, so ready to enjoy their envy at his place of honor, but he did not spot one glance in his direction. Even during the distribution of communion, he stole glimpses at those in line for the archbishop and Charlie; he observed eye contact and smiles; when he looked at those in his line, their eyes were lowered. *Why, O God, are you testing me? Have I not yet proved myself to you? I will save your church; I will not fail.*

Driving home alone that night Will could not let go of the scene of Bob, Charlie, Fran, Joan and Jennifer talking and laughing in the lobby when he left.

They were surrounded by so many that he knew no one even noticed that he had slipped out the door.

Arriving home just minutes before midnight he saw the answering machine blinking with one message. He became immobile as he heard his mother's voice saying, "Will, I'm so proud of you. Our local news station picked up the story about your archbishop and how you had this dinner for him; how thoughtful of you. I'm sure it took a lot of work on your part. I'm planning on coming to see you tomorrow; if I leave after morning Mass, I'll be there by noon."

"Oh. Mother," Will slammed his fist against the table. "How I wish I believed that you are proud of me, not proud that your friends heard about me on TV. Does it mean even more than grandchildren to you? What will we have to say to each other tomorrow? You try so hard to hide your disappointment in me, but I can see it in your eyes."

Dragging himself to his room, Will tore off his collar and black shirt. Throwing himself across his bed, he closed his eyes and turned his thoughts to Barbara. All he felt was his own hollow isolation. His barrenness cried out for an embrace beyond all his hope and longing, but he could never believe in an unconditional love, neither from a mother or the God he was so desperate to please.

Waking up an hour later, he massaged his aching head. Hearing the door open downstairs he checked the clock. *About time for you to be getting home.* An overwhelming but brief longing he had never before acknowledged engulfed him—a desire for complete acceptance by another human being, a real acceptance without judgment and without expectation. He refused this inviting opportunity for an honest look at the common call to fullness of life. *O God, I am sorry for being envious of Bob's admiration by others; I need no one's approval but yours. The time will come when all will know that I have been your faithful servant.*

He decided to change into his pajamas and get into bed. *I hope I can go back to sleep; need all my strength to deal with Mother tomorrow.*

When his alarm went off at 5:30, he realized he was in the middle of a dark dream. Remembering that he had been crying, he was relieved to be awake, though he groaned with the tiredness that slithered throughout his body and mind.

As he showered and dressed he thought about the wasted hopes of yesterday. Having to devise another way to get rid of Fran and Charlie, he prayed. *O God, I don't understand why you allowed me to fail yesterday.*

I know that you test people to prove who is worthy of you, but I believed that I was already your chosen servant. I know that my intention to save your church is even stronger now, and I trust that you will lead me to find another way to rid your church of these false prophets.

During Mass he reveled in unexpected high spirits while looking at Adam. Reminded of Adam's refusal of a polite interaction with Charlie yesterday, Will was positive that Adam—vulnerable, idealistic Adam—would be an instrument of triumph for him. Congratulating himself on an excellent homily even though his preparation took all of two minutes, he denied the nagging pull within him for surrender. Returning to the sacristy he recognized the agitation reminding him that his mother would be arriving in less than three hours.

In the kitchen he was pouring himself a cup of coffee when Bob walked in. "Good Morning, Will. I am so full of energy this morning; I can't remember when I felt so good."

"That's great, Bob. By the way, my mother is coming around noon."

"Wonderful. I've always wanted to meet your mother."

"She was watching TV and our dinner made the news."

"That must have made her proud of you."

"So she said."

"I'm heading over for the 10:00 Mass even though it's early; I have a great desire to meet and welcome people this morning, plus I need some quiet time to prepare. But when I get back, let's choose a restaurant; I think we should take your mother out for a nice lunch."

"Thanks, Bob. I'm sure she will appreciate that."

Will stared at his cup of coffee and poured it down the sink. He decided to try to get some rest before facing the afternoon.

Standing at his bed for a full minute, he chose the recliner. Closing his eyes he indulged in the picture of Barbara swaying to the music but was confused by the emptiness that crowded out the ripples of pleasure he expected. *Barbara, please wait for me; I will be your redeemer, and I am determined it won't be long now. You will know your savior, you will be....* His chin dropped into his chest as he fell into a deep sleep.

A ringing doorbell jarred him awake. His dazed eyes roamed around the room. *Why am I here? What day is this? Oh no, that's my mother; she's here!* Bounding out of the recliner, he ran to his bathroom, splashed cold water on his face, ran a comb through his hair, straightened his shirt and collar and raced to the stairs.

Hearing Bob's voice he waited on the second step. "Come in, Mrs. Owens. It's so good to meet you."

"Please call me Barb."

"Hello, Mother." Will walked over to her and leaned in with a stiff hug.

"Mrs. I mean, Barb, I had suggested that we take you out for lunch. We didn't have a chance to discuss a restaurant, but, Will, how about going back to the hotel where we were last night?"

"You want to go back there?" Will's fantasies leaped into his imagination.

"Of course; doesn't it hold great memories?"

"You're right. Let's do it."

Driving to the hotel the conversation between his mother and Bob was mere background noise. All Will could think about was how fortunate he was to see Barbara again so soon. He had already decided he was going to call her tomorrow to thank her for the superb job she had done for him. Believing they would be together after he had dismantled the curse of **Cry Justice**, he had no guarantee of the timetable now. Imagining the introduction of Barbara to his mother filled him with a bizarre edginess, associated in his mind with a boyfriend-girlfriend scenario.

Waiting for the light to turn green, he remembered the night of the accident; he was sure that God had saved him to complete the mission, but could not understand why God had spared Bob. Confident that nothing would deter him from his cause he rejected the hollow ache inside him as physical hunger, not the tug from his God of unconditional acceptance.

Hoping his mother and Bob were impressed when he tossed his keys to the valet his heart skipped several beats as they walked to the revolving door, his mother first, then Bob. Entering the lobby, he pointed them towards the restaurant, his eyes searching for Barbara. He nodded to Adam as the maitre d' took them to a table near the window.

Adam brought the huge menus to the table. "It's good to see you again so soon, Archbishop and Father Will." He made a slight bow to Mrs. Owens.

"Adam, this is Father Will's mother."

"I'm glad to meet you, Ma'm. Your must be so proud of your son; he's a wonderful priest."

"Thank you, young man. I am."

"I'll be back for your orders. Would you like something to drink?"

Mrs. Owens spoke first, "A glass of white wine, please."

"Red for me," said Bob.

"Same for me," said Will.

It took only a moment for Bob to find his favorite; Will also decided on steak, while his mother chose the salmon. In the middle of the table Adam placed a warm crusty loaf on a small breadboard with a knife and creamy butter shaped like a full-blossomed rose. Will found himself irked at that buttery rose—yellow and soft. He looked at Bob.

"Are you ready to order?"

Will was surprised that Adam's memory skills were so trained that he did not need to write down their selections. *Funny thing, memory,* he thought.

As Adam left the table, Bob lifted his glass and said, "To friendship."

Will felt another hunger pang, and dismissed it as before. He was paralyzed as he heard Bob say, "Barb, there's always something I've wanted to know. Why does Will insist on being called Will?"

Laughing she said, "We tried to call him Bill, but he kept shaking his head no when he was only 2, and by the time he was 5, he said, "You pay bills; I'm not a bill! I will do what I want. I am Will."

Bob chuckled, oblivious to Will's resentment. "So strong-willed at such a young age." Bob's amusement was clouded over by a threatening shadow that burst into his awareness. Shaken he realized he had ducked his head at something coming down on him. He felt Barb's hand grab his arm.

"Archbishop, what's wrong; you look as if you've seen a ghost."

"Bob, what is it?"

"I'm not sure. I've been having some strange flashes every so often; Charlie thinks my coma dreams may be coming back."

Of course, the dreamer would have all the answers. "You were in an accident; maybe it's just your nerves reacting to being hit."

"That's interesting—reacting to being hit. I did feel as though I was protecting myself."

"Here's our dinner," said Barb. "Thank you, Archbishop, for suggesting this place. Everything looks wonderful."

As Adam was placing Will's plate in front of him, Will said, "Could you see if Ms. Collins could come here to meet my mother?"

"I'm sorry, Father; Ms. Collins isn't working today."

"Oh, I see; that's fine; I just wanted my mother to meet the woman who did such a great job for our dinner yesterday."

Mrs. Owens saw a familiar twitch in her son's eye; she had seen it many times while he was growing up, and it always meant he was hiding something from her. An uneasy flutter in her stomach prompted a quick silent prayer. *O God, I could never seem to love him enough; he needs you to break through his isolation.*

Will was hungry but had no appetite for the steak he had ordered. If he didn't eat, his mother would start with her questions; he wasn't sure why her concerns for him always turned him off. He picked up his knife and fork. Bob had used Will's request for Ms. Collins to begin an animated review of yesterday's dinner. Grateful that his mother had turned her full attention to the archbishop Will tried to enjoy his meal.

Wishing he could join in the conversation all he did was force a smile and nod at what he hoped were appropriate times. His imagination was taunting him with what might have been.

"Will, are you enjoying your meal?"

"Of course, Mother. And how is yours?"

"Couldn't be better." She reached over, patted his arm, and let her warm hand rest there. "But, I know it tastes even better because I'm here with you."

That patting; he detested her fussing over him. Suddenly he saw Barbara Collins not his mother. Mumbling under his breath he said, "Barbara."

"Will, what did you say? You've never called me that."

"What? Oh, Mother, not you; I mean, I wasn't talking to you; I just realized that Ms. Collins and you have the same name."

"Well, if I thought about that, I would wonder why you didn't think of me when you first met her." Patting his arm again she laughed.

He was grateful that Bob changed the subject by saying, "Barb, I hope you are saving room for dessert."

"That's my one vice!"

Certain that he could not endure another minute Will excused himself and walked toward the men's room. On the way Adam caught up with him and whispered, "Father Charlie called me this morning after Mass; he said he wanted to talk with me."

"What did you say?"

"My first reaction was to say, 'No way!' but he sounded so sincere, so I said I would think about it."

"That's good, Adam. Keep walking with me towards the men's room." Will's imagination rocketed into high gear; the broad outline of a twisted plan was in his mind a response to a gift from God. "Call me tonight and I will help you decide how to set this up; what you need to say, and how to get to the truth."

"I knew you would be able to help me, Father. Things would have been different for my mother if she had met with you."

"Adam, don't dwell on what might have been; the important thing is to get justice for yourself, and your mother. But we can't talk now; I have to get back to the table." Will felt so much better.

When he returned his mother said, "Your color has come back to your face. Maybe you ate too fast; or maybe you're overtired; I know these last few weeks have been..."

"Mother, I'm fine, I didn't eat too fast," and with a smile to the archbishop he said, "and I never get tired working for God and our church."

"I know that's true" and his mother patted his arm again. This time Will brushed aside his usual annoyance, his thoughts soaring with anticipation of how he would use Adam to accomplish his goals; the Coordinator of Redemption was back in control.

"We're ready to order dessert; are you going to have something?" said Bob.

"Pie sounds good, don't you think?"

"You know what I like. What about you, Barb?"

"Sounds good to me, if they have apple."

"Well, that makes three!" Bob was so relaxed that Will was beginning to feel sorry for him, knowing how his life would change within a few days.

Asking for their dessert orders Adam's face lit up with a smile that had found a new home. Will caught the change; alarms bounced around his head. *What if he wants to tell everyone about our relationship? What if he forgets our agreement?* Will picked up the wine list. Adam looked at the archbishop.

"We're all in agreement, Adam. Three apple pies!"

"Would you like those a la mode?"

"Of course, right everyone? A great ending for a great meal! And three coffees." Avoiding eye contact with Adam, Will waved the wine list. "Anyone want another?"

"Not for me," said his mother.

"Nor me," said Bob.

Will was ready to celebrate but decided he needed to calm down. "I guess we'll just have coffee, Adam. Thank you."

Will's legs itched to dance under the table; he couldn't believe how easy it was now going to be to bring his plans to a glorious finale. *But I'll have to keep Adam's admiration from going overboard.*

As Adam served the desserts Will's excitement tempted him to wolf down his pie in two bites. Realizing the need for restraint, he hoped his mother wouldn't insist on enjoying every morsel the way she usually did. Checking his watch he picked up his fork.

Eager to signal Adam for their bill he watched his mother sipping her coffee, and then smiling at her last piece of pie floating in the remaining blob of vanilla ice cream. *Eat it already* he heard himself screaming at her. For an excruciating minute he bit his tongue while his mother dangled her fork above her last bite, laughing at some comment made by the archbishop. He glanced at his watch in disbelief. *Two hours for lunch!*

Finally, he sighed in silence. Observing her swallow he signaled Adam. She picked up the cup of coffee again. "Oh, Mother, I thought you were finished."

"It's fine, son. I'm not in a hurry to leave."

"But it does get dark early these days, and you do have a two hour drive home."

"Always the thoughtful son." Patting his arm with utter unawareness of Will's desire to push her away she said, "But you are right." She looked at her watch. "If I leave within the next half hour, I'll be home by 5:00." Patting his arm again she turned her attention to the archbishop.

Will knew his entire body had just groaned at the thought of another half hour. His mind was frantic with possibilities that needed to be decided upon before setting up the plot with Adam. Calming himself with the thought that he couldn't talk to Adam until he was off work and back home, the muffled voices of his mother and the archbishop faded into the background. Conjuring up various scenarios that would ensnare Fran and Charlie he promised himself meticulous discretion and detailed planning. *Adam can never know anything except that I am his redeemer.*

"Will, where are you?" Flinching he recoiled from his mother's intruding pat on his arm again.

"Sorry, Mother; I was lost in thought."

"I just wanted to say again that I am so proud of you, and I think we better leave. I'm glad that getting back to your place for my car puts me closer to the interstate; I'll be home before you have a chance to worry about me. Such a dear son." Winking at the archbishop she squeezed Will's arm.

Will waved to Adam for the bill and the archbishop pulled out his credit card. When Adam came to the table, he said, "Archbishop, Father, your bill has been taken care of." He smiled and signaled to a table behind Will. Turning to look, Will was stunned to see Barbara with a companion.

"Adam, who—I thought—didn't you say that Barb, Ms Collins was not working today?"

"That's true; but she came in about a half hour ago. I think it might happen today."

"Adam, what are you talking about?"

"Oh, of course, how would you know? She and Mr. Reynolds have been seeing each other for almost a year, now. We are all waiting for an engagement announcement, and I just have…'

Will smothered the scream within; he stood up and reached for his mother's hand. "Come, Mother, I want you to meet the woman I spoke about earlier."

Approaching the table, Will crumbled when Barbara looked up at him and smiled. *Barbara, how could you not realize that you belong to me? How could you not know that I am your savior?* "Ms. Collins, I would like to introduce my mother, Barbara."

"What a pleasure to meet the mother of such a dedicated priest." She put out her hand. "And, please, call me Barbara."

Remembering when those words had been directed to him Will ached to snatch her away and to himself right now. He reached for a chair.

Bob stared at him.

Barbara said, "Father, is anything wrong? You're shaking."

Feeling his mother's arm around him he squirmed out of her hug. "I'm fine; just a bit of lightheadedness." Regaining his composure he waved away their concerns. "I thank you for our dinner; we didn't expect such kindness."

"Think nothing of it, Father. I was telling Jim; oh, excuse me; my manners. This is Jim Reynolds." Tapping his arm just like his mother she said. "I was telling Jim all about you." Looking at Mrs.Owens she said, "You must be so proud of your son. I'm not a Catholic, but I was impressed." Turning her eyes to the archbishop, "You must be grateful to have someone so loyal to your church. And your sister looked so happy last night."

Bob smiled with "Thank you so much for everything, and for our dinner." A ripple of an abnormal chill caused him to shiver as he glimpsed a shadow pass in front of him. "Will, we should get going."

Seething with his violent craving to gather Barbara into his arms Will glanced at Jim. *She is mine, you shall not have her.* The revulsion stirring in his stomach shrouded the acute loneliness begging for his attention.

Stepping aside to let his mother and the archbishop go in front of him his mind brimmed with dreams of luring Barbara back to him. Turning around as they were walking out of the restaurant a cavernous hunger cramped his stomach as he saw Jim take Barbara's hands into his own; they leaned into each other and kissed.

Chapter 31

Gritting a smile Will held open the car door. His mother tapped her thanks on his arm and he hoped she and the archbishop would chatter away on the drive home. Their obvious relaxation with each other amplified his isolation while intensifying his resolve to rid himself of Fran and Charlie.

Barb fastened her seat belt with enough slack to let her sit with her face turned towards the archbishop in the back seat. In spite of the comfortable banter punctured by spontaneous laughing between the two of them, Will focused his mind on his developing scheme. Wanting Adam to set up a meeting with Charlie as soon as possible he thought, *in fact, tomorrow would be perfect.*

Arriving in the driveway, the sight of his mother's car triggered a relaxing of his grip on the steering wheel. Not wanting to risk any questions about his hurry to whisk her home, Will coasted to a standstill beside her car, switched off the ignition, and forced himself to hesitate before sliding out of the car.

"Thank you, Mother," he said as he leaned over to give her a fragile hug. "Drive carefully."

"It was so nice to meet you, Barbara," said the archbishop as he wrapped his big arms around her. "Do come again, soon."

Will's thoughts drifted off as his mother and the archbishop embarked on another conversation. Their effortless familiarity had annoyed and bewildered him all afternoon, and now he just wanted them to end it. Suppressing the urges to glance at his watch, to tap his foot, and most of all, to scream he waited. When he was sure he could not contain himself for one more second, he heard their mutual goodbyes.

Grabbing his mother's arm he opened her door; she insisted on another hug, and at last she slid into her seat. Biting his tongue as she turned the key and tugged on the seat belt he exhaled a sigh of relief when the tires began to roll back out of the driveway.

Waving a final goodbye he turned towards the archbishop. Bob opened his mouth but closed it, stunned by a dark shadow that flashed between him and Will.

"Bob, what's wrong?"

"I'm not sure; I think I'm still having flashbacks."

"I can't imagine what kind of dream you had, but maybe it's best to forget about it. I'm sure there's no message from God that you need to be concerned about."

"Well, I hope you're right, but I'll talk to Charlie if this continues."

"I'm sure he'll make you feel better." *If he lives that long. I want to go to my room, but if I'm too abrupt, he could get suspicious, or even worse, want to talk.* "I'm sure my mother enjoyed this afternoon; thank you. Maybe you want to get some rest, now."

"That sounds like a good idea, Will. Your mother did seem to enjoy herself. I think she loved telling the story of your name."

Will's obligatory chuckle stifled his loathing for Bob and for his mother. *You will learn the power of my will, but I do regret that you have been lost to the cause.* "See you later then." Will's relief as Bob left for his room turned into rousing excitement; Adam would be home in about a half hour.

Bounding up the stairs Will laughed out loud as he flopped into his comfortable chair. Rehearsing his scheme he made sure he accounted for all possible questions from Adam. He was so busy relishing his imagined outcome that when he checked his watch, an hour had passed. Grabbing the phone he pressed the speed number for Adam.

"Hello, Father; I've been waiting for your call."

"Adam, I want you to listen carefully now, so that you can get the justice you deserve, but first, what did Father Charlie say when he called you?"

"Something about wanting to tell me how sorry he was."

Perfect, thought Will. "He will try to convince you that he tried to help your mother; he might even attempt to tell you that he knew nothing of your mother's death. You do not want to get into that conversation on the phone. Nothing he could say will take away your loss of your mother or his guilt. You want a face to face meeting with him in my presence."

"Thank you, Father; I was afraid you would want me to confront him alone."

"Never, Adam; I would not subject you to that. In addition, I want you to invite Sister Frances Mary to be there, too."

"Why, Father? I like Sister Frances Mary and I don't have any problem with her."

"Because she supports Father Charlie, but I am sure she doesn't know what he did to you and your mother. In fact, she has the archbishop convinced now that Father Charlie can help him recover from some crazy dreams he had during his coma. So, I want her to see Father Charlie's true colors."

"If you say so, Father. I trust you."

"You will be doing a great service to the archbishop, too, and to the church. God will be so pleased with you."

"Do you believe that, Father? Sometimes I feel so unworthy."

"That comes from your bad memories of Father Charlie. Because he abandoned your mother, you felt abandoned by God, but I tell you that you are special in God's eyes, and He is going to give you all the graces you need; you have an important role in saving the church."

"So you think that Father Charlie is evil."

"I do not judge people, Adam, but I remember that Jesus said that a good tree does not bear bad fruit, and a bad tree does not bear good fruit. When you think about your mother's death, would you call that good fruit?"

"I understand, Father. You always help me to see the truth. So tell me what you want me to do."

"I think we should get Sister Frances Mary to meet with us first, because she has been under the influence of Father Charlie for quite some time now; maybe you remember all that happened when I and Sister Frances Mary and the other two sisters were at Sacred Heart. Father Charlie was in the background during that whole trial. It was the archbishop who saved me, and now I want to save him."

"You have so much courage, Father."

"It's God's grace, Adam. If you are a bit embarrassed to tell Sister Frances Mary about Father Charlie, I'll be glad to do that for you."

"I would be so grateful, Father."

"Now, I think it would be good if we could meet at the hotel; is there some room you could arrange for us that would be private?"

"Oh, I don't know about that, Father. I only work in the restaurant."

"But you know some of the maids who clean the rooms, right? A good looking guy like yourself? Maybe we could have a room that's not booked."

"You mean like a regular hotel room?"

"Don't you think that would be best? This could take two hours, and it would be private. We wouldn't want to embarrass Father Charlie at his own rectory, or Sister Frances Mary at her retreat house."

"I understand, Father. There are rooms that don't get cleaned until 1:00. So I think I could ask Maria if there's a room you could use; but the bed will not be made, and it might be messy."

"That's no problem. The rooms at that hotel have a little sitting room, right?"

"Most of them, yes, Father."

"We just need a place to talk. One other thing; it might be best if you just say you have two friends that need a meeting place without mentioning any names. Again, we don't want to embarrass anyone."

"Shouldn't I say three friends? You, Father Charlie, and Sister Frances Mary."

"I wasn't counting Father Charlie as a friend."

"You're so right."

"After you know that you have a room, then call Sister Frances Mary; now, even though I will be glad to talk with her for you, you must tell her that you want to talk with her."

"But that's not true."

"It will be true; after I persuade her to listen to the truth, and after Father Charlie gets there and we both show him the error of his ways, then I will call you to come to the room. And you can tell Father Charlie how he hurt you and your mother."

"I understand."

"I think you should ask Sister Frances Mary to come by 11:00 and Father Charlie about forty-five minutes later. I have a feeling that by the time Father Charlie gets there, it won't take long to have the problem solved."

"You sound so confident. You must have great faith."

"It's all God's work, Adam. Now, call me, on my cell phone, after you have set up the meetings with both Sister Frances Mary and Father Charlie. And remember, I'll call you when it's time to come to the room."

"I feel nervous even thinking about it. Do you think I'll be able to convince both of them to come? I get so angry just thinking about Father Charlie."

"But you must not express that anger; then he would refuse to meet you and all would be lost. I'm depending on you, Adam. Pray and ask God for the strength to do this work for him."

"And I will thank him for sending you to me. I can't believe that I will finally get justice for my mother. I'm going to call Sister Frances Mary right now."

"God bless you, Adam. I'll be praying for you."

Hanging up the phone Will shivered with anticipation as he visualized Fran's face when he greeted her tomorrow. Trembling with pleasure he pictured her squirming under his body. Roaring with satisfaction he watched himself stab her over and over. His enjoyment peaked when he imagined Charlie opening the door, finding Fran, and turning to see Will come at him. Closing his eyes he relaxed his neck and rested his head on the back of his chair, replaying the scene over and over again. He soaked up the gratification that drenched him from head to toe.

The ring of his phone jolted his fantasy to an abrupt halt. Grabbing his phone he tightened his grip when he heard Adam's quivering voice. *I hope he can stay just strong enough for my purposes.*

"Adam, you must have made contact; how are you?"

"I'm still shaking; I was so scared that Father Charlie would ask too many questions, and I wanted so much to scream at him. And Sister Frances Mary did want me to come to her place, but I stayed strong remembering what you told me."

"And so they are both going to the hotel?"

"Yes, just like you asked. Sister Frances Mary will be there at 11:00 and Father Charlie at 11:45. I have to call them back tomorrow morning when I have the room number."

"And call me first, please. Remember to use my cell phone number. God will take care of everything, Adam. I will go straight to the room, and will call you when it is safe for you to meet them."

"I can hardly believe that by tomorrow it will be over."

"It will be a first step, Adam, but you will see justice tomorrow."

Pulsing with wild anticipation Will said good night. Clutching the phone he whispered, *Fran, Fran, what a glorious end I have planned for you.*

The early darkness of December filled his room. Dropping to his knees he prayed, "O God, bring success to the work of my hands. I praise you for calling me to this great work as savior. I will restore your church to obedience and peace." Switching on the lamp and humming an Alleluia he peeled off his clothes and pulled on his pajamas. Looking at his clock he groaned when he realized it was only 8:30. *This will be a long night, and I don't expect to sleep much. But such is the cost of redemption.*

Dropping back into his chair, he became aware of a crushing emptiness in his stomach. He saw Barbara leaning into Jim and he squirmed with *No, No, No.* Rebuking the suspicion that her kindness to him had been only about business he squashed the emptiness calling to him from a Love he did not recognize. Reaching out and touching the night stand beside his chair he opened the bottom drawer. Grabbing the bottle of bourbon he lifted it to his lips.

Its smoothness oozed into every aching cell of his now sobbing body. Swallowing the last drop, he let the bottle slip to the floor.

At 12:30 a rare winter thunder awakened him. Squinting as his eyes adjusted to the light he realized he was still in his chair. His face fell forward into his cold hands as his thumping headache rebuked him. Rolling out of his chair he landed on his left knee; heaving a deep sigh he pushed himself to stand and fell back into the chair. Hearing another thunder roll and seeing a blurred image of Fran stirred him to stand again. Listening for another rumble, he was certain the thunder was a sign of approval from the God he was convinced was pleased with him. *O God, I am your loyal son and I will rid your church of the evil ones.* Moaning he stumbled to his bed. Pulling back the spread and covers he fell head first onto his firm pillow. He laughed once more as Fran's bloody body floated past him.

Chapter 32

Will shot upright and slammed his hand on the alarm. Rubbing his still aching head the realization that it was morning of the great day brought a wide grin energizing his drained body. Bounding out of bed, he jumped into the shower, and began singing his favorite Alleluia.

The warm suds streaming down his body stimulated images of Barbara. Gasping for air his surge of excitement caved into desolation as he remembered the kiss in the restaurant. With a vengeance he turned on the cold water at full force and howled with rage for a full minute.

Choking and shivering, he turned off the torrent and snatched his oversized bath towel. A vigorous drying off settled his furor, and he faced himself in the mirror. Sheer delight surged throughout his body and soul; raising his arms he shouted, "Hail, Coordinator of Redemption."

Scowling at the small clock he kept on the sink he threw on his clothes, ran a comb through his hair, and raced to the church congratulating himself for getting there ten minutes before Mass time.

All of a sudden he realized he needed to move his car to the other side of the garage where he could get it later without being seen from the office or hall windows. Running outside, gulping in a breath of cold air, he fumbled for his keys. A light snow covered everything, and he remembered the sign of thunder during the night. Opening the door, he jumped in, and swore as he turned the key, realizing he could not see through the snow on the back window. With a quick glimpse at both side mirrors, he backed up and swung around the tree next to the garage. Out of breath by the time he got to the church entrance again he had one minute to vest for Mass.

His spirits soared as he noticed Adam in his usual place; though defiant excitement engulfed him from head to toe, his outward demeanor was composed as usual. The one thing he had to do after Mass was make sure he told Bob and Annie that he was not feeling well and was going back to bed.

Adam would call with the room number while Bob was saying the later Mass, and he could leave without being noticed. Only Adam would know that he was to be at the hotel, and he had his cover story ready for him, too.

Complimenting himself on his homily given with such little preparation, he continued the Mass in his usual solemn manner. Aware of Annie's eyes scrutinizing him he did not look in her direction. Before distributing Communion he hesitated a bit before walking down the three steps from the altar. *She'll be sure to ask me if I'm feeling well,* he convinced himself. At the end of Mass he steadied himself for just a moment by resting both hands on the altar. *That should seal my story.*

In the kitchen he slumped into a chair at the table and waited. Annie was the first to come in. Keeping his eyes lowered, he was certain that her observant eyes were studying him. "Too much celebrating, Father?"

Not the response I expected. He looked up straight into her eyes. "Annie, sometimes the Lord's work is a bit overwhelming. It was a very intense weekend."

"I agree; the dinner on Saturday was wonderful. You must not have gotten any rest yesterday."

"My mother came to visit."

At that point the archbishop walked in. "Good morning, Annie. Yes, I finally met Father Will's mother."

Cringing Will heard himself screaming in mute fear that Bob was going to repeat the conversation about his name. The color had so drained from his face that its pastiness caught Bob's attention.

"Will, you look awful!"

Glad you noticed. "I am headed for my room; I don't expect to rise again until much later today." He congratulated himself on his choice of words—*rise again—how very appropriate,* he thought. Standing up he hesitated just long enough for Bob and Annie to notice. With slow, deliberate steps he walked past Annie and stopped in front of Bob. He turned to check if Annie was watching him, but she was busy getting a cup of coffee for the archbishop. Shaking his head he walked on.

Handing his coffee to the archbishop, Annie saw her hand shaking. She was glad the archbishop seemed too distracted to notice.

"I guess he just needs some extra rest; it was a very busy weekend."

"But you seem so alive, Archbishop. It makes me happy."

"Oh, Annie, everything is falling into place. I am so grateful. You know, that coma was the best thing that could have happened to me." Laughing he said,

"I guess I was finally quiet enough that God had a chance to speak to me. I'll see you after Mass, Annie."

Twenty minutes later, Annie clutched at her heart as she heard footsteps racing down steps, the door opening then closing like a whisper. *Sounds like someone is feeling better,* she murmured to herself. Berating herself for being judgmental, she shivered from an icy chill coursing through her whole body. The bright wintry sun sparkling around her whole kitchen disappeared. Gasping she made a huge trembling cross over herself from head to breast.

"Annie, what's wrong? Why is it so dark in here?"

"Oh, Archbishop," said Annie catching her breath. "I thought I heard someone, and I don't know what happened; do you feel cold, too?"

"I do, and I'm tired. I'm going to lie down for awhile, but I'm sure I'll be up for lunch. Maybe Father Will and I both have some kind of bug."

Annie did her best to smile. "I'll make some chicken soup; you'll be better in no time." Her heart ached as she watched the archbishop walk away, but *why* she asked herself; he himself had said how everything was falling into place. She couldn't shake the darkness growing inside her.

Chapter 33

Holding his breath Will grabbed the door the moment it slipped from his hand. He closed it with a resolve that ignored the cavity inside, opening wide to capture his soul. Glancing back at the window he was irritated with himself for worrying if anyone had heard him leaving. With his gloved hand he brushed off the thin layer of snow on the back window. Driving away, he delighted in the pounding pleasure in his heart.

Fran's face writhing in fear exploded in front of him. Striking the steering wheel over and over again, he relived the thrill of Adam's description of how easy it had been to convince Fran to meet him at the hotel. *So typical of people who think they are important and needed,* he thought, realizing at the same time how crucial her vulnerability was to his plan. *That Charlie has fallen for the plot just as easily is proof that the two of them have to be destroyed.*

Today he parked on the street and walked to the hotel; dressed in faded jeans and a dark brown jacket he slipped through the revolving door unnoticed. Taking the back stairs to the second floor, he opened the door to the hall looking to the left and right into an empty hall. Turning to the left he strolled past the closed doors to Room 235.

Shoving open the door his leer glistened in the morning sun. Checking out the unmade bed, its burgundy blanket twisted under the white sheet, the purple and blue diamond patterned bedspread on the floor, he tore off his jacket. Tossing it on the navy lounge chair, he walked over to the blue drapes, jerked them closed, and touched the sensor lamp.

A quick look at his watch fueled his excitement level. Fran should be walking through that door in a half hour. Pulling the knife from his jacket pocket his fingers tingled as they slithered over the blade. Fixing his eyes on the tip of the blade he vibrated with glee as he hid it underneath the Bible on the nightstand.

Hanging up the phone Fran brushed away the dampness moistening the corners of her eyes. Thinking about alerting Charlie, she smiled at how well she knew that he would respond to Adam with his habitual compassion. She considered calling her brother and then imagined how delightful it would be when she and Charlie could tell him together. Grabbing her white jacket with its matching scarf shoved into a sleeve, she stopped at Jen's office on her way out.

"Oh, Fran, a reconciliation between Adam and Charlie? And Adam asked you to be there, too. But why the hotel?"

"I asked him to come here, but he said he didn't want to take time off work to drive here. I'm just happy that he wants to do this; I know Charlie has been troubled about the whole thing."

"Does it seem to you that the fruits of your brother's Day of Recollection and Possibilities are yielding incredible results?"

"Bob told me the other day what a gift he believes his coma was; I think the Spirit was working even when they chose the name of that day."

"So true. I'll tell Joan and we'll celebrate this evening."

After Fran closed her door, Joan shuddered and clutched her stomach. *I knew I shouldn't have skipped breakfast this morning. I better go to the kitchen and get some hot cereal.*

"Jen, you don't look so good."

"I didn't eat this morning, Joan; I'm going to get something now."

"I'll walk with you. Have you seen Fran this morning?"

"Yes, such good news. She just left to meet Adam at the hotel."

"That's why the phone in her office kept ringing; I finally answered it. Charlie was calling, and said that Adam had asked to meet him."

Jen cringed with another pain in her stomach.

"Jen, are you sure you're just hungry?"

"Not really. I'm so cold."

Joan caught her breath as she felt a chilly breeze whip past. Grabbing Jen's arm she said, "I'm scared; something's wrong. Can we go back to your office? I think we should call Charlie."

"I agree. What's that shadow?"

"Where? I don't see anything, but why is it getting dark?"

"Joan, it's him; it's Will."

"Where?"

"I mean, the shadow; it's Will. This is all a trick."

156

Spinning around as one person they ran back to Jen's office. She had Charlie on speed dial, and when the secretary said that Father Charlie was on another line, Jen was heartsick. "Please tell him to call Sister Jennifer as soon as possible."

"Should we call Bob? I don't want to worry him, and I'm still afraid that Will has—"

"At least we could find out if Will is still there."

"Good point. Call."

Another secretary with the same message. "The archbishop is on another line."

Jen put the phone down; her whole body shaking. "His line is busy."

"What if he's talking to Charlie?"

"Let's drive over there."

"Charlie, this is Bob; I went back to bed after Mass and fell into a deep sleep, and had a terrible dream. But even worse; I remember it was the same one I had before I woke up in the hospital. I don't know what to make of it."

"Tell me what you saw."

"I saw Fran dead; she had been killed; and you were dead, too."

"What? How?"

"Actually, it was a second attempt; first Fran had been poisoned, then somehow she and you were at a hotel. The police…"

"Did you say that Fran went to a hotel?"

"Yes, and you were there, too. But the police found both of you dead, and they told me that it looked as if you had murdered Fran and then killed yourself."

"What else do you remember?"

"Something about Adam and your mother."

"Me and Mrs. Wetzer? This is all very strange, Bob. I just had a call from Adam this morning asking me to meet him at the hotel. Anything else?"

"When I woke up I was terrified and shocked, and yet all I could remember at first was screaming 'No'; in fact, my own yelling woke me up."

"That's how you woke up in the hospital."

"I know, so I started to pray for some calmness first, and then some images started to come to me. First, I saw Fran in the hospital and I remember being so sad because I thought she was dead. A doctor was saying something about poison. But she woke up; then I saw what I told you, about the hotel and the police; I still can't remember what made me scream."

"Take a deep breath, Bob. Think. Was someone chasing you?"

"No."

"Were you falling?"

"Not exactly; I was falling down, because—I was being hit!"

"Can you remember who or what was knocking you down?"

"It was large; I was looking up at it, and I was thinking of Fran. Wait. Oh, no; it was the sculpture—you know that sculpture she made for me. No! No!"

"Bob, what is it? Who is it?"

"But you said that we need to be careful about thinking dreams are literally true. So if I see a certain person, it could me a message about myself, right?"

"That's true, Bob, usually. Who was in your dream?"

"It was Will."

"Bob, there is such a thing as a warning dream."

"What do you mean?"

"Bob, I'm not sure how to say this, but I don't think Will is pleased with your new attitude."

Charlie's comment pierced Bob like an arrow. Bowing his head he did not answer.

"Bob, I'm sorry if that sounded harsh. Do you understand what I'm saying?"

"Charlie, this is hard for me but it's time to admit something I have been denying since I awoke. When I first announced the Day of Reconciliation and Possibilities, I was in a different place than I am now."

"I know that, Bob."

"Was it that obvious?'

"Not at the time. I had a dream the day after we received the invitation. I didn't understand it, but it made me sad, confused, and angry. I dreamt that you died, and I was so sorry that we had not renewed our friendship. In my dream I saw you and Will laughing while sharing a dinner with other priests. I had the wicked thought that you were planning on using that meeting as a way to discredit **Cry Justice**, and I was so upset with you. Then the accident happened, and I was afraid you were going to die without us ever having a chance to talk. When you were in the coma, I realized that my sadness from the dream went beyond the fact that you had died; I regretted that you had lost your vision. And I was ashamed of judging your reason for calling us together."

Bob was silent again. Clearing his throat he said, "Charlie, I need to ask for your forgiveness. You have no reason to be ashamed; your dream was giving you true information. I am so sorry. I know now that I have changed but I have refused to notice Will's opposition. I ignored his resentment when I changed the seating at the dinner. And when his mother came yesterday for dinner I sensed his dissatisfaction with me and with her, but I brushed it off."

"Bob, I'm just grateful we are friends again. I think I better get on my way."

"You're not going to the hotel after all I've told you."

"I have to; somehow Will has Adam convinced of something. If Will can put me under some shadow of wrongdoing, he knows it would kill me."

"I better call Fran."

"Find out if she had a call from Adam."

A car screeched to a halt; Bob spun around to see Jen and Joan racing towards his office.

"Charlie, hang on; Jen and Joan just drove up."

Dropping the phone Bob ran to open the door. "Where's Fran?"

"She went to the hotel to meet with Adam; Bob we are so afraid."

"I am too; Charlie's on the phone. Come with me." Jen grabbed one of Bob's arms; Joan held on to the other and they dashed to his office. Snatching the phone Bob said, "Charlie, Fran's already left for the hotel; we have to get there. I'll go with Jen and Joan."

"I'll meet you there." Charlie yanked his jacket off its hook and darted to his car. *O God, please take care of Fran; give her your strength.*

Chapter 34

Pulling into the hotel parking lot Fran's eyes roamed the first level but could find no empty spot. Following the arrow leading to the second level she noticed an empty spot three spaces away from the elevator to the hotel. A strong wind swept through the garage jamming her door. She shoved against it twice.

Words from the Bible flooded her mind: *"...there came a sound like a rush of violent wind..." And we had Pentecost,* she whispered. *Thank you, O caring Spirit, for offering us a new beginning.* "Now, please, let me open this door!"

The wind curtailed its power. Grabbing her purse she got out of the car brushing the static from her navy skirt. The crisp cool air made her wonder why she hadn't worn slacks today.

Her quick steps to the elevator and her thoughts of concern for Adam overpowered the queasiness in her stomach. She looked around the empty garage while waiting for the elevator door to open. Moving aside to let a young woman out she stepped inside. Placing her finger on the lobby button she breathed out a sigh.

When the doors opened to the lobby, she stepped out with a twinge of excitement, then backed away when a shadow jumped in front of her. Gasping she blinked her eyes and it was gone. Hugging her arms to herself she walked straight to the hotel elevator.

Shuddering from a quick icy chill when the doors opened she was grateful it was empty. Her hand trembling she pointed her second finger toward the second floor button. Her mind was crammed with doubts. *I should have called Bob and told him where I was going. Why didn't I check with Charlie before I left? Why am I shivering? What was that shadow? Why did that wind seem to be trying to stop me? O God, give me the right words for Adam.*

The elevator opened to an empty hall; passing a room where she could hear the hushed voices of a man and woman she continued walking. A TV was blaring in the room next door. Then she saw the door of Room 235.

Standing in front of it, staring at the number in silence with her fist in the air she lowered her hand and walked away. Taking a deep breath she shivered. The door of the room with the loud TV opened, and a woman in a navy pantsuit came out carrying a white wool jacket; a bellboy followed with her luggage. Fran turned back towards Room 235.

O God, I trust you to help me to know what to say. Again she stood in front of Room 235; this time she swallowed once and tapped on the door. "Adam? Are you in there?"

Hearing a faint "Come in" she pressed against the door. It was unlocked and opened a crack of two or three inches; she saw the unmade bed, and pushed the door to the wall. "Adam? It's Sister Frances Mary."

Terror seized her as the bathroom door opened. "What are you—Why are you—Where's Adam?" She spun around for the door but Will leaped in front of her and slammed it shut.

"Adam called you for me." Trembling she watched his hands move up his jeans and his fingers roll up the edge of his pale yellow shirt. She backed away as he began to pull the shirt over his head. Her eyes wandered to the bedside table where she noticed the Bible covering a knife.

All of a sudden his hands were around her waist squeezing her close to him. She twisted in vain. Releasing his right arm he tore off her jacket and dragged her to the bed. Shoving her down on the rumpled sheets, he jumped on top of her and stretched her arms above her head.

"Will, don't do this. Please think about what you are doing. Let me go! Let me go!"

"I'm doing this to save our church." He pressed his knees into her stomach.

Squirming under his crushing weight she said, "You're crazy, Will. What are you talking about?"

"Your death will be the beginning of the end of **Cry Justice**." Holding her wrists together with his left hand, his right hand reached for the rope he had laid on the bed. Jerking her hands to the bedpost he tied one to the left post and pulled the other one to the right post. Wrapping the rest of the rope around it, he looped a tight knot and yanked it with such force that Fran wailed in pain.

Tears gushed over her face. "You won't get away with this; how will you face my brother?"

He slapped her so hard she blacked out. "Oh no, you don't," he cried. "You're not getting off that easily." Cursing, he slid off her and went to the bathroom for a glass of water.

Fran opened her eyes. *O God, help me!* She heard the water running in the bathroom sink. *What's he doing now?*

She saw him, bare-chested still wearing his jeans, glide out of the bathroom holding a glass of water. "Oh, so you're awake again. Good, but I'll enjoy throwing this water at you anyway." Flinging it toward her Fran gulped as cold water flew into her mouth, over her face and trickled down her blouse.

He crawled on top of her again. She moaned. His bony body was squashing hers as he spread himself over her. Wrenching every muscle nausea ballooned within her. "Keep struggling, Fran; I love the futility of it all." Raising himself he slid down beside her nuzzling himself into her side; she jerked her head away.

Rolling on top of her he clutched her face in his hands. "Look at me!" he said yanking her by the chin.

Fran shut her eyes, and as soon as his hand let go, she turned her face away again. He backhanded her cheek. "I said, look at me!" She stared straight up at the ceiling.

His laugh was so vigorous he began choking. His pulsating body dug into Fran's abdomen. She twisted under him straining her back; warm blood began oozing from her tied wrists. Sitting up he doubled over as he said, "You're trying to make a show of power even now. But you'll soon find out who is in charge here."

He slithered off the bed. Fran heard his belt fall to the floor, then his jeans. "How do you feel, Fran, knowing what I'm going to do and you can't stop me?" Shaking he pulled off his shorts; he froze as his mother's face burst in front of him. "You can't stop me either," he said.

Fran turned her head to see who else was in the room. Shrieking she closed her eyes.

Naked and shaking, he leaned over her face, pressing his hands into the pillow around her head. He blew his warm breath over her eyes. Skimming his tongue over her ear lobe he plunged it into her ear. He roared as she twisted her head away.

Pulling himself up to his full height he stared at his quaking body. He had dreamed of his first performance being with Barbara; *I would have been superb with her,* he told himself; *I would have thrilled her with ultimate ecstasy, but this revenge will be a supreme delight for me.*

Fran felt the bed sag as he crawled over her, sealing his legs around her thighs. "How does it feel, Fran, to be completely, totally, and absolutely in my power?" Stroking her cheek while she buried the side of her face into the pillow he whispered in her ear. "My body yearns for yours." Running his finger over her lips he said, "Do you like this, Fran? I want you to be pleased with me." Licking the tears streaming down her cheeks with his cold wet tongue his hands massaged her stomach. Cringing as he ripped open her blouse she cried as the buttons popped to the floor. She pulled and tugged her roped arms as his fingers fumbled with the clasp of her bra. The hook stung her back and he slid the bra upwards to her neck.

Chapter 35

His forehead creased with worry, his voice straining to sound brave Bob turned to Jen in the back seat. "Can you try Fran's cell phone? I left without mine."

"Of course." Jen's eyes filled with tears. She had tried twice on their way over to Bob's, but she pushed the redial button. Wiping her eyes, she said, "It went to voice mail; she must have forgotten to turn it on."

Heaving a sigh Bob prayed. "O God, please protect her."

"Amen," said Joan and Jen in unison. Slowing down as she approached the red traffic light she tapped the steering wheel. Checking Bob out of the corner of her eye she said, "Just a few more miles, Bob."

"I appreciate your driving, Joan. I hope Charlie doesn't get caught in traffic. How I wish I had recalled my dream sooner. How could I be so blind?"

"Bob, you can't blame yourself. Let's be grateful that you remembered it when you did."

"Did Fran ever share a prayer with you called The Un-Magnificat?"

"Yes," said Jen. "She wrote it. How did you know?"

"It was a guess. Some words have been swirling around in my head since I awoke from that dream, something about being cursed, or crushed. Did I cause her such misery when all that sad business happened at Sacred Heart?"

"Bob," said Joan, "she always understood that you did what you had to do. We all did. That prayer was how she dealt with her anger and hurt, but believe, me, it was not directed at you. She loves you."

Wiping the tear that rolling down his right cheek Bob said, "Do you remember the prayer?"

"I think so," said Jen. "The first part came out of the pain. Are you sure you want me to say it?"

"Please; I need to hear her thoughts."

Jen inhaled. "My soul wilts before you, O Lord, and my spirit weeps in your presence." Hesitating as Bob wiped away another tear she took a deep breath. "Do you want me to continue?"

Bob nodded.

"Why have you looked away from the misery of your servant? Surely from now on all generations will call me cursed, for your might has crushed me with sorrow, and terrible is your name."

Covering his face with both hands Bob began sobbing. Reaching over Joan stroked his arm; from the back seat Jean squeezed his shoulder.

"Bob, listen to what comes next; it will show you how deep is her faith; may I?"

"Yes," he said raising his head.

"But your remoteness is an illusion for those who seek you from generation to generation. You show strength with your arm; you gather..."

"Sorry to interrupt, Jen, but there's the hotel."

"Who would have guessed how that night would change everything. This intersection, the traffic light, the glare of twinkling lights that had been designed to welcome us." His voice cracking Bob bowed his head.

Turning left Joan drove towards for the garage. "I see a spot in the first row. Look around and see if Charlie is here yet." Bob and Jen opened their doors before Joan had turned off the ignition.

His eyes skimming the first parking level and the ramp leading to the second Bob said, "I don't see him." Grabbing for Jen's arm, he pulled her with him. "We have to move fast; we have to find Fran; Adam must know where they would be; he likes Fran; he'll help us find them."

Catching up to them Joan said, "Bob, take some deep breaths."

"We're almost at the lobby; I can't stop now."

Once inside, Joan insisted. "Bob, sit here; Jen and I will find Adam."

"There he is; I see him in the restaurant."

"Stay here," said Jen. She and Joan raced to the restaurant entrance. "Adam! Adam!" they shouted in unison.

"I'll seat you," said a hostess trying to block them from running to Adam.

"It's a matter of life and death," said Jen. "We have to talk to Adam."

Seeing Jen and Joan, Adam turned back to the people whose orders he was taking. The hostess said, "Please; wait here; I'll see if Adam can talk with you."

"Please believe us; I'm Sister Joan."

"And I'm Sister Jen; Adam can help us; we are trying to save someone's life."

"You must stand here; I'll get Adam."

Jen wiped tears from both eyes; Joan wrung her hands as they watched Adam shaking his head no to the hostess.

Jen screamed, "Adam, Sister Frances Mary needs help."

At that Adam handed his order form to the hostess and darted toward them.

"What makes you say that? Archbishop, why are you here?"

Joan and Jen turned to see Bob a few feet away.

"Adam, if you know where my sister is, you must tell us."

"Have I done something wrong? Father Will said I was helping the church; that God would be pleased with me."

"Adam, where are they?"

"Room 235; I can take you."

"No, just point us to the closest elevator. And keep an eye out for Father Charlie; tell him where we are."

Pointing to the right Adam said, "There's the elevator, just past the restaurant."

Jen and Joan each took one of Bob's arms and raced to the elevator.

Her eyes squeezed tight Fran squirmed as Will leaned over and fondled her breasts. Her stomach heaved and she gagged on the vomit caught in her throat. "Stay calm, my darling; you can't spoil this for me."

Glancing at the bedside clock, he said, "As much as I'd enjoy prolonging this pleasure, I'm going to complete your rapture soon. Charlie will be there in twenty minutes .But you'll never be able to tell Charlie how I delighted you, because—." Shrieking he slapped her and said, "because you'll be dead."

Yelling Fran jerked the ropes holding her captive. Flattening his hand over her mouth he said, "Oh yes, my dear Fran, that's how Charlie will find you; stabbed, bloody and violated. Then I'm going to kill him; when you're both found it will look like a lover's quarrel. Think what that will do to your brother, and your **Cry Justice**." His fingers crept up her legs to her waist. "I'm so glad you're in pantyhose today." Fran plunged into darkness as he began pulling them off.

"Fran! Will!" Jen was the first to burst into the room.

Blocking Bob with her arm across the doorway Joan said "Don't go in yet."

Will froze. Charging at him Jen flung her arms pounding his chest and shoving him backward. Falling off the bed, he dragged a piece of the bedspread over himself. Rushing over to Will, Bob dropped to his knees, grabbed him around the throat, and shook him. Moaning, his arms flailing left and right, his fingers grasping for more of the spread he said "Bob, stop. Stop!"

Bob let go. "How could you do this?"

Lunging for Fran Joan tugged at the sheet and blanket. Pulling them up to Fran's chin, she touched her face. Screaming and tugging at the ropes she heard, "You're safe now."

She opened her eyes and started whimpering. Spying the knife, Jen ran around the bed, grabbed it and sliced the ropes. Biting her bottom lip she observed the rope burns and the blood. Fran's arms dropped to the blanket; her whole body began convulsing. Rolling on her side, she swung her head toward the floor and threw up. Shoving Will's head to the floor, Bob scrambled to his feet. Sliding through her vomit, he landed on the bed. He lifted Fran's head and cuddled her to himself. "I'm so sorry! I'm so sorry."

"Oh, no. No!" Darting from the doorway Charlie slid to Fran's other side. Burying her head deeper into her brother's arms she sobbed.

Standing in the doorway, Adam's eyes moved first to Fran and the archbishop, then to Father Charlie. He stared at Jen standing behind Fran with her hand squeezing the pillow. Glancing at Joan standing near the bedside table his mouth fell open as his eyes fell on Will. "Father Will, what have they done to you?" Ducking his head under the spread Will crouched down on the floor.

"Adam," said Father Charlie, "please call the police."

Adam looked at the archbishop. "Yes, Adam, do what Father Charlie said."

Taking one last look at Father Will, Adam bowed his head and left the room.

Rocking Fran back and forth in his arms Bob felt the tension receding from her body. He nodded to Charlie, who reached over and laid his hand on top of Fran's. Looking into his eyes, she burst into tears.

Drawing back Charlie said, "Fran, forgive me."

She pulled him toward her. "I'm the one who's sorry; I should have been more careful." Her tears flowed.

"Fran, none of this is your fault. You are the innocent one."

"So why do I feel guilty?"

"Fran, I'm so sorry. Just believe that we are here for you; you know we all love you."

Joan wiped tears away; Jen fluffed the pillow and propped it against Fran's back.

Everyone except Will lifted their eyes toward the knock at the door. Two detectives, a man and a woman, walked over to Fran. Following them were two other people carrying black cases and cameras

"I'm Detective Kim Hudson."

"And I'm Detective Phil Roberts." Pointing to a tall woman with blond hair tucked behind her ears, and a lanky man with short wavy gray hair, he said, "And this is our forensics team, Lisa and Al. They'll take some pictures first." He yanked off the bedspread covering Will, who cowered as the cameras flashed twice.

Detective Hudson dangled the handcuffs in Will's face. "Turn over." Securing the cuffs she motioned to Roberts. "Get his clothes on him."

Tempted to embarrass him further Lisa and Al looked away from each other as Roberts dragged Will across the floor. Al picked up Will's jeans, rolled his shorts and shirt together, and threw them into the bathroom.

Detective Hudson turned her attention to Fran. "Sister, may I call you Fran?"

Gazing into gentle, understanding eyes, Fran forced a feeble smile, and nodded yes.

"Thank you, Fran. After they remove him; I'd like to ask you some questions. Are you up that?"

"Can I get dressed first?"

"I'll need some pictures." Discerning terror in Fran's eyes she said, "The men will leave." She touched Fran's arm.

Kissing her on the forehead, Bob motioned for Joan to come and sit beside her. "Come, Charlie, let's go out to the hall."

The cameraman and Detective Roberts, holding on to Will, followed. "I'll meet you back at the precinct," said Roberts. "I'll have him booked and in a cell when you get back."

"I'll see you soon." She turned and saw a glimmer of relaxation in the three women now seated on the bed, Fran still clutching the blanket around her. "Fran, tell me first about your arms."

As Fran described how Will had tied her, the camera flashed. Detective Hudson lowered the blanket. Shivering Fran lowered her head. Her bra hung from her shoulders under her button-less blouse. The camera flashed one more time.

"That's enough; you can get dressed now." Joan and Jen put their arms around her and helped her stand. Pulling her bra down and back she fastened it. Overlapping the right side of her pale blue blouse over the left, she tucked it into her skirt. She shuddered as she remembered Will's fingers crawling up her legs.

"Can you talk some more? Maybe you'd like to sit over there in the chair."

Fran nodded yes and held onto Jen as she made her way to the chair. It felt so good to sit down on something clean.

Chapter 36

Returning to the hallway Adam walked over to the archbishop, his eyes avoiding Charlie standing beside him. "Archbishop, can you explain what happened to Father Will?"

"Adam, do you know why he was in that room?"

"Yes, he was meeting with Sister Frances Mary and Father Charlie to help me solve a problem."

"But my sister was asked by you to come first."

"I know; Father Will said he needed to talk to her first and make her understand what Father Charlie had done to my mother."

"Your mother?" said Father Charlie. "I only found out on Saturday about your mother; I never knew, Charlie, and I am so sorry."

Backing away his eyes filled with tears Adam said, "She did it because you left her."

"Adam, what are you talking about?"

"Remember," Adam sobbed, "how you used to come to our house; you even made dinner sometimes, and then you left her."

"Adam, I was counseling your mother; one day she told me she had met someone else, and she didn't need to talk with me anymore."

"But I thought she was going out with you."

"No, Adam, that never happened."

"But she was going out with someone. I even heard her on the phone one day asking him something about a will; why he wanted a will, or had to have a will, something like that."

"Oh no," said the archbishop. "I think I know what you heard; but it wasn't Father Charlie on the other end of that line."

Adam looked at Charlie who shook his head. "That's true, Adam. I thought your mother was happy when I said last goodbye to her; then I was assigned to a new parish far away. I never heard from her again."

Adam started to cry. "You know who it was, don't you, Archbishop? How could I have been so stupid? It was Father Will, wasn't it?"

"I'm afraid so, Adam. I think what you heard your mother asking was not that he wanted a will, but why he had to be Will—to be called Will."

"How could he have lied to me all this time?"

"Adam, maybe we can sort this out soon."

The door opened and Detective Hudson came out; Jen and Joan followed with Fran in the middle her head bowed.

"Sister Frances Mary, I am so sorry; it's all my fault."

She touched his arm. "No, Adam, it wasn't."

Her eyes downcast she said, "Bob, Charlie, would you come home with us?"

"Of course, Fran" they said in unison.

Noticing that Adam's bottom lip was quivering she said, "Adam, you're welcome to come, too."

"I'd like that; if it's OK with you, Archbishop, and you, Father Charlie. I'm so confused right now, and upset." Running his fingers through his hair he said, "But I'll have to see my boss; I know I can't work anymore today."

"Adam," said Charlie, "I'll wait for you; we can go together, and I'll bring you back later for your car."

"I don't know what to say." Adam looked Father Charlie in the eye. "Thank you, Father."

"Before you all leave," said Detective Hudson, "I need to say something. I know you have all been through so much today, but I would like you, Fran, to come down to the precinct tomorrow to discuss the arraignment and how we are going to proceed with this case. You can bring anyone with you that you like."

Looking at her brother Fran said, "What are we going to do; how can our diocesan lawyer be involved? I don't want anyone to know."

"Detective, isn't there another way we can handle this?"

"Archbishop, first, I want you to know that I am a Catholic, but you could not mean that we can't go forward with this case. Father Will is a criminal— attempted rape, attempted murder."

"I can't even begin to explain the pain I am experiencing now; but even if he pleads guilty and there's no trial, putting him in jail will not help."

"My only suggestion right now is for you to meet with him tomorrow."

Bob's eyes met Fran's. She mouthed the words, "I can't do that."

"I'll be there," he said, glancing at Charlie.

"I'll come with you."

"Fran," said Hudson, "remember what I said to you, call me anytime.
"Thank you very much. Is it OK for us to leave now?"
"Of course."

On the way home, Fran did not close her eyes; fresh snow covered everything and was still falling. Allowing her body to be mellowed by its cleanness she wished her mind could relax. *Why did I go alone? How could I have been so naive?*

Sitting in the back seat with Jen Bob lamented the day he made a place for Will in his life. Full of regrets for the time separated from his sister he examined his journey from that Tuesday dinner to his present change of heart. Reproaching himself for mistaking Will's rage for zeal he searched for answers. *How could I have been so blind? O God, what have I done? How did I let power come between me and Fran?*

Jen kept reliving the scene when she had opened the door and saw Fran tied, bloody, and unconscious. She recalled the words of Fran's prayer she had been sharing with Bob as they arrived at the hotel. *You show strength with your arm; you gather*—that was as far as she had gone. Now she tried to pray the rest of it, but all she could murmur in her silence was *you gather the heartbroken into your eternal embrace.* A single tear rolled down each cheek.

No one felt a need to break the silence and Fran was grateful. Not even when they reached the turnoff for Sophia's Blessings did anyone attempt to interject a sound into the soul enveloping quiet.

Joan pulled into the driveway. The afternoon sun, the falling snowflakes, and the Christmas wreath on the door shattered their silence. Fran burst into tears, fell forward covering her face with both hands; her shoulders heaved with her sobs. Joan stroked Fran's arm, using her other hand to brush away her own tears.

Jen, blinking away the sting in her eyes, wiped away the stream flowing down her cheeks. Crawling out of her seat she balanced herself against her open door. Blowing his nose Bob dragged himself out of the car. Trudging around the front of the car to get to Fran's door he pulled it open, bent down and put his arms around her. "Come, with me; let's go inside."

Clutching his arm Fran cried. "Why did I go? Why did I go?" Pulling her close to himself he rocked her in his arms.

Slipping twice Joan made her way around to Jen. They wrapped their arms around the sister and brother locked together in anguish. *Our souls wilt before you, O Lord, and our spirits weep in your presence,* prayed Jen in her hushed agony.

Time maintained its usual pace but they were immobilized in the horror of the now. A heartbreaking comfort with each other ignored the cold, and the snow hurried to blanket them with its gentleness. The sound of an approaching car jolted them. Grateful that Charlie had arrived, Jen pointed to the house. Nodding he opened his door, and motioned Adam to follow him. Pushing his hands into his pockets Adam plodded along behind Charlie up the sloping hill to Sophia's Blessings.

Inside, Jen took Fran's jacket with hers; collecting a coat from Bob, and jackets from Charlie and Adam Joan hung them all on the rack. "Please," said Jen, "go on into large living room; there's no group on retreat today, so it's empty. We'll be right back."

Putting his arm around Fran Bob walked her to the maroon couch in front of the large window. Guiding her towards the middle, he fluffed the gray and maroon pillows, sat down beside her, and entwined his fingers with hers. Charlie set himself on her left.

Scanning the room Adam headed for the straight-backed cushioned chair near the wall. A large framed snow scene on that wall matched his bleak mood. After settling himself in the chair his eyes roamed the other three walls; to his left he saw summer, and spring landscapes above the TV, and on the opposite wall was autumn.

Jen came back with a tray of mugs and a carafe of coffee. Joan carried a plate of chocolate chip and oatmeal cookies. Placing the cookies on the oblong glass-top coffee table Joan waited as Jen served the coffee.

"These are home-made," said Joan as she held the plate in front of Bob first. Shivering Fran glanced at the red poinsettia sitting in the center. Taking a cookie she placed it on a napkin. Looking up at Jen and Joan, Bob's eyes brimmed with his gratitude. Charlie waved Adam to the table but he winced and shook his head no.

Jen poured coffee for herself and Joan, took a cookie, and pulled a chair closer to the couch beside Charlie. Joan picked a chocolate chip cookie and moved to the lounger next to the end table. Squeezing Fran's hand Bob said, "Fran, do you feel like talking?"

Gazing at his hand holding onto her and into his eyes, she surrendered a fragile smile. Shifting her eyes to Joan, then to the wall where Adam was sitting, she turned her head to Jen and with her other hand reached for Charlie. "Thank you for finding me." Pulling her hands from Bob and Charlie, she covered her face, and sobbed."

Weeping Bob said, "Fran, please forgive me; if I had only…"

"Bob, how could you have known? I do not blame you. How could I have been so foolish?"

"That was my fault, Sister," said Adam.

"Adam, come closer," said Fran. "Please. You can't blame yourself."

Adam dragged his chair next to Joan. "I can't believe what he did. I can't believe how he lied to me. Now I think he was setting me up to take the blame."

"He used your pain, Adam; you were a victim. Listen to Sister Fran," said Charlie. "You can't blame yourself. In fact," Charlie took Fran's hand again, "we have to concentrate on two things—healing first,"—he squeezed her hand—"and how we are going to deal with Will." Charlie's candor plunged them into a fog of fear, questions, and nervousness; the ringing of Jen's cell phone pulled everyone back to the present.

"Yes, the archbishop is here. Yes. I'll tell him. Thank you, Father." Jen's eyes darted from Bob to Fran to Charlie. "That was Father Ed. He said we'd better turn on Channel 7." Joan had already picked up the remote. Adam gasped as the picture filled the screen.

Standing in front of the Cloister Royale Hotel a reporter was saying, "Though we will not reveal the name of the victim, Father Will Owens, a priest from this archdiocese was taken into custody today charged with attempted rape and murder." Staring straight ahead, Fran dug her fingers into the hands of Bob and Charlie.

Charlie's phone rang. "Yes, Mike. I am watching." Fran's fingers dug deeper. "No, Mike, I can't tell you anything else right now." Shoving the phone into his pocket he said, "This is only a hint of what's coming."

Still glued to the set Adam said, "Look who the reporter is interviewing."

"Didn't you work with Father Owens planning a huge event here at the hotel?"

"I did," said Barbara. "It was a wonderful event, and our hotel was pleased to accommodate the Catholic Church."

"What did you think when you heard that the police were taking Father Owens into custody?"

"I was shocked beyond words; he seemed like such a fervent priest. How this happened today, I have no idea. I can assure you that we will have our own internal investigation."

Moaning Adam said, "There's goes my job; and they'll want to know who helped me get that room."

"Try not to worry, Adam," said Charlie. "I'll go with you when the time comes."

"Is anyone getting hungry? It's almost 5:00," said Jen. "We gave the cook the week off, but I can whip up something for us."

"I'll help," said Charlie. Fran released her grip on his hand. Leaning over he said, "You may not feel like it, but we would like you to eat with us."

"I will try."

Chapter 37

Waking for the fifth time, Fran dreaded closing her eyes again even though the expected nightmares had not come. In fact, she could not remember anything, dream or nightmare. The longest uninterrupted span, an hour and a half, was after midnight, but the sporadic sleep left her exhausted. She was relieved that it was finally morning.

Wiping away a tear she remembered that Bob and Charlie would be talking with the police at 10:30. Hearing a light tap at her door she turned on the lamp beside her bed. "Come in. I knew you two would be checking on me."

Jen carried a tray on which were three cups of coffee and three glasses of orange juice. Joan had a plate with slices of banana bread. "We thought we could have breakfast here this morning," said Joan straightening the pale yellow blanket.

"Good idea." She covered her yawn with the palm of her hand.

"Maybe we should have let you sleep," said Jen.

"No, it wasn't a good night; this coffee hits the spot. Thanks." She sighed as she broke off a piece of the banana bread. "I need to talk about it." The tears began; Jen set the tray on the floor and both scrambled on to the bed to hold her.

"Take your time, Fran," said Joan. "We have the whole house to ourselves, and all the time you need."

For the next two hours Fran cried, sighed, screamed, described her thoughts of despair, panic, and anger, and sat for long moments in silence. After an hour and a half she asked if they could all go to the chapel and share a communion service together. In their pajamas and robes they prayed, and after the final Amen, she surprised herself as well as Jean and Joan. "I have to go to the precinct."

"Are you sure?" said Jen.

"Do you want us to go with you?"

"Yes, to both," she said. "If I don't face him, then I'm still the victim. Can we be ready to leave by 10:00?"

When Joan opened the door, the winter sun danced with hope as the three of them skidded through the snow to the car.

"Joan, if you would drive, I'd appreciate it," said Jen.

Grabbing the ice scraper Jen hurried to clear the windows. With two wide sweeps Fran cleared the snow off the car roof. Joan turned on the heat, and as soon as the two climbed in and fastened their seat belts, she backed out.

Each one struggled with her own imaginings of what might take place in a half hour. Fran tried to visualize looking Will straight in the eye. She shivered at the thought of his turning to glare at her.

Joan enjoyed the guilty pleasure of remembering Will as he cowered underneath the blanket but conceded that continuing to concentrate on that was not a Christian response. However, she also admitted she was not yet ready to forgive him.

Gazing at her fists Jen relished the picture of pounding him again. Aware of the improbability of that prospect, she conjured up scenes where she would trip him, kick him, and slap him. Scolding herself for being so absurd she reminded herself, *I should be thinking of Fran and how difficult this is going to be for her.*

"We're almost there," said Joan. Fran's heart leaped into her throat. She stared at her fists, her knuckles turning white, her fingernails cutting into her palms.

Reaching from the back seat Jen massaged her shoulders. "God will give you strength, Fran."

"And all of us," said Fran.

Parking next to Charlie's car Joan whispered a silent prayer. Holding tight to the door handle Fran sighed and bowed her head. *Please, help me, O God.* Inhaling a deep breath Jen opened her door. Scrambling out of the driver's seat Joan gulped the crisp air. Linking arms they marched up the two steps and then single file through the door.

Charlie and Bob were sitting with Detective Hudson, their backs to the door. Noticing a satisfied expression cross her face, they looked at each other. At the same time, hearing the footsteps behind them they both stood up.

"Fran," Bob said, "you decided to come. How are you this morning?"

"I realized I will never get better until I face this—face him."

"You are so right, Fran," said Hudson.

"But I can't do it alone."

"You don't have to," said Charlie.

Clasping her hand Bob said, "Whatever you need, I'm here." Jen and Joan nodded their heads in agreement.

"He hasn't said anything since we brought him in yesterday," said Hudson. "It might be overwhelming if you all go in at the same time; how would you like to do this?"

"Well," said Bob, clearing his throat, "since he worked with me, I could go first."

"No," said Fran, "I should be the one; besides, I'm afraid I'll lose my nerve if I wait. Just so I know you'll be nearby."

"They can be in the observation room with me; we'll be able to see and hear everything that goes on."

"Let's do it."

"I'll take you to the interrogation room first, so you can be seated and prepared; then I will come in with Father Will. If you decide you want me to stay, I will." Opening the door, Hudson, said, "Try sitting on that side of the table; that way you'll be facing him when I bring him in."

Fran nodded her head. Tiptoeing away Hudson closed the door.

Caressing her in serenity, silence and stillness seeped into every cell of Fran's body. She drew in slow deep breaths of calmness and composure; minutes passed. The peace was shattered with Will's yell, "Why did you come? What are you trying to prove?"

Looking up at him, Fran panicked but her terror evaporated in a spontaneous embrace of tranquility accompanied by strength. Without flinching she said, "I came to ask you why."

"Why! Why! Do you still not understand? I was chosen as the Coordinator of Redemption."

Staring at him her mouth dropped open. Gulping, swallowing, and jamming her fist into her mouth, she stifled her scream. Releasing a slow breath, she said, "You were chosen as what? By whom?"

Her questions opened the gates stirring Will to spew out his madness. "I was chosen to redeem the Church by God. **Cry Justice** is an abomination to our Church; it has to be destroyed. I chose you and Charlie as the first sacrifices; my hope was your deaths would be the only ones needed; once those devoted to the Church saw two leaders so disgraced and humiliated, the movement would die."

"But you were going to rape me!"

The outrage on Fran's face egged him on. "That was a bonus; not only would I reduce you to a whimpering woman in my control, thus having my own personal revenge for all you did to me, but it would trash Charlie's reputation."

Behind the two-way mirror, Bob wiped away tears that would not stop. Charlie gasped for air. Joan's head was swimming. Jen hit the window with both fists.

Detective Hudson said, "Good work, Fran. We got him."

Fran infuriated Will by saying," I was so angry at you yesterday that I didn't think I would ever be able to face you. Now, I am so sorry for you."

Flashing his eyes at her Will said, "Why? Because you think I am disgraced? This is a test of my steadfastness. Like Jesus on the cross, it only seems that I have been abandoned."

Will became a blur. The room began spinning. Fran gripped the table.

Looking at the archbishop and Father Charlie Hudson said, "I hope you're thinking about how to proceed with his case. Now, I think it's time to take Father Owens back to his cell."

Fran relaxed when Detective Hudson opened the door. "Father Owens, it's time to return to your cell."

Sneering at her he stood and leaned over to Fran. She jerked her head away. Jerking his arm Detective Hudson pulled him to the door. Throwing his head back, he roared and said, "I will succeed."

Walking him back to his cell, Hudson stopped dead when she heard a female call out, "Will!"

Recognizing that voice Will spun around and saw her standing beside Hudson's desk. "Mother, why are you here?"

"You are my son! I want to know why you are here."

"I am God's servant, Mother. You would not understand. You are fixated on earthly things. You want grandchildren; that's all you cared about, not me; you never understood me."

"Will, what are you talking about? I have always been proud of you. I only wanted you to be happy."

"Go home, Mother." Will turned on his heel and with his head held high marched past her.

She began crying when she saw the archbishop, Fran, Jen, Joan, and Charlie coming towards her. Running towards them, she reached out for Bob. "I don't understand. How could all this have happened when everything was so good on Sunday?"

Wrapping his arms around her Bob said, "Barbara, let's go somewhere quiet where we can talk. But first, I have to speak to the detective. Stay here with my sister; this is Sister Frances Mary; she will introduce you to the others."

Walking to Hudson's desk he sat down in a chair. When he saw her coming back from the cell, he stood. "Detective, I would like to take Mrs. Owens back to my place; she is in shock. I promise we will come back tomorrow and talk about what to do."

"Another day won't make any difference, Archbishop. Do what you have to do. I'll see you tomorrow about the same time. I hope your sister will feel up to coming back."

"Oh, I'm quite sure you will see all of us tomorrow."

Chapter 38

After three hours sleep, Bob woke up feeling a tear rolling down his cheek. The hollow pit in his stomach reminded him of the anguish Barbara Owens had shared with him as they talked until 2:00 that morning. His own agony united them in mutual grief.

Checking the clock he groaned thinking he needed to get up in another hour; then he remembered that Charlie had come back about 9:00 and offered to say the early Mass. Having spent the afternoon and evening with Fran, Jen, and Joan at Sophia's Blessings Charlie had news to share.

Sighing Bob knew their plan of action was fitting; whether Detective Hudson agreed, and if she did, would Barbara understand were questions that confused his anger, cluttered his worries and challenged his faith. Rolling over he closed his eyes, praying at the same time. *It's almost Christmas, God. Show us that you are Emmanuel, God with us.*

When Charlie came into the kitchen after his Mass, Annie had coffee and toast ready. She thanked him for being there for the archbishop. "Everything will work out, Annie," he said to her, clasping her hand in his.

"How's Sister Frances Mary?"

"She will get through this, and she has all of us to help her."

"Sometimes," she began, her eyes meeting Father Charlie's, "I saw terrible shadows when Father Will was here. I prayed but I should have said something. I was often afraid and…" She pressed her lips closed as Mrs. Owens walked in.

"Annie, I didn't say thank you yesterday for dinner and for your kindness to me. I'm sorry if my son frightened you; now he frightens me." Her bottom lip quivering she brushed away a tear. "And so, maybe you will continue to pray for both of us."

"Mrs. Owens, I am so sorry; and I will pray."

Leaning over Barbara gave her a hug. "I'm going to Mass now, and then after breakfast the archbishop and I will be leaving." Turning to Charlie, she wiped away another tear, and said, "I'm so sorry that Will…"

Charlie interrupted her. "No need for you to apologize for anything. Know that I believe that God will help all of us to get through this; your son, too."

She began weeping. "I hope so."

"There you are. Come with me, Barbara." Bob glanced at Annie. "We'll see you in a half hour."

"I'm going to call Sister Frances Mary," said Charlie. "I'll see you before we leave, Annie."

Watching him leave her kitchen Annie wrestled with her mixed up feelings: she was so happy to see Father Charlie and the archbishop as friends again; she was overjoyed that the archbishop and his sister were reunited, but she did not know how to explain her feelings about Father Will. If he hadn't been stopped, all that made her happy would have been destroyed; for that she didn't know how she could forgive him. Yet her conscience said she must. *I'm sorry, God, but I can't do it, at least not now,* she whispered. She hurried to make a sign of the cross.

Her thoughts returned to Will's mother. She had seen the torment in her eyes. She wondered if during the night Barbara recalled when he was born, how he must have made her laugh with his toddler antics, how he must have run to her when he fell and skinned his knees. She understood that his mother would still love him. Somewhere deep within, she realized for one brief moment that this was also a picture of how God can love everyone. With her fleeting delight in this new image of unconditional love, Annie was confused and angry. *It's too much to believe. What if God loves us that much? What if, in the end, everyone gets saved?*

Hearing the archbishop and Mrs. Owens coming in, she broke off the questions that both bewildered yet soothed her. Rushing to get their coffee and orange juice she had two places ready when they walked into the kitchen. Annie smiled at Mrs. Owens and hoped that her face did not betray her disconcerting feelings.

"Barbara," said Bob "have some coffee while I make some toast."

"I don't think I can eat anything; I'll just have the coffee."

"We'll go soon. Annie, is Father Charlie upstairs?"

"He said he was going to call your sister."

"Here I am. Fran said that Tess called her last night after I left. She had been having terrible images both while awake and in her dreams on Sunday.

She said she woke up screaming Monday morning. Now she's upset she didn't call Fran that morning."

"I was afraid of that," said Bob. "Those two are so connected. But I did not want to worry her just in case that this time…" Charlie's cell phone rang.

"Adam, yes I did say I would go with you. Give me the number and I will try to change the time with your boss. I'll call him right now before we leave for the precinct." Charlie walked into the dining room.

"Poor Adam," said Bob.

Annie noticed that Mrs. Owens bowed her head. *All this sorrow and trouble that her son has caused; her pain is beyond my imagination.* Another question rose up within her. *Is God also suffering?* With a shake of her head she dismissed that intriguing thought.

Closing his phone Charlie came back into the kitchen. "I've set up a meeting with Adam's boss for 2:00; I hope that, after agreeing to a solution today with the police regarding Will, I can also help Adam. And, by the way, Bob, Tess understands why you did not call her. She said to tell you that she will talk to Tim, and for you to concentrate on taking care of Fran."

"I will do that." Bob took Barbara's arm. "Let's go."

Watching them leave Annie detected a calmness seeping into her. She raised her eyes expecting to feel a gentle waterless shower falling on her. She found herself relaxing into a quiet peace. Even the puzzling questions didn't matter now.

At the car, Bob opened the passenger front door, but Barbara said, "No, Archbishop, I'd rather sit in the back seat. You and Charlie can talk; I need to retreat inside my head for awhile."

"I can tell I won't be able to change your mind. Know that we are going to do what's best for Will."

"I have no doubts about that." Settling into the back seat she closed her eyes.

Charlie looked at Bob and with a nod, he put on the classical station as they backed out of the driveway.

The soft music took Barbara back to her all-night conversation with Bob. She told him how she worried about Will even as a child. She sighed. *He was so driven, then and even now. Maybe if his father had not been drunk so often, maybe if he had lived long enough after he was in recovery, maybe if I had not pushed him into dating. Is that when he got the idea I was only interested in grandchildren? Michelle was such a nice girl and she would have been a calming influence on him. Or Vivian, she was crazy about him. And Paige—I thought she would attract his attention because she was into all kinds of church activities. But he never seemed to have much fun with any of them. Why was he so intense? What made him think he had to prove himself to God, or that he had to do so much to please God? Why did he feel so unloved? If he could have only believed how much I loved him. And yet, I always knew he couldn't return my love. What did I miss? How could I have prevented all this insanity?*

She felt the tears welling up again. *What will happen to him, to my boy? I don't know him, my own son. I knew he was not telling me the whole story when he was moved form Sacred Heart; I had heard rumors but when he was called to live at the Chancery with the archbishop, I believed—I wanted to believe—that he was unfortunate enough to be caught up in something beyond his control. I wish we could have talked about it. How did he become so violent? Even when his father was drunk, he never hurt me or him. I'm afraid he will hate me for coming to see him again.*

As Charlie slowed to a stop in the precinct parking lot, Barbara's stomach coiled itself into a tight knot. Her arms aching with a mother's yearning to snatch her child she longed to hide him from the world. At the same time she shuddered at the picture of her son shoving her away. She would have collapsed in despair but remembered Bob's words. When he opened the door she peered into his eyes inhaling a gulp of trust as she crawled out of the car.

Seeing Fran getting out of a car two spaces away Barbara lowered her eyes feeling the knot in her stomach twisting tighter. Bob's hand took her arm; looking up she fixed her eyes on the steps that would lead to her son.

Chapter 39

Arriving at the bottom step at the same time Bob reached his other hand out to his sister. Grasping it Fran flashed a quick smile to Barbara. Charlie nodded to Jen and Joan as they fell in behind Barbara, Bob, and Fran.

Detective Hudson, on her phone as the six came through the doorway, waved them to her desk. Completing her call, she stood up. "Good morning," she smiled. "Let's go to the conference room."

Keeping her head down Mrs. Owens walked past the desks of other detectives staying beside the archbishop. Focusing her eyes straight ahead Fran walked behind her brother with Charlie. Passing by the first few desks, Jen noticed Detective Phil Roberts, and pointed him out to Joan. They both stopped at his desk. "For our sister, Fran, we want to say how grateful we are," said Jen.

"Sometimes I say that nothing surprises me, but I must admit, that scene at the hotel, shook me. I hope Sister will pull through this."

"She will," said Joan. "She has great strength, and she has us."

Racing to catch up with the others they came face to face with Hudson ushering everyone into the conference room. She motioned for them to sit at the table where there were eight chairs. Bob took the first chair facing the door and Fran sat down next to him. Charlie placed himself beside Fran. Jen took the seat at the far end of the table, and Joan took the seat across from Charlie; Barbara sat down beside her.

Hudson remained standing and asked "Can I get coffee or a cold drink for anyone?" Taking the time to look at each one, she had no takers. Pulling out the chair at the head of the table she sat down. "I know you are nervous about the media attention a trial would generate. By pleading guilty, Father Will can be sentenced by a judge; he should understand why that would be the sensible thing to do since he was caught in the act."

Barbara stifled the sob that rose within her. Joan touched her hand.

Taking a deep breath Fran said, "Detective Hudson, we want to discuss a different approach. Sending Father Will to prison will not deal with the problem. He is suffering from a tormenting disorder that…"

"Sister," Detective Hudson bit her lip. "Fran, I respect your faith, and your belief in forgiveness, but…"

"I have not yet forgiven him, Detective. This isn't about what I think I should do. This is about my taking charge of my life and refusing to be a victim." Hesitating long enough to swallow she said, "This was not a quick decision or an easy one. I am angry; I am hurt; I am afraid of sleeping for fear I will keep dreaming about him. But I want real justice, and it seems to me that a true and just sentence requires my insistence that Father Will be given the chance to become whole, and well."

Detective Hudson looked around the table; the archbishop nodded his agreement and she noticed his eyes were glistening. Charlie's face flushed with admiration. Jen and Joan clasped each others hands. Barbara wiped her eyes. "I'm not sure how to respond. I can't even suggest how this could be done."

Bob spoke up. "The archdiocese can send him to a facility, a hospital facility, in another area of the country. There he will undergo psychological treatment until he is better, and if he cannot be healed he can be confined where he can never do such harm again."

"You would be taking the responsibility for this?" Detective Hudson said.

"Yes, but the legal system can make his treatment a requirement, right?"

"It's not the solution I had in mind, but yes, I'm sure we can make this official—if Father Owens agrees to accept this consequence. Are you ready for me to bring him in?"

Inhaling a deep sigh Fran gazed at her clinched fists under the table; she unfolded the left one, reached for her brother's hand and they both nodded yes. Charlie looked at Joan and Jen; Joan squeezed Barbara's hand, and said, "I think we're ready."

After Hudson left the room, no one spoke, but a presence in the room left no doubt they were not alone. Marveling at the stillness that had wrapped itself around her Fran remembered that Christmas was a week away. A prayer swelled within her. *O Emmanuel God, you are with us.*

Her stomach twitched as Hudson opened the door; seeing Will with his wrists handcuffed jolted her out of her quietness. Looking at Barbara she recognized the agony of love. Bob closed his eyes; Charlie glared at Will cringing at the revulsion that burst into his soul. Jen choked on the nausea that mushroomed within. Joan dug her fingernails into her corduroy slacks.

Pulling out a chair Hudson motioned for Will to sit down. "I prefer to stand."

Hudson heaved a sigh. "Will, I am going to offer you the plan we have agreed upon; you must accept it, or I will have no option other than charging you with attempted murder and attempted rape."

"I am only interested in God's plan."

"Will," his mother pleaded. "Please, listen. You need help, and I don't want you to go to prison."

Will stared at the wall. "O God, I will complete your mission."

Dropping her head into her hands Barbara cried. Will said, "I am the Coordinator of Redemption."

"Will, sit down," said Bob.

"You have no authority over me. I take my orders from God." Without warning a surge of isolation overcame him and he shrieked. "O God, why have you abandoned me?" He sunk into the chair across from Bob and next to his mother.

"Will," said Bob, "God has not abandoned you. We all are here to help you. You did a horrible thing, but we do not believe that justice will be served by sending you to prison."

Will began rocking to the left and to the right. "God, let this cup of suffering pass; but whatever is your will, I am prepared to suffer." The emptiness within engulfed him; a spark startled him, and his heart was thumping. Twisting and turning, he made every effort to break the hold of an embrace that would not let go. He collapsed to the floor. "Why, God? Where are you?"

Tumbling off her chair his mother knelt beside him. Putting her arms around him, she cuddled him, brushing his hair from his face and whispering in his ear. "My son, accept the plan; you will find God, I promise."

Will's tears spilled over her arms. She kissed his forehead again and again.

Pushing back his chair Charlie walked over to them. Bending down he spoke to Barbara. "Let me help you pick him up." Releasing her hold she let Charlie put his arms under Will's armpits pulling him to his feet. Will wobbled and his head fell on Charlie's shoulder. Staggering over to the chair Charlie placed Will in it.

Grabbing hold of the chair Barbara stood up. "Will, please say yes."

Banging his head on the table Will shouted a mixture of curses and warnings. Finally exhausted he said, "All right, Mother. Yes, yes, whatever you say."

"Is that enough?" Bob asked Detective Hudson.

"Yes, and I'll call for the paramedics to take him to the local hospital for now. You can get back to me when you make arrangements to have him committed." Turning to Barbara she said, "Mrs. Owens, if you want to go with him in the ambulance that will be fine."

"Do you want to do that, Barbara? I'll come and pick you up later," said Charlie. Patting his arm she whispered her gratitude. "I'll call a cab; I need time to be alone."

"Let's go home," said Bob. Fran went first and tiptoed past Will. Joan followed Jen around the table; Charlie waited at the open door and accompanied Bob into the hall.

Hurrying past all the desks Fran was grateful the morning was over. Bob and Charlie strode behind her. Jen and Joan darted around a desk and caught up with her.

Shoving open the door to the outside she collided with an onslaught of cameras and microphones. Bob and Charlie ran up behind her. Bob whispered, "You do not have to make a comment."

Eying the crowd from left to right she heard shouts of "Sister! Sister!" A woman reporter jostling her way to the front shoved a microphone in Fran's face. "Why did you go to that hotel alone?"

A male reporter at the far edge in the back yelled, "Hey, Sister, I bet you wish the death penalty was an option for attempted murder."

Hearing Bob whisper again, "You don't have to say anything," the stillness that hugged her tight earlier embraced her once more. A desire to speak surged through every cell of her body. "We are called by justice to do the right thing. And what is right in this matter is becoming whole, becoming healthy, both for me and for Father Owens. Punishing a sick person makes me another oppressor. In consultation with my brother, the archbishop; my friends, Sister Jennifer, Sister Joan; and Father Charles Fletcher, Father William Owens has agreed to enter a care facility for treatment."

"Not enough!" came a bellow off to the right. Fran turned to see a throng of women on the sidewalk. One, in a white leather jacket with a fake fur collar and hat, persuaded the others to join in the chant. "Not enough! Not enough!" Other voices from the main group merged with theirs.

Fran searched the faces of her support group. "I'm not going to argue about this; let's go to our cars."

As if on cue, they charged off the first step together, their arms linked to one another. The crowd divided in front of them. A lone reporter leaped out. "What are you hiding, Archbishop? Where is he being sent? How can you protect him after what he did?"

Again, as if they had planned their response, the group froze in their steps. The archbishop raised his voice, "A complete report will be released at 4:00." They kept on walking to their cars. Bob said, "Fran, let's go to your place. I'm sure all these reporters will be racing to their vehicles to follow us. I think it will be appropriate to speak to them from Sophia's Blessings, don't you think?"

"Perfect setting," said Fran. She tilted her head towards the crowd. "They're ready and waiting." Bob and Charlie escorted Fran, Jen, and Joan to their car.

"We'll see you soon," said Charlie. "And let me make a little something to eat for all of us when we get there. Bob and I will stop at that new market on the way. But first, we have to go to the hotel and save Adam's job. We'll see you later."

"Sounds great," said Joan turning on the ignition and pressing the button to close her window.

Fran heaved a great sigh as they drove away. The Christmas decorations in the stores and hanging from the street lights seemed so out of place. "You were great," said Jen.

"Thanks. I do feel as if tons of lead have been lifted away. But I think many are going to be disappointed."

"That's because some people, like those women, are going to accuse you of showing mercy instead of justice," said Joan. "But you were right about the meaning of justice; it doesn't mean condemning Will to punishment, but getting what is right for you and for him."

"What many people do not realize is that I'm not sure I could show mercy to Will. I wonder what I would have done if he had refused treatment." Fran gazed at her fists, clenched for the second time today.

Jen chimed in from the back seat. "Fran, you know how we share at some of our retreats—that forgiveness takes time; you have believe that for yourself."

"I guess you're right, but I'm too tired to think about this anymore. I wonder what Charlie is going to make for supper."

"Whatever, it will be fabulous."

"Time to be soothed by music" said Joan. "We have some of your favorites on the CD."

"Sounds good to me." Closing her eyes Fran leaned back against the head rest.

Seeing Christmas wreaths on a house and a Santa Claus in the next yard Jen reflected on how these sights always brought bubbles of joy inside her, but today drought. She sighed as they arrived at the driveway. Looking at her watch she said, "It's already 12:30; do you want a quick lunch? Then I'm going to lie down when we get inside."

"Me, too," said Fran opening her eyes. "But I don't feel like eating."

"I'm too hyper," said Joan. "I'll wait for Charlie and Bob to get here."

Fran was the first one out of the car. Catching her breath as the cold air swept across her face she gasped as she felt Will pulling at her.

"Fran, what's wrong?" said Jen trudging beside her.

"A flashback. I know it's been only a few days, but I'm scared I'll never get over this."

Putting her arm around her, Jen waved Joan to Fran's other side. Once inside, she took Fran's jacket and hung it with hers. "Sure you don't want something? Not even a drink?"

"I am so tired. Call me when Bob and Charlie get here."

Standing in her doorway, Fran looked at the bed she had not made that morning. Dragging herself across the room she rubbed away the chilliness in her arms. Tugging on the bottom sheet she tucked it under the mattress, smoothing away the wrinkles with both hands. She let herself sink into the featherbed topper, and within minutes had dropped into a deep slumber.

When Bob and Charlie arrived, Joan looked in on her, and decided to let her sleep until their meal was ready. Jen had heard them come in and was already on her way to the kitchen. Peeking into one bag Jen saw a container of crab bisque soup, wheat rolls, and ground turkey. In another bag she noticed ingredients for a tossed salad, and a green and red box.

Like a TV cooking show, Jen and Joan, Bob and Charlie produced, in twenty minutes, a tossed salad of lettuce, red cabbage, onions, red and green peppers with a Dijon dressing, and honey-mustard turkey burgers on warm wheat buns to go with the steaming soup. Charlie opened the red and green box, and Jen smiled as he arranged cookies shaped into wreaths around an eight inch chocolate Santa. Charlie gave her a wink; they both knew Fran's love of chocolate.

Skipping a step or two Joan went upstairs for Fran. Hearing a low moan as she got to her door, she pushed it open. Tapping three times she jumped when Fran bolted upright with a cry. Rushing from the doorway Joan wrapped her arms around her. "I'm so sorry, Fran."

"Are Bob and Charlie here?" Looking at the clock on her bed stand she said, "It's almost 2:00!"

"You were fast asleep when they got here, so I didn't wake you. Everything's ready; are you hungry?"

"I am. Let's go."

The aromas floating from the kitchen snuggled into her soul teasing her into swift footsteps. When she walked in to the cluster of devoted, smiling faces the chains protecting her heart broke apart. Tears trickled down both cheeks as she extended her arms. Hugging Bob first she went around the circle wiping away tears and smiling at the same time. "Thank you all so much." Everyone was happy to hear her next announcement. "I'm starving."

When everyone was seated, Bob offered a brief prayer. The soup was passed around first, and soon the chatter buried their worries and fears. By the time Fran was handed the chocolate Santa, Bob took a quick glance at his watch. It was 3:15. Turning his attention back to Fran, he was aware of the gratitude stirring inside him.

Picking up a knife to cut the Santa Fran started trembling. Everyone realized the connection. Sitting next to her; Charlie snatched the knife, saying "I'm sorry, Fran. Let me just break it."

"I didn't mean to spoil this."

Bob, Jen, and Joan chimed in together. "Fran, nothing is spoiled."

Bob said, "Please, we understand."

Fran managed a smile. Charlie handed her a piece of chocolate. "We're all here for you, Fran. And I bought this chocolate guy especially for you."

"You know how to lighten up the worst situation, Charlie. Give me his sack of toys!" The laughter around the table, delicate to their ears but hearty to their souls, held the promise of healing.

Bob glanced again at his watch, and Fran noticed this time. She looked at hers. "It's 3:30; are you ready?"

"I am. If you're up to it, I think you should repeat your message from this morning first; I could not improve on that. And then I'll give the facts about the facility."

"I can do that."

"Charlie," said Bob, "are you planning on saying anything?"

"Yes, but not much."

Joan said, "Jen and I will clean up the kitchen; why don't you three get refreshed and prepared for the cameras?"

Fran took a quick peek as she passed the window on her way to her room. Snow was falling, being more than a nuisance for the crews of five news vans setting up cameras and microphones. Before a moan made itself audible, a now familiar embrace comforted her.

Walking by her still unmade bed, she shook her head. She held a cool wash cloth to her eyes for a full minute. Putting on a little blush she patted her face with a light powder. Pulling down a few hairs of her bangs, she inhaled a slow deep breath. She ran her fingers along the blue flowered bed sheet and headed downstairs.

She met Bob and Charlie in the foyer. "Two minutes to go." Without a word their hands joined and they bowed their heads.

"O God," said Bob, "let our words reflect your unconditional love."

"Amen" said Fran and Charlie.

Bob opened the door; a blast of December air jolted all three. The snow had stopped. The last rays of the sun glowed. Fran was swept up into an encounter of connectedness to all of creation.

Facing the glare of lights she realized she had no fear. "Good evening," she said. Her words from the morning flowed with the ease born of integrity. "And now my brother will give you the details of Father Owens' journey to wholeness."

Stepping forward Bob stated that Our Lady of Victory Medical Center, five hours away, was the facility where Will was being sent, and gave his word that monthly reports would determine when Will was suitable for ministry again. "When Father Owens is healthy, he will be accepted in another diocese by mutual agreement between that bishop and Father Owens. He will not return here."

Charlie moved to the front. "Because God created both of us, Father Owens is my brother. Though I am still learning how to love all people as my brothers and sisters, my prayer for Father Owens is that he will discover that I am his brother. Thank you all for coming."

"Father," said one reporter, "Can you tell us how you felt when you saw Father Owens in that hotel room?"

"Sister, what made you decide to come forward?"

"Archbishop, when did you figure out what was happening? How did you get to the hotel in time?"

Bob held up his hands as a winter wind picked up a spray of snow. "I think it's much too cold to continue today. Be assured you can ask us for updates as our journeys continue. We wish you all the special blessings of Christmas."

"You owe us one answer, Archbishop. When is Father Owens going to Our Lady of Victory."

"Today at 6:00." Opening the door he ushered Fran inside first and then Charlie.

Father Jim bit the inside of his cheek as he sat in front of his TV. He was stung with a sense of remorse unlike any he had experienced before. His fidgeting when Charlie talked about being a brother forced him to face his tenacity, which he had believed was a virtue. *How will I change when I no longer believe religion is all about rules?*

When Father Pete heard Fran he recalled a moment during that Day of Reconciliation and Possibilities when he caught a hint that **Cry Justice** was a call to new energy in the church. *Maybe God will bring something good out of all this evil.*

Father Joe watched Bob and thought, *What ever made me think I would want to be a bishop?* And *I'll never joke again about real Catholics.*

Father Ed prayed, *O God, forgive my weakness; if only I had been strong enough when he was at Sacred Heart; if only I had trusted Fran. I will ask her, Jen, and Joan for forgiveness tomorrow.*

Father Mark called Father Mike. "Want to watch the 6:00 news over here—in case Charlie comes back?"

"Good idea; I'm not sure what to say to him at this point."

"Well, we know that Will's transfer will be the first story at 6:00," said Charlie.

"This seems like the worst time of the year for this to happen," said Fran. "Yet, I keep hoping that somehow, the message of Christmas will become real."

"Emmanuel, God with us," said Bob. "Charlie, will you stay until the news is over?"

"Of course. I need to do something creative while we wait." Winking at Joan he said, "Do you think you have ingredients for bread, plus some nuts? I'd love to bake my mother's Christmas bread."

"I'm sure we do. You know our kitchen; do your thing, Charlie. I'm going to the exercise room."

"Me, too," said Jen.

"Fran, do you feel like spending some time with your brother? And I think we better call Tess and Tim."

"Let's do that." They walked towards the living room together.

By 5:55 Fran and Bob joined the others gathered in front of the TV; Charlie's bread had just come out of the oven promising a comfort treat after the news.

At 6:00 Father Nick heaved a heavy sigh as he turned on the TV. *I never thought I'd see something like this in my old age.* Watching Will being lifted into an ambulance and hearing a repeat of the 4:00 special report, a light surrounded him. Becoming aware of a new energy he realized he was smiling. *I am looking forward to Christmas this year.* Grabbing a note pad he began scribbling. Ideas were swarming—words of hope for the future, trust in new directions, and peace.

Fathers Mike and Mark looked at Will, strapped to the gurney. Visions of the archbishop's dinner exploded before them. They glanced at each other in silence. When Charlie spoke Mike bowed his head. "I guess I have a long way to go."

"You know what I've been thinking—I'm going to join **Cry Justice**."

"I'm glad you said it first; I was planning on doing the same thing."

Seeing Will brought a gasp from Fran; squeezing her hand Bob held it tight. Charlie lowered his eyes when he saw Barbara climbing in beside her son. Jen bit her lip and Joan looked away from the screen. Reaching for the remote Fran pressed the OFF button.

"Fran," said Bob, "I've heard parts of your prayer that you composed after leaving Sacred Heart. Would you say it for us now—your Un-Magnificat?"

Swallowing the lump in her throat Fran wiped away a tear. She recalled what Joan said to her back in October, *you will see him turn back to the real person trapped under all that clout.* "My soul wilts before you, O Lord, and my spirit weeps in your presence. Why have you looked away from the misery of your servant? Surely, from now on all generations will call me cursed for your might has crushed me with sorrow, and terrible is your name."

She swallowed again, and wiped away another tear. "But your remoteness is an illusion for those who seek you from generation to generation. You show strength with your arm; you gather the heartbroken into your eternal embrace; you cuddle the anguish of the grief-stricken and lift their faces to you; you fill them with longing for eternity but send them to complete their work on earth. You are a constant help to your servant who remembers your promise: I am with you always. Surely from now on all generations will call me blessed."

Bob hugged her first and the two of them gathered Charlie, Jen and Joan into a group hug. For a full minute they savored the comfort and luxury of friendship. *O God, how blessed I am but I know the tears are coming.* She broke the embrace. Tongue in cheek she complained, "I thought someone made a treat for us—didn't I hear something about a special mother's recipe for nut bread?"

Charlie was as pleased as a Santa. "Ho! Ho! Ho! Come into the lounge and see what my elves have done."

Following Charlie out of the living room Fran was stunned to see a glow of lights twinkling in the lounge. Coming to a standstill in the doorway, her mouth dropped open as she stared at the tree. Peering into the room her eyes sparkled with awe—on the table sat a bowl of green punch in the middle; the Christmas cookies left from lunch were off to the right; on five small white plates were two slices of bread crammed full of a sweet nut filling.

Walking up behind her Bob leaned his chin on her shoulder. "Charlie, when did you do this?"

Jen and Joan broke into applause. Charlie waved them all into the room.

"Christmas is next week," Fran whispered. "God is with us."